MW00856965

BEST FRIENDS FOREVER

CATHRYN GRANT

INKUBATOR
BOOKS

Published by Inkubator Books
www.inkubatorbooks.com

Copyright © 2022 by Cathryn Grant

Cathryn Grant has asserted her right to be identified as the author of this work.

ISBN (eBook): 978-1-915275-25-7
ISBN (Paperback): 978-1-915275-28-8
ISBN (Hardback): 978-1-915275-31-8

BEST FRIENDS FOREVER is a work of fiction. People, places, events, and situations are the product of the author's imagination. Any resemblance to actual persons, living or dead is entirely coincidental.

No part of this book may be reproduced, stored in any retrieval system, or transmitted by any means without the prior written permission of the publisher.

PROLOGUE
NOVEMBER 12, 2010

The room was utterly dark. She liked it that way, for now. Even though her brain felt as if it were sloshing around inside her skull, taking wild dips, skidding sideways, she'd never felt so loved and content in her life. Her eyes were closed, her body still warm from the half-naked boy who had lain on top of her a few minutes ago. Or was it longer? An hour? The night before? Was it a dream?

Her sense of time had dissolved. But that didn't bother her either because the bliss was incredible. She still felt him inside her, although she knew that was a blur of memory and imagination, not an actual physical sensation.

Was this what it was like to be drunk, or was it something else? Until tonight, she'd never had more than a single beer or a few sips of champagne. Other kids partied, but she thought it was stupid to choose to deaden your own brain. She liked thinking about things. She liked the intricacies of her mind and her sharp, clear awareness of life.

She wasn't sure how many Jell-O shots she'd eaten. They were so good—like eating candy. At some point she drank a plastic cup filled with soda that might have had alcohol in it.

No one had ever told her that alcohol made you feel calm and loved, at peace with the world. As if no one could ever hurt you again.

A wave of nausea passed through her. She willed it away, remembering the feel of his lips and the way he'd looked directly into her eyes the entire time they were making love, as if he could see through the lenses into her soul. As if she were the only woman in the world. As if she'd been made for him. She sighed and felt a smile ease across her face.

He was so cute and charming. The most charming boy she'd ever known. He was funny and, best of all, smart. He knew what he was doing with her body, and he'd made her feel things she would never be able to describe. No wonder people went crazy over sex. Why on earth had she waited so long to try it? She laughed softly, her voice sounding like it belonged to someone else.

She wasn't sure where he was right now. He'd gotten up and left the room, maybe. Had he? She'd drifted to sleep or even passed out. She couldn't remember. He would come back soon.

The door opened. See! She'd thought it, and he appeared. Just like that. Magic. She smiled, her eyes still closed. The nausea pushed against her, demanding she pay attention.

After a few moments of silence, she tried to ask him to lie beside her, but she couldn't seem to make the words come out. She felt like she was falling asleep, but different. That sense of absolute bliss was growing, filling every crevice inside her body, making it seem as if each cell had a life of its own, thrilled with its own existence, bathed in an unimaginable awareness of love.

Making out the shape of the other person in the darkness was impossible. It wasn't him after all because there was a faint scent of weed. He never smoked. He liked to drink, but not go *too crazy*, he'd said. He never wanted to pass out or forget what he'd done. That made her feel secure, as if he wasn't with her simply because they were drunk.

She tried speaking again, wanting to ask who was standing near the foot of the bed. Why wouldn't her tongue work? Or was the problem her vocal cords?

She was lying on the bed where everyone had left their coats and purses. She was surrounded, almost buried in jackets and sweatshirts. She still couldn't speak, and now the nausea had grown more intense. She was pretty sure that if she opened her mouth even a fraction of an inch, her dinner and all those Jell-O shots would bathe her face, soak her hair, and splatter across other people's belongings. She imagined the disgust that would come her way as members of the fraternity and the kids from her dorm complained that she'd spewed all over their nice wool coats and leather purses.

The visitor stood beside her now. She felt their weight against the side of the mattress. The heat of the coats was smothering her, making her skin feel like it was dissolving. Another coat was tossed over her upper body, the feather-stuffed nylon cool on her skin.

"Help me. Please. I can't…"

Her silent companion, impossible in the dark to tell if it was male or female, pulled another coat across her body. Too hot. The stuff that had roiled in her stomach rushed up her esophagus without warning, her stomach heaving before thrusting its contents out into the previously sweet-smelling air. She gagged and coughed hard. Vomit burned her throat. "Help me. Please help me. I…"

She couldn't breathe. Why couldn't she breathe? She tried to cry, but nothing came out. Some of the vomit had rushed into her lungs, where the burning was so intense that she thought it might tear a hole in the fragile tissue. It was the most awful feeling ever—her mind still blissfully happy as her body screamed with agony. Her arms and legs trembled.

Her stomach twisted violently, trying to expel more. She needed to sit up or turn onto her side. She tried to push herself up, but her hands slipped on soft fabric, and she wasn't able to lift even her head off the pillow.

It felt as if there wasn't enough room for oxygen in her lungs. She coughed, a hard stinging attack. Her mouth opened wide, trying to get air, but her lungs were tight and on fire with the presence of thick liquid that shouldn't be there.

Why wouldn't they help her? Why weren't they helping her sit up, moving the coats, speaking to her? They should be telling her it would be alright. But it wasn't. Something was wrong. How could they just stand there?

Was she dying? Was this what it felt like? This strange ecstasy and blissful unconcern blended with absolute physical torment? She *was* dying. She was sure of it now. There was no air in her lungs, and she was so unbearably hot. She'd never been this hot in her life.

Gagging, unable to grasp even a wisp of air, she felt her thoughts dissolving. Her head seemed to sink even deeper into the pillow. And then she felt nothing.

1

ABBEY

Before taking the picture for Instagram, I'd gotten a professional manicure. I chose dark purple polish. On the ring fingers of each hand, the glossy purple was slashed with a strip of gold glitter. At home, I placed my hand on the pale gray kitchen counter. Light streamed into the eating area and across the counter from the sliding glass doors of my new condo.

With the phone securely wedged in my right hand, I gently arched a few fingers of my left hand so it didn't look splayed like a piece of meat. I made sure all the nails were captured in the frame and snapped eight shots, one after the other, two with the flash, the rest without. I wanted the picture to be perfect. It was meant as an important announcement, maybe the most important of my life.

I scrolled through the photos I'd taken, chose the best one, and uploaded it to Instagram. I typed my caption, although it was more like a little speech than a caption:

After almost ten soul-destroying years, I'm a single girl again! My life is starting over! Today. It's time for a road

trip, because I can't wait to see what happens next. The
past is gone. Dead to me.

I followed this with a bunch of emojis—confetti, champagne, balloons, over and over in a string that took an entire line. I added hashtags about freedom and divorce, taking back your power and following your bliss. I used travel hashtags and party hashtags. Then hit the share button. All the things I'd lost when I was twenty, when I'd decided it was a good idea to marry my boss, were waiting for me now.

My wedding to Dave hadn't even been a real wedding. We repeated our vows in front of a judge with three other people standing beside us—his best friend, my mom, and my cousin. Our wedding couldn't be *splashy* because Dave's divorce hadn't been final until two days before. But I was so in love it didn't matter.

I honestly believed that at the time.

Even though I became his wife, Dave continued to act as if I was still his personal assistant. After a few years of marriage, he started to get that I wasn't the always-agreeable, hot twenty-year-old he'd promised to love. A mind of my own was not what he was expecting, I guess. Pretty soon, it was easy enough for him to find new twenty-year-olds who didn't want anything but him.

When those rings slid off my finger, I knew I'd severed the worst part of my life. Soon, I'd be ready to figure out how to dump the second-worst part—my job as a go-fer for a successful Realtor. Of course, she didn't call me a go-fer, but when you're buying ibuprofen and hand lotion on your way into the office and dropping off another girl's dry-cleaning on your way home, it's hard to see yourself as a professional. I thought working for a woman would give me a chance to move outside the box of college dropout. I thought I'd be respected and told to expand my aspirations. I was wrong.

The photo of my hand without its rings had only been live for five minutes and I already had 134 likes and ten comments. Most of them said stuff like *you go, girl.* I had over three thousand followers on Instagram because my account was open. Between my ex-husband and my boss, I'd felt as if I was living a tiny, fenced-in life. On Instagram, I could be fabulous and filled with dreams. I didn't want to shut myself off from anyone the world might bring to me. It wasn't as if I posted really personal things, just fun stuff. There was nothing to hide, so I didn't.

I knew I'd probably get some comments about the purity of marriage and trying harder to make it work and not giving up and how tragically sad it was to celebrate the end of something that was meant to last your whole life. People shouldn't pretend to have opinions about something they never lived through.

I'd grown up very fast after a bunch of people decided they knew all about me a long time ago. It seems old-fashioned to say I was shunned, but that was what it was. I read a little bit about shunning, just what I could find on Google, but still, it's probably solid information. Shunning is abuse. Cults use it to control people. Maybe college kids in dorms and fraternities are cults. It sounds dramatic to think that way, but I bet they fit some of the points on the list of what characterizes a cult.

Shunning makes you feel like you don't exist, like a ghost. I didn't read that online, I lived it.

Walking across the campus of the University of Washington when I was nineteen years old, I felt like flames were licking my body. Even in early December, when most people wore hats to keep out the cold, my skull was on fire with shame. And the sick part was, it was shame for something I didn't do. It's funny how other people thinking something about you can make you feel shameful for something you haven't done. Maybe it's because you're looking at yourself through their eyes instead of through your own.

When I spoke, no one answered. When I smiled, they stared as if they were looking at empty space.

When I first learned they were whispering behind my back, I tried to ignore it like the experts tell you to do. *Don't worry what other people think of you.* That's what we're told. Anyone who thinks you never have to consider what others think has probably had a lot of people yielding to their will.

I never told a lie in my entire life. Ever. Some people would say that's a lie because everyone lies, and if you say you don't, you're automatically a liar. But I always tell the truth. And when you do that, and everyone still says you're lying, it messes with your head. Now, after being accused of lying when I wasn't, it no longer seems so important to be truthful.

After a few weeks of feeling as if I didn't exist, I couldn't take it. That's the power of shunning. I felt like I wasn't even a real person, and I couldn't figure out whether I belonged in the world or not. I had no idea whether my personality was a real thing or a figment of my imagination. I was no longer sure what the words *I* and *me* were supposed to mean. Thoughts like those really mess with your head too. I felt like I was seriously going crazy. So I dropped out.

At first, I felt free. It was the awesome freedom of being an adult. Earning money. Decorating my own apartment. Pretty soon, dating an amazing, slightly older, successful man. An engagement ring. A disappointing wedding. And then, real life.

It wasn't freedom at all. And without a college degree, my dreams of a career as a publicist became fantasies that would never come to pass.

Now, I'd learn what freedom is. I was truly free.

To celebrate, I was planning a road trip. I'd rented a BMW convertible! Thanks to Dave. I would drive up the coast, then inland through Oregon north to Washington State. A perfect end-of-summer celebration of my new life, free from the past. The fact that my former classmates from the University of Washington, all those kids who had sucked the life out of me, were having their ten-year reunion had nothing to do with it. I didn't even find out about the reunion until after I posted the news about my road trip.

2

RAVEN

Emmett gave me a look of love mixed with far too much pity as he stared down the length of our dining room table, looking into my eyes until I was forced to turn away. We ate at our dining room table every Sunday evening. I'd started that tradition for several reasons. I wanted to be sitting at that table every Sunday as our family grew, adding several children until the room was alive with laughter and teasing arguments and reminders about table manners. It would be one of our traditions.

I didn't have family dinners when I was growing up. We had Wiccan coven meetings, run by my mother. She said that was better than family. It was a family you chose, a family with respect and love instead of grudges and rejection. I loved the coven, until I hated them, embarrassed by their unconventional beliefs and the simple fact they weren't like other people. Once I discovered how other families lived, that crowded family dinner table became the holy grail for me.

So far, it was just Emmett and me, with too much space between us. The serving bowls huddled at either end, as if they were taking sides.

"Don't say it." His tone was even. He wasn't trying to criticize me or control me. Just a calm reminder that what he called my *slightly inflated enthusiasm* for subjects both good and bad was not helpful here.

I couldn't stop myself. I had to say it. "I feel like I'm cursed."

"Please don't talk that way. It doesn't help anything. Besides, this is about both of us, not just you."

"I know that, but I'm the one who appears to be at fault."

"It's not about fault, Raven. Please don't keep blaming yourself. You're creating so much negative energy around this. You're only thirty. It will happen."

That was always the phrase that never failed to push me over the edge. I guess he'd forgotten that. I began sobbing, the shaking of my body causing the cutlery to rattle against our ceramic plates where they rested among the remains of our dinner. "How can they say they don't know why I can't get pregnant? It means I'm just not capable. It means they can't fix it."

Emmett stood and walked toward me. When he reached my chair, he put his hand on the back of my neck and rubbed it gently. He bent over, and I felt his face pressing into my hair. Normally, I loved it when he made these spontaneous moves to show me how much he needed me and cared for me. But now, I wanted to punch him in the stomach so he'd move away from me. He didn't know anything.

Finally, I forced myself to appear calm, and we started to clear the table. I put on music—loud and driving and designed to prevent any conversation. The beat and the volume made me feel better. The intensity of it numbed my thoughts so I could stop crying, which made Emmett feel helpless and sometimes frustrated, bordering on irritated. It hadn't been that way when we were first married, but after eight years, four of them trying to conceive a child, some conversations tended to repeat themselves. And when something repeats too often, we get bored. Then impatient.

Emmett didn't get it. The grief every single month...for years. The irrational feeling of inadequacy. He complained that the spreadsheet I'd introduced into our sex life was intolerable. We were not in a good place with each other. Each living an almost separate existence from the other, side by side in the same bed and across from each other at the table, and walking into the homes of friends, carrying a bottle of wine and a plate of cookies, and smiling as if we were the happiest couple alive.

I hadn't told him that my ten-year college reunion was coming up. There was no way I was going to meet up with my classmates, bumping into bellies swollen with life, smiling at pictures of their children. It was easier not to tell him some of these things. It hurt me that a gap was growing between us, but trying to explain was too hard. The doctors couldn't find any reason that we weren't pregnant, and that was that.

When the dishes were finished, Emmett went into our home office to catch up on email, and I went into the bathroom. I closed and locked the door, lit the candles surrounding the tub, and started running hot water. I poured lavender bath salt into the water. The bathroom filled with steam, and a few minutes later, the room was warm enough for me to strip off my clothes and slide into the water. I gazed at the three candles at the foot of the tub and visualized a child taking shape inside my womb.

This practice had become more and more difficult over the years, but I refused to give up. That would be the worst. I couldn't give up. It was desperately unfair that I might be denied this basic human desire. I would be a wonderful mother, a supportive mother, a wise and tender mother. I deserved to have a child. It wasn't fair.

Later, in bed, Emmett asleep beside me, I picked up my

phone and opened Instagram. I scrolled through pictures of cats and whales, book recommendations and food and vacation pics. When I saw friends' live stories or pictures of their kids, my finger moved at lightning speed to sweep all that stuff out of view.

I clicked over to the search bar for the few people I stalked on Instagram. People with public accounts. People I was curious about but didn't follow for a variety of reasons. For one, I didn't want to seem like a celebrity seeker. Not all of them were celebrities, obviously. One was my college roommate.

Abbey Parker Young.

The first thing I noticed on her page was that *Young* was missing from her name. And then I saw her latest post, already liked by 984 of her thousands of followers. The photograph was bathed in natural light—a shot of her left hand. The skin as supple as that of a college girl. I supposed that was what came of being slightly pampered. I didn't have those thoughts in a bad way, it was just reality. Every week or so, I looked at the photographs Abbey posted—the vacations she and her husband took, the decorating projects, the dinners out with friends. It all looked pretty amazing.

This time, I didn't need to read her accompanying comment to know that the ringless left hand meant her marriage was over. The clearly-larger-than-one-carat engagement ring, the diamond-encrusted wedding band, and the clean, upscale French manicure were gone.

Instead, there was purple and gold polish and very naked-looking fingers. The colors made me think of our college colors. I was sure that hadn't crossed Abbey's mind. Maybe the color choice had been subconscious. She'd dropped out in the middle of our sophomore year. Revering those colors was not part of her mindset.

We hadn't spoken since the day she moved out of our

dorm room. Not even a text message or an email or a Christmas card.

I stared for a long time at that picture. My phone went dark. I tapped to wake it. She didn't know I stalked her, obviously. That's the point of stalking. The other person isn't aware. At first. Stalking has a dark connotation, but I didn't know how else to think about it. But I wasn't keeping an eye on her life as it was filtered through social media for any evil purpose. I did it because I missed her.

I believed, from the moment Abbey and I exchanged names at the start of our freshman year, that we were kindred spirits. I knew Abbey felt it too. Something clicked. It felt as if we'd always known each other. We started talking right away, and the conversation just flowed, barely stopping until the day she disappeared. We would go to class and come back to our room and keep talking as if we'd been together all day. For our sophomore year, we requested each other as roommates. There was a third roommate, of course, and even though she wasn't like us, we co-existed without too much drama.

Our third roommate was not a kindred spirit. She probably felt left out at times, but you can't control that sort of thing. Abbey and I had the kind of connection that makes you think you knew that someone in another life. There's a history between you before you even have a chance to build one. You know what the other is thinking with a little sidewards glance. You can say anything to her, and she'll understand.

Abbey was the only person in my life who made me feel like that. I'd had friends in high school, but we drifted apart when we all went off to various colleges around the country because we were only friends due to proximity. I had other casual friends in college, but they'd never been close. I had friends at work, and Emmett and I had couple friends.

Among all those people, there was never anyone like Abbey.

When she left school, a hole opened up inside me. Despite being completely in love with Emmett, and even though he filled a large part of that gaping wound, that empty space remained. Every relationship I had with other women felt like playacting. I hated that, but I still tried to make the best of it. My mother tried to be helpful, like she'd always tried—by casting spells for the creation of meaningful friendships. But the spells never took, no matter how hard she believed in them.

I stared at the picture of Abbey's hand and read the comment for the fiftieth time. If I clicked *like*, would she block me? She didn't know I looked at her posts. If she blocked me, I'd never know what was going on with her again. How much did she want me out of her life, even after all that time? Maybe she never even thought about me. Maybe she wouldn't notice I'd liked it because she had so many people following and commenting on every post.

I got out of bed and walked through to the living room and out to the back patio. I wanted to click *like*. I needed to click *like*. I needed her to know I cared about what was going on with her. But I didn't want Emmett to ask what I was looking at. This was private, between Abbey and me.

Emmett had never heard Abbey's name. He had no idea I had a best friend who dropped out of college. He knew nothing beyond a few deliberately vague memories I'd shared from my second year of college. I'd placed an overlay of stories from my final two years at UW on top of everything, as if that time before had never happened.

I looked at Abbey's ringless finger and read her comment again. I tapped the little heart and immediately felt my own heart clutch as the emoticon filled with life, turning vibrant red. When I'd steadied my breathing, I tapped the comment box and wrote, *Miss you.*

Then, to keep myself from freaking out, I plugged my phone into the charger in the office and went to bed.

The next morning, I forced myself to wait until I'd finished two cups of coffee, a slice of toast and scrambled egg with a bit of salsa, and taken a shower and blow-dried my hair until it was thick and wavy. I put on my makeup, and then I checked Instagram. She hadn't liked my comment.

Fear squeezed my lungs, although I wasn't sure why. Our friendship had been dead for almost thirteen years. The significance of that number was not lost on me. I'd hoped she missed me as much as I missed her. I wanted to believe the void between us had been painful for her as well.

Finally, two days later, after I'd checked it a thousand times, she clicked the little red heart on my comment. Below it she wrote, *Are you still in the Bay Area? Maybe we should meet for a glass of wine.*

My eyes filled with tears of happiness. I felt more excited and hopeful than I had in a very long time.

3

ABBEY

I wasn't sure why I posted a response to Raven's comment saying she missed me. After all those years? And what did she miss, exactly? The shadow of me that I turned into during my last two months of college? The idea of missing that person was ridiculous. At the same time, I was curious.

First, how had she found me? Obviously, she could search and find me easily since my account was open. It made more sense to ask myself, *when* had she found me? Did she follow the divorced hashtag? I had no idea if Raven was married or single, had kids, what kind of career she had. I knew she'd been studying marketing and PR, just like me, but who knew what had happened after I left. She could have become an entirely different person.

It was unbridled curiosity, an asset and a flaw of mine, depending on how you look at it. Gnawing curiosity. I wanted to know what direction her life had taken. I wanted to know why she'd decided to jump back into my life at that moment. And I had to admit, despite everything that went wrong, part of me did miss her. We'd been the kind of friends that had some inexplicable, mysterious chemistry. We liked the same music and TV shows and food; we disliked the same people. We wanted the same things out of life. And we could say whatever we thought to the other and feel immediately like we weren't alone in the world. Someone else thought the same thing.

Raven owed me an apology. An epic, down-on-her-knees, tears-on-her-cheeks apology. Raven Sanders had abandoned me during the worst time of my life. Maybe she now thought I needed support in my divorce, and she had the idea she could make up for how she'd abandoned me. Maybe that was why she clicked *like* and wrote that comment. But I didn't need support. I was doing absolutely fine. I was excited about my future and the chance for a do-over. Not a do-over exactly, but a making up for what I'd missed. Turning in another direction.

Even though she had completely failed as a friend, I missed her. I hated admitting that, but the feeling was there like an inflated balloon in my chest. It was complicated. Maybe she was getting in touch because she'd finally realized what a truly horrible friend she'd been. Maybe she wanted to apologize. It was better to have low expectations, but it wasn't impossible.

While I waited for the date of our meetup to arrive, I decided to see what I could find about her online. Her Instagram profile was private. That shouldn't have surprised me. There was no way I was requesting access, so I abandoned that idea. Needing information, even though I wasn't sure what kind of information, but something to keep me from feeling I was going in blind, I searched for the University of Washington reunion website. It had been ten years since Raven and the others graduated. Not me, obviously. Of course, I hadn't received any information about the reunion because I wasn't invited. It did make me wonder if there was something subconscious that prompted me to plan a road trip to Washington State. I hadn't thought about the reunion or even the year and a third that I'd lived in the UW dorms. I'd been more focused on choosing historic hotels in California and Oregon. The logical path was to go all the way to the top of the country.

The reunion consisted of a weeklong blowout with fraternity and sorority open houses, a family picnic, and a golf tournament, ending with dinner and dancing at a lavish home on Lake Washington. The Greek open houses were truly that—open invitations to undergraduates, alumni from other years, prospective students, and even the ungraduated, like me. I laughed at the thought of seeing all those people again. I wondered if they'd even recognize me, if they remembered me at all. I clicked through to a page that displayed the class of 2012, their reunion attendance status posted below their graduation photo. Raven had marked herself as not attending. Her tiny status update told me nothing except she was married and loved her career. I scrolled through the pages—the smug face of Lance Mitchell stared back. Lance, Jane Stuart, Devon Craft and all the others displayed a status of not yet responded. I closed the page. I didn't want to think about any of them.

RAVEN and I met for wine and appetizers on a warm, bright evening in late July. We sat outdoors at an Italian restaurant in downtown Palo Alto.

She looked the same, but different. Her hair was still long, but it had some red highlights among the blond strands and was wavier than I remembered. She was thinner than me, possibly thinner than she'd been in college, and not in a completely healthy way. She wore a lot of mascara like she always had, but nothing on the rest of her nearly perfect skin.

We smiled at each other across the table as if we were meeting for a job interview. It was clear to me that she was taking the role of the applicant. That felt kind of good. After the way she'd hurt me, I liked knowing that she seemed to want to impress me a lot more than I wanted to impress her, which was not at all. She looked hopeful, as if she wanted me to start the conversation.

We both turned our attention to our menus. "Should we order wine?" I asked. "And some arancini?"

"Sure. Or maybe champagne." She looked up with an expression that was even more hopeful, but also slightly sad.

I laughed. "What are we celebrating?"

"Being together again."

I gave her a cool smile, signaled the server, and ordered two glasses of champagne and our appetizer. I scooted my chair another inch away from the table. "Obviously you saw that I'm divorced."

She nodded. "I'm really sorry to hear that."

"Don't be. I wasn't happy. Being married to someone who is always looking for a newer model is a lonely experience." I glanced at the rings on her left hand. "How long have you been married?"

She twisted her engagement ring from side to side. "Eight years. It seems like yesterday."

"Any kids?"

She shook her head, turning to look at people walking past on the sidewalk. Her attention remained there for several seconds, as if the two couples followed by a man walking his Lhasa Apso was the most thrilling event she'd seen all week. When she turned back, her eyes were teary. "I can't have kids. At least so far, and maybe never. Emmett says I shouldn't stress about it. We have plenty of time, but—"

"You do."

"We've been trying for four years. And they've done tests,

and there's nothing medically wrong." The tears grew thicker, but they didn't fall. "It's been hard on our marriage. Not divorce hard." She laughed nervously. "Just, there's this huge space between us, and it feels like it's getting wider and deeper every day." She blinked rapidly. "Sorry. You and I haven't seen each other for twelve years, and the first thing I do is dump out all my problems." She laughed again. "I'm a little raw. It doesn't take much to get me started. Sorry. Especially since I can't talk to Emmett about it anymore. He gets upset, a little angry. And I cry, which he doesn't like."

Our champagne was delivered. Raven raised her glass toward the center of the table, and I clicked mine against hers, waiting to hear what she considered an appropriate toast.

"To reconnecting," she said.

I smiled. "Cheers." I was withholding judgment on the reconnecting part.

"Anyway. It's hard. It consumes me. It affects my work, our marriage, our friendships. Emmett is upset about our sex life. He says it feels like he has to do it on demand. But he just doesn't understand that maternal longing. It hurts like..." She gasped, then took a quick sip of champagne.

"I get it."

She smiled, all that hope returning to her lips and eyes.

"I wanted kids," I said. "I still want them. But I assumed Dave did too. That's how it is when you're twenty, right? You don't know how complicated people are, how they can tell you things, but you don't realize they're not telling you everything. So you only think you know what's going on."

Raven nodded. The arancini arrived along with a bottle of Pellegrino Raven had asked for. The server poured some into two glasses half-filled with ice, thin slices of lemon clinging to the rims.

"That's hard," Raven said.

"It's for the best. He wasn't a good guy to have kids with, so I'm probably lucky. But I absolutely get how you feel. My heart squeezes up every time I see a baby or a little child. And I wonder...will I ever?"

She nodded, whipping her head up and down. I had a sudden spark of that feeling we'd had years ago. That feeling of knowing someone else on the planet gets how you feel. You don't have to explain, and you don't have to wonder if they're just pacifying you or not really listening. In that moment, I knew Raven and I felt the same thing, and that made me sort of glad she'd gotten in touch. Even though reconnecting, as she said, was going to take a lot more than a glass of champagne and knowing that we both lived with the same ache.

"Not having children is part of the fallout from having to drop out of school," I said. "It changed my whole life. I ended up in a job where I'm basically a go-fer. I got married too young because it seemed more interesting than my crap job, and now I'm divorced, and now I don't know if I'll be too old to have a child by the time I meet the right guy. I'm back at the starting line. All thanks to one single night."

"Do you think you'll move out of the area now that you're divorced? Or go back to school?"

I stared at her, wondering if anything I'd said made her feel guilty, or sorry, even. "It was so awful when Lily died. I hated looking at her bed every night after she was gone. It made me feel weird, like she might not really be dead and would be sleeping there when I woke in the morning."

Raven shivered at the image. "Remember how beautiful her eyes were? It was impossible not to look at them. They were mesmerizing. I always wondered if she had powers."

I laughed.

"That's what they say about people with two different eye colors, remember? Witch's eye."

"Don't go down that road. Please."

She took a sip of champagne and said nothing.

I was thankful for that. But I was also slightly unbalanced. It felt as if my head were mimicking the champagne, bubbles steadily rising to the surface and popping, creating a fizzing sensation as I tried to think about what she'd said. Raven was talking about Lily's eyes as if she'd loved them. It had been the opposite. We used to spend hours discussing those eyes and the effect they had on people. Raven was almost scared of them. I found them unsettling. You weren't sure where to look. I was always staring into her eyes, never able to relax. When you look at people whose eye color matches, you sometimes don't even pay attention to their eyes.

You were almost forced to look at Lily's eyes. They *made* you look. They were so unfamiliar. Surprising. Shocking.

"You and I had some crazy times," Raven said. "You were always my favorite person to party with. I didn't have as much fun after you were gone."

I smiled. It sounded as if she was not at all in an apologetic frame of mind. She almost acted as if we'd simply lost touch. She didn't seem to remember anything, and certainly didn't appear to be looking for an opportunity to offer an apology.

"I loved Sunday afternoons when we ate Doritos and Skittles and drank soda and talked and laughed and danced when a song we liked came up."

"Yeah." I swallowed the last of my champagne.

"Should we order another glass?" Raven asked.

I shrugged.

She laughed. "We can't leave already. We're just getting started. We have so much to catch up on, so many great memories."

"I'm mostly future-focused now. This is my do-over. The

first thing I need is to clear my head. Figure out who I am and what I want. I want to forget about the past."

"Are you in therapy?"

I laughed. "Nope. I'm taking a road trip."

"That sounds fun."

"There's a 1920s hotel in Ashland, Oregon, that I read about. And when I was a teenager, we worked on the stage sets for a Shakespeare festival at the Benbow Inn. We never got to go into the hotel. We stayed in a campground. The hotel is a little pricey, but it's also almost one hundred years old and really beautiful. So I'll stay at both those places. I'm still working out the rest."

"Sounds nice."

"I rented a BMW convertible."

She laughed. "A midlife crisis."

"Absolutely not. I'm not anywhere near midlife." I took a few sips of water.

"I'd love to go on a road trip with you," Raven said.

I tried to smile over my shock. I glanced toward the street. I wasn't sure if she was serious, and I wasn't sure how I felt about it if she was. It was my turn to change the subject. "Why aren't you going to the reunion?"

"The *family* picnic? The dinner where everyone passes their phones around, filled with baby pictures and cute kid videos? All the girls I knew who are pregnant with their first? I can't handle that. Maybe I'm weak. Maybe I'm too full of self-pity and small-minded when I should be happy for others, I don't know, but I just can't. It hurts too bad."

I nodded. "It's hard when it's right in your face. I didn't think about that part of it, since I'm not invited." I laughed. "But don't you want to go and show Carter how happy you are?"

She gave me an angry look. "I don't need to prove my happiness to Carter. I never even think about him anymore."

"Okay." That was probably a good thing. It had been more than a decade, but she'd been so crazy in love with him and *so* broken up when he dumped her, I thought there might be a small part of her that wanted to show him she was doing great.

"Although, it might be cleansing to visit the open house where she—" Raven picked up her champagne glass and took a long, almost gulping swallow.

"That would be weird," I said. "But also...maybe we should go anonymously to some of the open houses. After, we could stay in a swanky hotel and have our own party. The divorced dropout and the infertile graduate." I laughed, maybe harder than I should have.

"Does that mean I'm invited?" Raven asked.

I picked up my champagne glass and held it between us, letting my eyes focus on the bubbles. Did I want her coming along? The idea of doing whatever I pleased was part of what made me decide to take a road trip. But having another person is always more fun. And it was still my trip, so I didn't think she would make a lot of demands. "Sure. Why not?"

"Thank you. That makes me so happy." She gave me a watery smile. "This is just what I need. We'll have an awesome time. I won't feel so alone in my nonpregnant state."

I smiled. I ate the last arancini half, chewing slowly, thinking about my own non-baby limbo. It's an empty feeling that's difficult to describe.

"You know what would be fun," Raven said. "What if you went to the official reunion dinner as me? Dye your hair. Change your makeup." She giggled.

"Why?"

"You can talk to people you used to know and make them feel bad for turning against you. But they won't know it's you." She giggled again.

I stared at her. Was this the extent of her awareness? That

other people had *turned against me*? I could pretend to be her and make them feel bad? It sounded like something two high school girls would come up with. It also sounded like she was clueless about what my life had been like back then. But I'd already known that.

"How much do I owe for my half of the car?" Raven asked. "And I need the dates for the hotels so I can book my room."

I pulled out my credit card and gestured at our server. "Don't worry about that. You can share my room. I already reserved the car, so it's money already spent."

"I can't—"

"Honestly. I'm serious. My ex-husband might have hurt me in more ways than you can imagine, but he isn't stingy. I'm in a good position, and I'm happy to pay." It was the truth. Sharing the trip with her made me feel less like I needed something from her and more like I was in charge. All those years ago, I'd felt absolutely powerless. Everyone blamed me for Lily's death when it was nothing but a tragic accident. That was what the police said—too much alcohol, topped off with Ecstasy. But thanks to vicious rumors, all lies, it somehow became my fault.

There were so many worse injustices in the world, but this was my injustice, and it felt earth-shattering.

4

LILY'S JOURNAL
SEPTEMBER 13, 2010

The minute I stepped into my new dorm room and saw my roommates sprawled on the beds closest to the window, already claiming the best dressers and desks with their possessions, I knew how things were going to go. They didn't bother to introduce themselves or apologize for not waiting for me before deciding who got what. It turned out they had been lucky enough to share one of the double rooms the year before, and they were BFFs. Gag.

The next thing they did, which was not a shock, since it had happened to me a thousand, maybe ten thousand, times before, was they stared at me without bothering to hide their reaction to my eyes. They were freaked out.

One hazel. One blue. It's something I can't hide unless I wear dark glasses twenty-four seven. All my life, I've been *lucky* enough to notice as people smile and say *hi* to me as they do to everyone else, and then watch the look of shock freeze their faces. When their expressions unfreeze, either curiosity, fascination, or revulsion remains. My new roommates are in the last category.

As I lifted boxes off the dolly, stacking them near the foot of my bed, I decided to be the bigger person. I introduced myself. They told me their names, then glanced at each other with an unspoken wariness. I ignored the unsubtle exchange and asked what they were majoring in. They both said marketing and PR. How cute. They didn't ask me what I was studying. I had to tell them it was forensic entomology.

They wanted to know what entomology was, which told me a lot about them.

When I told them it was the study of insects, they let out identical, theatrical shrieks. One of them, I forget which one, said, "That is so, *so* disgusting."

The other one said, "What does forensics have to do with insects?"

I knew they weren't going to like my answer, but there was no reason not to creep them out further and enjoy watching them squirm. It's the only choice sometimes. "Forensic entomologists observe the developmental stages of arthropods in decomposed cadavers. It helps investigators solve crimes by giving an accurate time of death."

"Oh my God. That's revolting. I feel like I'm going to puke."

In that moment, I decided to rename them—Roach One and Roach Two. As I'd learned when I was ten years old and my cousin read my diary, then told my other cousin what I'd written about her, it's safer not to name names in a journal. Even though I keep my journal safely hidden, you never know.

The names are fitting. I'm fascinated by bugs of all kinds, and young roaches are called nymphs because they don't change much as they mature. Which was clearly the case with these two. And a nymph is also a beautiful young woman. I'm smiling as I write this. It always helps me deal with stupid people when I put them in a category and catalogue them in my mind. It makes me feel like I'm in control, even if they're being awful to me, even when I know I'm not in control.

I knew then that things were not going to get better, but I hoped that if I kept to myself and didn't touch their things and didn't try to pretend we were friends, or even expect them to be polite to me, it would work out okay.

Instead, it's already worse. When Roach Two saw me writing in my journal, she laughed and said, "Are you twelve, writing about the meanies in your secret diary?"

I gave her a snarly glance. At least she had the awareness to look sorry for saying it, but she didn't apologize. After that, I decided I'll only write in here when they're both out of the room. Besides, I can think better when I'm alone and they aren't playing music or talking their heads off about this or that guy or the next party. Their ratio of parties to classes, based on how much they talk about it, is five to one. Maybe six to one. Ha ha. Insects have six legs. I love my little bug analogies.

Roaches One and Two are in college to party. Obviously, lots of kids are in college to party, but I've never spent so much time around that type. I've never seen up close how they live day-to-day. I can't get my head around it. They're disgusted by insects, which are incredibly complex creatures, upon whom our lives depend because they keep nature in balance. I'm disgusted by their deliberate destruction of their bodies. Especially their brains. Maybe that's why they say such ridiculous things. Didn't they learn in high school health class that alcohol affects the function of their brain cells? Why do so many people not care about that at all? Especially supposedly smart people who are in college?

Of course, they think that makes *me* the freak. But what is the point of being a human being if you spend all the years you're supposed to be acquiring knowledge ripping out pieces of your brain until your thoughts are on a level with insects?

Last night, the Roaches came crashing into our room at two in the morning. They didn't care if I needed to get up early to work on a paper. They laughed and talked nonsense, which made them laugh harder, as if they were the cleverest comedians of all time. They danced without music, shaking and twisting themselves around like pole dancers. I'm not a prude, but I was raised to respect myself and my body. They just want to *go crazy*. Party. I know this because they say it every weekend, as if it's some brilliant new idea.

Guys come into our room all the time. Roaches One and Two never ask if I want all these guys in our room. They sit around on Saturdays and drink beer and talk. I try to study with my headphones on, but they're so loud, I can still hear them. And it gets so hot in here. Dorm rooms are not designed for seven or eight people to throw a party. If I leave the room to pee, Roach One flops on my bed. When I come back, she rolls around like she's having sex. When I try to get her to move off my bed, she opens her eyes really wide, like bug eyes. Yesterday, she said, "Maybe I should get a green contact lens and look freaky like you. Then all the guys would be staring at me all the time like they stare at you."

I'm not aware of any guys staring at me. Mostly they don't talk to me unless they find out I'm studying forensic entomology. They're really interested in that. But they only like it because they think it's creepy.

After two weeks of school, I asked to be moved to a different room, but I was informed that part of the college experience is learning to get along with people who aren't like you. And besides, there's a waiting list for all the dorms, so I should be happy I have a spot.

Also, I don't like writing this, but I'm human, and the point of my journal is to tell the truth. They make me feel left out. Sometimes, it really hurts. A lot.

5

RAVEN

Going on a road trip with Abbey, spending twelve days with just the two of us, felt like a dream. I'd thought about her so much over the years, it was strange seeing her in the flesh. She looked about the same—super-straight hair the color of espresso, huge dark blue eyes, and the kind of breasts that attracted guys. Sometimes more than she wanted, as she used to remind me when we were nineteen.

Hearing her voice was almost like hearing my own voice. That sounds impossible, but it's how I felt. Her voice was a part of me, and even during all those years when we were estranged, when I had a decision to make, I imagined talking it over with her. I felt like I still knew how she thought. Of course, that wasn't true at all. I had no clue what was going on inside her head now that we were adults. I hoped I would find out on our trip.

Taking two weeks off work would be good for me. Nearly two weeks away from Emmett, two weeks when I didn't have to track my ovulation, avoid alcohol, or study more articles about natural methods to help me conceive. The thought of it made me blissful. It was a vacation from my current self. I could be who I used to be—ready for fun, not worried or anxious or sad, just free.

As we drove across the Golden Gate Bridge, headed north, the roof of the car was down. The sun was out, and there was a light, warm breeze because the temperature in San Francisco was an unusually warm eighty-two degrees. There was a lot of traffic on the bridge, so we were going about thirty. Even so, the wind whipped our hair across our faces whenever a strand broke free of our ponytails.

Basking in the sunlight, feeling her presence beside me, I was having a hard time believing all this was real.

Abbey had started a playlist of alternative rock. We hadn't talked much. Abbey said she liked to think while she was driving. It was her trip, so I didn't argue. I was already a little uncomfortable with her paying for everything. It made me feel like she was in charge, but I tried not to dwell on that. She was being nice, generous. That was all. I didn't need to make something dark out of it.

I reached over and turned the music down slightly.

"Why did you turn it down?" Abbey put on her blinker and slipped into the lane to our left, which was going about one mile an hour faster than we were.

"I wanted to thank you for inviting me on the trip."

"Don't keep thanking me. It's annoying."

"I'm just so grateful."

"Okay. Awesome."

"It was a brilliant idea to take a road trip. Getting away from your usual experiences gives you such a different perspective."

"It does."

She didn't turn the music up, which I was glad about. Just because she was paying didn't mean she got to have everything her way. What fun would that be anyway? Part of having another person along is working out your plans together. Surely, she knew that.

I hated feeling like I owed her, but she'd refused to let me pay for anything. We were going to book flights home when we got to Seattle, and she was paying for that too. Waiting to book our flights meant we weren't locked into a schedule, although I did have to be back at work in just over two weeks, and I didn't really want to spend all my time off on the road trip. After it was over, a weekend for Emmett and me would be nice too.

"I'm so lucky I'm one of the top performers at Richardson PR," I said. "They had no problem giving me two weeks on the spur of the moment. They don't want to lose me, so they give me a lot of freedom."

Abbey didn't say anything. I wondered if she'd heard me.

After a few minutes, she said, "Some of us never had a chance to pursue a dream career where your boss values you and gives you all the flexibility you want."

"You got time off from work."

"Not the point."

"What is the point?"

"I should have had the same career as you. I should be at the top of my company." She said this in a very catty voice.

"It's not my fault you dropped out."

She didn't say anything more.

Once we were across the bridge and winding our way past Sausalito, she turned up the volume. Was she going to sulk now? I didn't remember her being that way in college. She was so friendly from the moment I met her. She liked to go with the flow. Everyone loved her, until they didn't, of course. But that part wasn't her fault. In our freshman year, she'd kind of taken me under her wing. That makes me sound weak, but it wasn't that. It's just that growing up with a mother whose family and friends were all members of a witches' coven didn't give me a lot of skills in the friend-making arena.

I turned the volume down again. "I'm sorry you decided to quit school. It's so terrible what happened to you."

"Yup."

I decided it was best to change the subject. It would be easier to get her laughing again if we talked about the trip. "I've never been to the Benbow Inn."

She warmed up immediately. "You'll absolutely love it. We have a suite overlooking the river. It's so peaceful, but there's also a lot going on. There's an amazing outdoor patio for eating. Live music. They have an awesome bar that feels like you're walking into the 1920s."

"I checked the links you sent. It looks amazing."

She turned up the volume again. About twenty minutes later we hit stop-and-go traffic. I didn't need to turn the volume down for her to hear me now. "It already feels good to not be thinking about babies every minute of the day."

"Party time, right?" Abbey said.

"Definitely."

Abbey tipped her head back slightly, looking at the sky, letting the breeze brush across her face.

"I should tell you, I told a little white lie to Emmett," I said.

"Oh?"

She didn't look at me, but she smiled, like we were co-conspirators.

"I told him I'm visiting my mom."

"Why?"

It was complicated, and I wasn't sure how much I wanted to tell her. But she needed to know what I'd told him, in case there was an emergency or something like that. If he called at the wrong time, she would need to know she had to be quiet. I didn't want to tell her all the reasons I'd lied, but the main reason was that Emmett had no idea who Abbey Parker was. He didn't know the names of my college roommates or anything about my first two years of college at all. He never asked, and I never volunteered. I kept the stories I told him about school focused on the sorority I joined in my junior year. "He thinks I need to relax about getting pregnant, and then it will happen. If I told him I need to clear my head or need a change of scenery, he wouldn't understand. It would make him feel bad." I laughed. "And annoyed."

Abbey nodded.

"Don't judge me."

"I'm not. I mean, someday, I want the kind of marriage where we're totally open with each other. But I know that's hard to find."

"I have a great marriage. I adore Emmett. And he loves me so much. But wanting to have a baby has been hard on us. I tell him everything, but with this—"

"You don't need to explain."

I still felt I did, but I wasn't going to. Although we both felt cheated out of having children, so far, our situations were completely different. Starting with, I adored my husband. He didn't cheat on me, and he didn't treat me like his PA. Emmett was sweet and incredibly devoted to me. Thinking about him made my heart melt.

The traffic cleared, and she started driving fast, obviously loving the wind and the feel of that fancy little car buzzing along wide, recently paved, gently undulating roads that were ideal for a sports car.

We reached the Benbow Inn just before three o'clock, right at check-in time.

Before she drove up the curving drive toward the entrance, Abbey stopped the car. She jumped out and took a picture on her phone, the hotel looking stately and massive behind her. She got back in the car and continued up the drive. I felt a little hurt that she didn't want to take a photo with me to remember our trip, but maybe it was too soon. After all that time, we needed time to reconnect. That was the whole reason we were here. It was going to be an awesome trip, and I wouldn't sour it with hurt feelings.

We checked in and were shown to our suite. It was stunning, with two queen beds, windows that actually opened, unlike a lot of modern hotels, and solid, elegantly classic furniture. The plan was to spend three nights here, so we took the time to put our clothes in the dressers and hang nice tops and jackets in the closet. Abbey said she wanted a catnap, so I went out to walk along the river while she slept.

Later, we went to the lobby for the complimentary wine and cheese served on antique marble-topped tables. The side doors were open to the dining patio with gardens and redwood trees beyond, allowing guests to wander in and out. We each got a glass of red wine and went outside, where we found a table at the edge of the garden.

Abbey went back inside for a plate of appetizers, and I pulled out my phone. There were two messages from Emmett. I responded to both, telling him my mom was doing well and clicking a thumbs-up on his *I hope you're relaxing*. I opened Instagram for a quick check. Nothing specific drew me to look at the stream of photos, but it was such a habit, I did it almost without realizing what I was doing. Always craving something new. Maybe that was all it was.

Right at the top of my feed was a picture of Abbey smiling and looking gorgeous in front of the Benbow Inn. Her caption said, *Our road trip begins! Let the good times roll*. Already she'd received over four hundred likes and fifteen comments.

Abbey returned to our table, and I slid my phone into my purse. I took a sip of wine. "You posted your photo on Instagram."

"I did." She smeared blue cheese on a flatbread cracker.

"I didn't think about...is that safe?"

"Safe?" She laughed.

"People know your condo is empty. Someone could break in. I read you should be careful about posting when you're clearly not at home."

"No one from Instagram is going to break into my condo."

"It just seems risky."

"That's what social media is. You risk exposing a bit of yourself, and that leads to making connections."

"Okay, but I don't want anyone to know I'm on this trip. I told Emmett and my manager I was—"

"I know what you told them. That's why I didn't include you in the picture."

I took a few sips of wine. I didn't want any of the cheese or even a grape. My stomach felt queasy. I knew for sure it wasn't the queasiness I longed for because my period was just ending. "I know it sounds paranoid, but it makes me worry that Emmett might somehow find out I lied."

Abbey laughed. She laughed so hard I thought she was going to knock over her glass of wine. "Are you serious? How on earth would he find out?"

"I said it was paranoid." I tried to laugh with her, but it sounded fake.

"Yes, it is."

"Why do you have to post about our trip?"

"I don't *have* to post. I like sharing my life."

"Will you please not post any more during the road trip? I know it's impossible he would see it. He's never even met you." I stopped before telling her he didn't know she existed. It was over-the-top paranoid, but when you're keeping something hidden, you can't be too careful.

"Does he even know I exist?"

"Of course he does." I ate a grape, hoping it would settle

my stomach. "I just don't want to take any chances. I don't feel good about lying to him. It was necessary, but I don't like it."

She must have noticed that my voice caught in my throat. She gave me a smile that might have been understanding, might have been full of pity, I wasn't sure. "No worries. I won't post anything else during our trip."

"Thanks."

She took a long swallow of wine and looked out toward the trees on the hill that sloped down to the riverbank. It seemed like there was a chill in the air, but the sun was still above the trees, the air still heavy with late summer heat, so it wasn't that.

6

ABBEY

Except for Raven's crazy paranoia, we had a decent afternoon drinking wine on the patio. For dinner, we got dressed up, high heels and all. The evening air was warm, almost sultry. Dinner music was provided by a local jazz group that made you feel like it wasn't necessary to talk, the volume just loud enough to keep the silence from feeling awkward. I liked that. I'd realized I needed more time to adjust to the reality of Raven back in my life. I didn't want to talk every single minute, digging through each other's lives like sand crabs. The purpose of the trip was to revel in freedom from my previous life, without lots of baggage. There was something about Raven that made me feel heavy, chained down at times.

It had been a long, slightly stressful day. I'd expected a relaxing drive out of the bay area, crossing the glorious Golden Gate, flying toward the calm of the northern California redwoods. I thought I'd managed to let go of my need for an apology. I thought I was focused on the trip, but Raven had triggered me with the humble brag about her job. She was so valued she could take time off whenever she felt like it.

No begging and bargaining. No lying about a vague medical issue that required several lengthy tests so two weeks off were *unavoidable*.

Maybe it was an illusion, but I knew that when you had a successful career, you weren't handcuffed to a boss the way I'd been ever since I walked off the University of Washington campus for the last time. I had been only nineteen, feeling lost and more alone than I'd ever imagined possible, and not well-prepared for adult life.

It was all because I was the unfortunate person who found Lily Mitchell's body.

The luck of the draw. Circumstances unfolded around me because I'd been the one who decided it was time to leave the party. Raven wasn't doing all that well. She'd rushed to the downstairs bathroom, telling me to get our coats, thanking me for dragging her out of the frat house and back to our dorm.

It had already been a strange night.

Our misfit roommate had shown up at the party. Until that night, Lily hadn't gone to a single party. When kids came to our room, she made it clear that even those little groups were too much partying for her. She looked down her nose at the beers we opened, getting unbelievably upset if we teased her even a little bit.

I never knew why she went to the party that night. I'd been dancing with a guy I'd just met when I noticed her. She was watching me. The only difference was, this time she didn't have that disapproving look all over her face. She seemed relaxed. She was smiling and obviously a little tipsy, which I thought at the time was good for her. For once, she was going to let go and have some fun instead of acting as if she were the only person in the world who understood the potential dangers of alcohol, never understanding that drinking was fun if you didn't overdo it. She was too much sometimes.

While Raven was in the bathroom, I went upstairs to the room where we'd dumped our purses and coats, scarves and hats, because in November it was getting pretty cold at night. At that time of year in the northwest, night came early. So at one o'clock in the morning, it felt more like 3 a.m. because the sun had been down for nearly eleven hours and seemed to have forgotten her promise of reappearing.

The room was dark when I stepped inside. There was no light switch on the wall near the door. The only table lamp was on the other side of the bed, so I left the door open, thinking I could find our coats and purses with the light from the hallway. The room smelled like vomit, which made me feel sick myself. Someone must have been rushing to leave, digging for their coat, and lost it before they could make it down the length of the landing and around the corner to one of the upstairs bathrooms. I tried not to breathe through my nose and kicked the door open wider to let in more light and clean air.

I'd underestimated the amount of winter clothing and large purses that fifty or sixty college kids brought to a party. I felt like I was digging through a dumpster, looking for something I'd accidentally thrown away. The stink of vomit that I wasn't successfully avoiding did not help.

I found Raven's purse right away. My purse was on the floor near the nightstand, where it must have fallen off the bed because my hairbrush and a tube of lip gloss had spilled out. I picked it up and felt through the bag to make sure my wallet was still there.

I started grabbing coats and sweatshirts, tossing them to the side, turning to hold them up to the light to check the color as I looked for Raven's green wool coat and my pink jacket. I thought my jacket would stand out, but apparently a lot more girls than I'd realized had pink jackets or sweatshirts.

Finally, I found Raven's coat. I placed it on top of our purses near the door and started throwing stuff with more force, frustrated because I wanted to get away from that awful smell, and it shouldn't have been so hard to find a jacket. I realized I was digging through the same pieces of clothing over and over.

Then I saw a cowboy boot. I knew immediately it was Lily's because the leatherwork was black and red. No one else had boots like that. I wasn't sure I'd ever seen anyone but Lily wearing cowboy boots on campus. It seemed strange she would have taken off her boots. I tried to remember if she'd been wearing them when I'd seen her from the dance floor, but it had been that blissful look on her face that had grabbed my attention. I couldn't have said what she was wearing, much less what was on her feet.

I threw a few coats to the side and saw my pink jacket wedged under the cowboy boot. Finally. I grabbed the boot to toss it aside, but it didn't move. It felt like there was something solid inside. I pushed more coats out of the way, realizing as I dug that the boot must be on her foot. She'd passed out and was half-buried in coats. She was the cause of the reeking vomit that was now making me gag.

"Lily, wake up." I shook her leg gently. "Lily!"

There wasn't even a groan or the sound of snoring.

I stood up from where I'd been leaning across the bed and went around to the other side. I switched on the bedside lamp, wondering why it had seemed like too much work to take a few steps around the bed in order to provide more light for my search.

Turning back to the bed, I saw that her right arm was dangling over the side. Then my attention moved to her face.

I screamed, a long, loud wailing, followed by hysterical

shrieks. I felt vomit swirling in my own stomach. I spun around as alcohol and half-digested potato chips and cookies spilled out of me onto the carpet. I spit out the rest of it, not caring about the mess on the floor.

Lily's eyes, one hazel, one blue, were staring at me, empty of life. Now that my stomach had cleared itself, I screamed again, the sounds pouring out of me. It felt like I screamed forever.

ALL OF THIS came back to me, passing through my mind like a movie sped up ten times, while Raven studied the menu and tried to decide what she wanted for dinner. I grabbed my wineglass and took a long swallow of cold Pinot Gris. It felt good going down. It wiped my memories clean and helped me focus on my dinner selection. Being around Raven had invited the memory of that horrible night to shove its way to the front of my mind. It was something I hadn't thought about in such vivid detail for years. I hated that it was tormenting me now. I took another sip of wine.

After a few glasses of wine, dinner became a pleasant escape into the music and amazing food. We didn't talk much, letting the music wash over us. Things felt easy. Maybe we were getting back in sync.

After dinner, we hung out in the lounge for a while. "Should we check out the bar?" I asked, trying to drag Raven's attention away from a half-completed jigsaw puzzle set up on one of the game tables. She was holding two pieces in her hand, eyeing the design.

She placed the puzzle pieces on the table without figuring out where they belonged, and yawned. "I'm really tired."

"It's only nine thirty," I said.

She shrugged. "I'm tired. What can I say?"

"Just one drink?"

"Not tonight."

"Do you want to see the bar? It's really cool."

"I saw the pictures online."

"Well, I'm going to have a drink. I'll see you in an hour or so."

"I'll be asleep." She stepped closer and gave me a light hug.

When she was gone, I walked slowly toward the bar, excited to see whom I might meet, wondering what drink I should order. Going in alone was no different from what I'd originally planned. It didn't matter that Raven was ready to sleep so early on our first night. It was as if she'd never joined me on the trip. I was free to meet whomever the universe dropped onto the seat beside me.

Most of the tables were occupied by groups of two or three. Only five people sat at the bar. I took a stool in the center and ordered a Manhattan. While I waited for my drink, I glanced to the side. To my left were two women having a very intense conversation. On the other side of me was a guy with dark hair and a mustache. He was drinking some kind of whiskey without ice. He wore a sport coat and a white shirt with jeans.

Feeling my not too subtle attention on him, he turned. He gave me a smile that wasn't at all predatory and returned to tapping at his phone, which was lying on the bar.

My drink came, and I shifted my position on the stool, wanting to look more approachable, wanting someone to toast with, but he was still staring at his phone. I whispered cheers inside my head and took a sip. I turned and looked around the room behind me. There was a huge fireplace near the door where I'd entered, with old books and some copper vases arranged on the mantel. Turning back, I admired the dark wood framing the bar itself in a series of arches with intricate carvings. The craftsmanship of every detail felt old and filled with history, yet modernized enough to make it sleek and classy.

I took another sip of my drink, then turned again to the area behind me, hoping I wasn't looking too squirmy. I had the prickling sensation someone was watching me. I glanced around the room, but no one was looking my way. The sensation must have been the result of sitting alone, feeling conspicuous and hyperconscious of my body. I resisted the urge to take another sip of my drink because I didn't want to slurp it down too fast.

I took a slow, calming breath and spoke to the guy with the mustache. "Are you checking work email or just browsing social media?"

He looked up. He smiled and clicked his phone. The screen went dark. "Busted. It's work." He raised his glass toward me. "Cheers. I'm supposed to be relaxing. Why does work have such an ability to suck us into it?"

"I think it's FOMO."

He laughed. "Could be."

"I'm Abbey."

"Dirk. What brings you to the historic Benbow Inn?" he asked.

"Road trip. With an old college friend. What about you?"

"My sister's wedding was Sunday afternoon. I'm heading back to San Francisco first thing tomorrow."

"So you need to get back up to speed."

"Sad to say, I've checked it all weekend, not just tonight." He took another sip of his drink.

He wasn't wearing a wedding ring, and he was absolutely warming to me, so I figured he'd come alone for the wedding. As we talked, the creeping feeling started up again, like ants in my spine, whispering that someone was staring at me. I turned again. No one. The longer Dirk talked, the more the feeling grew until I had to force myself not to look every few seconds. When I did check, I never caught anyone even half-glancing in my direction, but the feeling was overwhelming. Finally, after a second Manhattan, it started to fade. But by then, I'd formed a habit of looking around the room every time I took a sip of my drink, hoping I wasn't giving Dirk the impression I was scouting for a better opportunity.

Dirk looked like he was about ten years older than me. He worked in high tech but was cagey about revealing the name of his company. We talked through three Manhattans and three shots of whiskey. Mostly he talked—telling stories of all the places he'd traveled around the world. I found myself slipping into the person I'd been when I met my ex-husband, the wide-eyed inexperienced girl listening to someone else's tales.

He was very cute. He leaned slightly closer with each drink, and soon our knees were brushing against each other under the bar. Then his hand was on my leg. Then mine was on his.

"A fourth round seems a little excessive," he said.

"I agree."

He moved toward me and kissed me gently. It was so nice. I felt warm and soft and noticed. His kiss wasn't hungry and demanding. Just...perfect.

"How about a drink in my room?"

"That sounds very nice."

He paid for our drinks. I thanked him, and we walked out of the bar. I resisted the urge to look back, even though the desire was quite strong.

In his room, he opened a bottle of champagne, courtesy of the wedding party. We drank a glass, then moved slowly and inevitably toward the bed. He was a much better lover than my ex, which I shouldn't have been thinking about, but I couldn't help it. The comparison was there, uninvited. We drifted to sleep with our legs wrapped around each other. I woke an hour later to hear him snoring softly.

I got out of bed. The champagne was still sitting in icy water, so I poured a bit into my glass. Taking a sip, I wandered around the room, checking out the bathroom and closet, studying his things, trying to figure out what they said about him. I opened his suitcase on the closet floor. Going through his things was way out of line, but there was something about all the alcohol I'd consumed and the anonymity and the very unsettling situation of being on a road trip with a woman I hardly knew that had shifted my brain to a different place, separating it from its usual boundaries. I considered whether I should take a souvenir to help me remember him. The temptation was so strong, I knew I couldn't fight it.

He was snoring more heavily now and had turned his back toward the room. I got dressed and wrote a note on the pad of paper on the nightstand. I left it on my pillow, telling him he was just what I needed and thanking him again for the drinks. I didn't sign my name.

When I opened the door to my room, all the lights were on. Raven was sitting up in bed, her arms folded across her chest. "It's two a.m.! Where were you?"

"I told you I was going to the bar."

"For five hours?"

"Four and a half. And I wasn't there the whole time." I gave her a satisfied grin.

"I know. I went down there to look for you."

I laughed.

"It seems like you've forgotten the purpose of this trip," Raven said.

"I haven't forgotten at all. The purpose is to celebrate my freedom and make up for lost time. I did that. And I'll continue celebrating."

"I thought we were hoping to reconnect with each other."

"The two aren't mutually exclusive."

"It's crazy to go have sex with some guy you don't know."

"It is. But life is risky if you want to experience everything you can."

"It's better not to experience some things. Especially the repercussions of sex with a total stranger."

"Okay, Mom." I shoved my purse into the shelf of my nightstand, conscious of its bulk with my souvenir buried inside. I wouldn't tell Raven about it. She was wound up enough. I went into the bathroom, brushed my teeth and hair and washed my face. Changing into a cropped T-shirt and stretchy shorts, I climbed into bed and turned out the light. "Can you get the other lights?"

"That's it? You don't think we should talk about this?"

I turned on my side, my back toward her side of the room. "I'm tired. I planned this trip to have fun. That's all I want. I hope you want the same."

I didn't say any more and neither did she, but I fell asleep before she turned out the other lights.

7

RAVEN

When Abbey came back to our room at two o'clock in the morning, the smell of a man's cologne and alcohol along with a light aroma of sweat was bleeding off her. In that moment, I realized we were not going to return to how we used to be as easily as I'd hoped. She was more troubled than I'd thought. She'd been deeply damaged by what those kids did in college—refusing to talk to her, treating her like a murderer.

At the time, I thought she needed to be stronger. That she should stick it out and not let them get to her. Instead, she allowed them to force her to drop out of school. I didn't see why she would let a bunch of people, most of whom she hardly knew, do that to her. I tried to talk her into staying in school. I even half-suggested we could move out of the dorm and rent an apartment, although I knew I couldn't afford that, and I doubted she could. She'd also grown up with a single mom, and usually when it's just you and your mom, money does not flow like a river through your life.

After breakfast, Abbey said she had a headache and was

going to lie down for an hour. I wasn't surprised by the headache. She didn't seem surprised either.

I changed into hiking shoes and went out for a walk along the river. Following many years of drought, the Eel River was more like the Eel Creek or Eel Stream. Still, it burbled nicely over rocks, and there was a wide pebbled shore on each side, and an embankment covered with trees, which kept the air cool.

I walked west, setting the exercise app on my phone so I could check how many miles I went.

It was quiet except for the birds calling to each other and the sound of water flowing beside me. I felt peaceful and so glad that I'd come on this trip, even if things between Abbey and me weren't as smooth as they could be. It would get better once we got used to each other, once we went hiking and shopping and ate together at lots of interesting restaurants. The next time she wanted to go out for a drink in the evening, I would join her.

After walking for almost two miles, I turned back. Now that it was close to noon, the trees no longer provided as much shade. I wiped the back of my hand across my forehead, and it came away damp. Making my way through the thick ground covering of pebbles, I thought about taking off my shoes and socks and cooling my feet in the clear, gurgling stream. As I stood looking at the water, trying to decide if a few minutes of feeling the water lapping at my toes would be worth trying to yank socks over wet feet, I heard the crunch of someone walking on stones.

I turned. A man stood near an outcropping of rocks where the stream curved, leaning against the boulders. His head was shaved clean, and his skin was tanned with a leathery quality that was obvious even from that distance. He was tall and lean with lots of well-defined muscles. He didn't wave or acknowledge me, but stared right at me.

I turned and walked with more purpose. He hadn't done anything threatening, but it felt unsettling knowing he was back there, that he might have been standing there for a while, and that he was now watching every slight misstep that caused me to stumble on the loose stones. I tried to take longer strides, but I didn't want him to notice and think he'd scared me. I wasn't sure why. It wasn't as if he were a wild animal and I needed to be sure he couldn't smell my fear, to avoid prompting an attack.

Knowing he'd been watching me, it didn't seem smart to turn and see if he was still there, giving more evidence of fear. Why was I so concerned that he not know I was afraid? Why *was* I so afraid? He hadn't done anything. It felt like a lifetime of conditioning and bad experiences were controlling me, silencing any rational thoughts. I wanted to cry.

I walked faster, moving closer to the embankment, which gave me a moment to turn naturally and look. He was still there. Still watching. He hadn't shifted his position near the boulders even a fraction of an inch. Now I started walking so fast, I was tripping and stumbling, grabbing overhanging branches to keep from falling, no longer caring what he might be thinking.

The next time I turned, he was gone. I felt the tension slide out of my shoulders along with a bead of sweat that oozed down my back. I wiped my forehead again and continued walking as fast as I could. Why had I let him spoil my peaceful walk? I was angry at myself for letting a simple glance upset me so completely.

I walked up the trail that led to the lower garden of the hotel. As I turned to take the steps up to the patio, I saw the same man. He was sitting on a bench among a cluster of flowering trees, looking at me. As I stared back at him, he stood and walked along the path and through one of the side doors of the hotel. He was a guest? Or trespassing? Could this be the guy Abbey had had sex with?

I hurried up the steps and went into the lounge. He wasn't there.

When I opened the door to our room, Abbey was on the floor, doing yoga. She wore black exercise shorts and a black sports bra, her hair wrapped into a tight bun at the very top of her head. I was impressed by her skill. She'd obviously been practicing a while.

She ended her complicated pose and sat up straight, crossing her legs into the lotus pose. "How was your walk?"

"Nice, until the end."

She stood and stretched her arms overhead.

I sat on the chair near the door and began to untie my shoes. "What did the guy you had sex with look like?"

"Why?" She laughed. "Did you hook up instead of walking?"

"No. This creep was staring at me. He came out of nowhere and was standing near some rocks, just watching me. Every time I turned around, he was still there. He didn't move or come toward me, just stared."

"Did you ask him what he wanted?"

"He was quite a way away."

"Maybe he was just surprised to see someone else down by the river."

"When I got back to the hotel, he was sitting in the garden."

She shrugged and undid her bun, letting her hair fall around her shoulders and arms.

"So what did your guy look like?"

"He left this morning."

"How do you know?"

"He told me."

"That doesn't mean anything. He might have lied."

"He had dark hair and a mustache." She bent over and shook her hair. "He's very cute."

I wasn't sure if it made me feel better or worse that it wasn't the same guy. "Okay. Then this wasn't him. But you need to be more careful. Are you planning to have more hookups on this trip?"

"I'm not planning anything except the hotels where we're staying. And having fun. I do plan to have a lot of fun. And meet new people."

"It's dangerous to have sex with someone you don't know."

"People do it all the time. And I'm not naïve. I listen to my gut."

"What if that guy has dangerous friends? If nothing else, maybe they think the women in this room are hot to jump into bed."

Abbey laughed. "I doubt that. It's not like there's a bulletin board in the lounge announcing who's slutty."

"It's not funny. This guy was very intense and scary. If he saw you go into Dirk's room..."

"Okay. Yeah, it was probably a little irresponsible of me. Maybe I shouldn't be so open to any guy who clicks with me, but you don't seem to get how lonely it is to be married to a man who doesn't want you. It guts you. And every so often, I think about all the things I wanted but never had...I've lost ten years of my life to a guy who wasn't into *me*. This is pretty much my last shot at enjoying how men notice me."

"I just think you should be careful."

"I don't want to be careful. What's wrong with a little fun, with feeling the attention of men after being shoved in the corner for all those years?"

I tried to look sympathetic because that was honestly what I felt. But she was risking a lot. "You can't get back what you lost with a one-night stand. Besides, I thought this trip was supposed to be about girlfriends, about getting back what we had, right?"

Abbey shrugged, but she didn't argue with me.

"We never let guys get between us when we were in college," I said. "Remember how free we felt? How we talked about keeping our power? My husband doesn't even know where I am. Maybe we should declare this a guy-free zone." I heard the words come out of my mouth, sounding a little contrived. I knew how ridiculous and probably self-serving they sounded, especially after what she'd said about how it felt to be rejected. But, they were out there, so hopefully she would understand what I was trying to say.

"I'm not going to invite a guy to our room or to eat dinner with us, if that's what you're worried about. But I can't promise I might not meet someone else who seems nice and kisses like a god."

I tugged off my shoes and shoved them under the chair, then peeled off my socks, which I carried to the bathroom and dropped into my laundry bag. I washed my hands and face and returned to the room. Abbey had resumed her yoga without putting up her hair. As she bent forward, her head resting on her knees in a pose of utter relaxation, her hair covered the sides of her face.

"Have you noticed anyone lurking around?" I asked.

She shook her head, her hair waving across her arms and the sides of her legs. "I haven't been out except for breakfast."

"I'm going to take a shower," I said.

She still didn't lift her head. "Enjoy."

I stood in the spacious shower. Water poured over me, lukewarm to cool my skin, which was on fire from the sun and the discomfort of feeling threatened but also slightly embarrassed that I'd felt so threatened, and still did. I vowed, for what seemed like the hundredth time, to be more chill. I desperately needed this trip, and I didn't want to spoil it.

8

ABBEY

We stayed two more nights at the Benbow Inn. The second morning, we took a walk along the river together and didn't see a single person. We took off our shoes and waded around in the shallow, gently flowing water. We spent almost an hour trying to resurrect our skill at skipping stones and did better than I thought we would.

After lunch, we walked around the town of Garberville and checked out the shops. We ate another awesome dinner on the patio, later this time, with the stars starting to twinkle over us. We sipped champagne and walked among the fairy lights after dinner. All that time, we talked only about what we saw around us, what we were doing. It made me relax. Raven didn't seem to want to work so hard at creating whatever she was hoping for. Our conversation was easy, filled with silly comments and jokes, most of them lame, but still funny.

We slept late the last morning and ordered breakfast in our room. We barely checked out before the deadline. Raven wanted to hang around and work on the jigsaw puzzle.

Apparently, it had been nagging at her that it had been sitting incomplete the entire time we were there. She imagined it remaining unfinished for months, possibly years, and she couldn't live with that.

Because the puzzle took a while, we ate a late lunch and lingered over that, sipping a glass of wine, but limiting ourselves to one since we'd be driving. Raven said she wanted to drive this leg. I hated giving up the wheel of that adorable, speedy little car, and the feeling of power and freedom that came with it, but she was so eager, I agreed.

It was a five-hour drive to Ashland, Oregon, where we'd be staying for the next eight nights. We drove toward the coast and then started north toward Eureka. The sun shimmering over the Pacific Ocean in late afternoon was stunning. It glittered like diamonds bobbing on the water, which everyone says, so it didn't seem that remarkable to point out, but it's the only way to describe it. The blue was intense and rich and soothing. Raven scrolled through my playlists and chose one, which made me smile, because it seemed she now understood why I liked music instead of conversation when I was the one driving. It helped me get into the flow of the journey and the scenery gliding past.

The route would take us along the coast, inland to the Oregon border, and then bring us in north of Ashland before turning south for a few miles. It was the fastest way, and I loved driving along the coast. For a girl who had lived almost all of her life in California, I didn't see the ocean nearly enough.

"Someone is following us," Raven said.

I'd noticed her glancing in the rearview mirror more than necessary, and now I knew why. All the ease of our drive so far evaporated. She was going to spill her anxiety all over me again.

"There are only two lanes right now," I said. "They don't have a choice."

"But I can sort of see the driver, because he gets too close sometimes. I think it's that guy."

"The one who was watching you by the river?"

She nodded.

"Highly unlikely," I said.

Raven slowed as we came to Crescent City, where we would turn inland. "He's still there."

"Where?" I turned in my seat.

"Don't look."

"Why?"

"I don't want him to think we're scared. We can't slip away from him if he realizes we know he's there."

"I don't think it's the same guy. There are hundreds of thousands of small blue SUVs on the road."

"You wouldn't know if it's the same guy because you haven't seen him," Raven said. Her tone was peeved, as if the guy somehow belonged to her.

I picked up my phone and started flicking through apps, looking for something interesting to distract me.

"He's still there."

"Stop looking."

"He's scaring me."

"Your imagination is out of control. I doubt anyone's following us at all. Even if someone is, you can't possibly tell if it's the same guy just by looking at the rearview mirror."

"I would recognize that shaved head anywhere. And you can tell he's big."

"Do you hear yourself? There are millions of large men with shaved heads. Literally millions. Possibly tens of millions."

"I know it's him."

"Even if it's the same guy, and even if he is following you, or whatever, what's he going to do? Run us off the road?"

"Maybe. Look, he's closer now."

I turned and looked. To me, the distance between our cars looked the same as it had been. I did have to admit he appeared to be following us, because Raven had slowed, and now that we were on a four-lane highway, he still wasn't trying to pass us.

"See. You're worried. Otherwise, you wouldn't still be looking," Raven said.

I didn't respond. Maybe if I quit giving her airtime, she would let it go. We drove for about seven or eight miles. It was dusk now, and the air cooler, but still not enough that we needed sweatshirts.

"I'm really nervous now that it's starting to get dark," she said.

"Why?"

"It's more upsetting in the dark, easier for him to do something."

"Please calm down. It's almost impossible to believe it's the same guy. If by some remote chance it is, we'll be absolutely safe at the hotel in Ashland."

"We should have started earlier," she said.

"Too late now."

Without warning, she veered off the highway onto a frontage road. Ahead, a cluster of deserted buildings stood in the fading light.

"What are you doing?" I asked.

"Forcing him to keep going."

"You can't force him to do anything." I turned. "Anyway, it didn't work. He's right behind us." I had to admit I was a little worried now, but it wouldn't have been a problem if she'd stayed on the freeway. We were only about two hours from Ashland now.

In another abrupt move, she pulled onto the gravel parking strip.

"What are you doing?"

The small blue SUV slowed and then drove past, picking up speed. As far as I could see, the driver didn't even glance in our direction.

Raven was almost crying. Her body was shaking. She clutched the wheel as if she were maneuvering the car around a racetrack. I put my hand on her shoulder. What was wrong with her? This seemed like more than the grief of not being able to conceive. Her overreaction was so extreme, I couldn't imagine what she would do if we were in a truly threatening situation. There was no man following us; it was a coincidence. The fact that she believed he'd been watching her at the hotel seemed very close to something imagined, a projection of her fears onto an innocent person.

Her memory was off too—the things she'd said about loving Lily's eyes and that guys had never come between us. Did she really believe that? Or was something broken in her mind?

9

LILY'S JOURNAL
SEPTEMBER 21, 2010

I spend a lot of time alone in my dorm room, but considering the situation, I'm okay with that. Roaches One and Two go to parties every Friday and Saturday night. Sometimes there are pop-up parties in our room on Sunday afternoons, and that doesn't count the *study groups* that turn into gossip-fests, and then out comes the beer. I really prefer it when they're gone.

Yesterday something happened that made them maybe hate me a little more. Just what I need.

They were not in the room. I was stretched out on my bed, loving the quiet, and totally focused on the research project I'm supposed to summarize for Ecology and the Environment. It's due Tuesday.

Without even knocking (my bad for not locking the door after Roach One and Two scurried out of the room on their skinny little legs), a guy from the floor below ours opened the door and rolled on into our room as if I'd invited him.

He flopped on Roach One's bed and said *hey*. I glanced at the door, which he'd left hanging open, and saw his posse coming in after him. I'll call them Predators One, Two, and

Three, to stick with my promise not to write any names in here. I guess it's not fair to call them predators since they probably are not actually predators, but anyone who walks into a woman's room when he wasn't invited is a little predatory, IMO.

"They're not here," I said.

"Who?"

"My roommates."

"Yeah. I saw them go out."

"What do you want?"

"We never get to talk to you, Ms. Lily Mitchell. And we think you're an interesting person."

I could feel him staring at me. Were my eyes *interesting*? Was this the circus freak show again, or was he actually being nice? It was hard to tell. I kept asking myself those questions every few minutes while he rambled on about football and his classes. I gave myself a different answer every time I asked. He didn't seem all that interested in how remarkable I was, because he did all the talking. Even his friends mostly said *hmm* every few minutes, or *no shit*, and looked around the room as if they were working on a lab study themselves —*How do college women decorate their rooms?*

They sprawled on the other beds—Predators Two and Three had taken Roach Two's bed—for over an hour. They talked a lot. They finally asked me about entomology and what I was working on. They actually did seem interested. I wished I'd had more fun talking to them. The whole time I kept wondering if it was a setup. Did the Roaches tell them to be nice to me, making me think people in the party group liked me, to make me seem gullible later when they told me it was all a joke? It seemed so strange that these guys would just stop by. They've hardly said three words to me before yesterday. It seemed planned, as if they'd waited for the Roaches to go out.

Then, just like that, the Roaches were back.

Roach One walked into the room first. She flopped onto the bed beside Predator One, snuggling up to him like he was her boyfriend, but he is not. "You had a party without me."

"There is no party without you," Roach Two said. All the predators laughed as if they'd never heard anything so witty and hilarious.

The Roaches started talking. They asked the Predators if they wanted beer. The Predators said no, they had to get back to studying, and they left. They disappeared as fast as they'd appeared. Blink and they were in the room, blink and they were gone.

"Lily has herself some boyfriends," Roach Two said.

"We were just talking," I said. Which I knew I should not have said. I would never win a verbal battle with either one of them. They're both pretty smart and a lot faster to think of clever comments than I am. Maybe because there are two of them, and they bounce off each other. And that might be part of the problem. They don't have to put in a lot of effort to get decent grades. Since they aren't driven to get the parade of As like I am, they can slack off and still do well in school.

Then they started with their *teasing*.

"I'm shocked you took a whole afternoon off from studying to talk to *boys*."

"Did you flirt? Do you know *how* to flirt?"

"Which one do you like the best?"

I tried to ignore them.

"Hey!" Roach One said. "I asked you a question. I'm trying to be friendly. Why do you have to be such a bitch?"

"I'm not."

"Always studying, acting like we're slackers. And you never talk when people come in to hang out. It's a little embarrassing. You make everyone feel awkward."

"Why is my not talking embarrassing to you?" I asked.

"It's rude."

"They aren't my friends."

"Maybe they want to be your friends. Maybe that's why they came by."

"They're party people. I'm not."

"You could be. Parties are fun. Most people agree on that fact."

"I don't like drinking."

"Everyone drinks. The whole world drinks. Every culture in the world has some kind of custom around alcohol."

"Not true," I said. "In the Maldives, for example, alcohol is only served at the resorts. It's illegal for residents."

"This is what is so off-putting about you. Why do you have to be such a know-it-all?"

"I'm not a know-it-all. I just happen to know that random fact. I don't claim to know everything about everything, or even a little about everything, or..." I paused, "...everything about a little." I thought that was clever, and I was replaying it in my head. The Roaches were still talking, but I tuned them out.

"They sure were into you," Roach Two said. "They almost looked like they were drooling when we came in."

They really were clueless. The guys might have liked talking to me about school. But mostly they wanted to stare at my eyes. Maybe they thought they would bring good luck. People have a lot of superstitions about heterochromia. Those guys did not want me to be their girlfriend, they wanted to look at something weird. I knew I was the circus freak show to them.

RAVEN

After the guy who'd been following us drove past, Abbey and I sat in the car in front of a boarded-up diner surrounded by the other deserted buildings. The car was completely silent. Her hand was on my back, and I wondered what she was thinking. Maybe she'd decided I was a burden, and she wished she hadn't invited me on her trip. What she should have been thinking was that she would have been so much more exposed to this creepy guy if she were alone!

Finally, she spoke. "See, he wasn't following us."

I didn't understand why she didn't believe me. I flung open the car door and got out.

Abbey shouted after me, "Where are you going?"

I didn't answer.

"It's getting dark," she shouted. "We're already not going to get to Ashland until almost nine. We'll be starving if we don't get going."

I walked toward the diner. I didn't think I could drive, my hands were shaking so badly. I stepped onto the porch and tried to look through the grimy windows. I couldn't see anything but dirt smudges on the outside and a thick, greasy film on the inside of the glass.

A moment later I felt Abbey standing behind me. If she put her hand on my shoulder in that condescending way again, I would scream. At the same time, I was constantly aware that I wanted to fix our friendship more than she did, so I felt like I had to keep giving in to her. But this was too much.

"You never respect me," I said. "You're trying to keep me from trusting my gut."

"If we're going to throw around accusations, then you never consider anything from my perspective," she said. "Everything from wanting to get back the years I lost to how it felt when I was shunned. You can't imagine what that was like. It really messes with your head. It's not just about feeling lonely."

"I tried to be supportive, but it was—"

"You didn't support me at all. If you'd stood by me, I wouldn't have needed to drop out because I was starting to have an actual breakdown. I honestly felt like I was losing my mind. Do you get that? It's an awful feeling having people look at you and pretend they can't see you. After a while, you wonder if they can't."

"I tried to get you to stay in school. I told you they'd move on. They would have gotten bored. You were too impulsive. You still are."

"Well, if you want to rebuild this friendship, you'd better understand why it blew apart. And the reason is—you abandoned me."

"So you just cut me out of your life? Cancel your cell phone and email? Tear up my snail mail cards, or whatever you did with them. I know people were terrible to you. I knew that then, but they were upset too. Everyone was upset. It was horrible, but I tried to help. I *told* them you were freaked out from finding a dead girl's leg on your coat. *Anyone* would be. I told them that proved she was already dead, and you had nothing to do with it. But they didn't believe me, and that's not my fault. You can't *make* people believe you, even when it's the truth. Not if they want to think something else."

I stopped talking. She looked really upset, almost as upset as the day she moved out of our dorm room. I guess she didn't like me bringing up the memory of finding Lily's body. I wondered if that night had traumatized her a lot more than I knew. Maybe that was why she got married so young, looking for some kind of security or comfort.

She was staring at me, starting to back away, as if there were something scary about me.

"Are you okay?" I asked.

She turned around and ran to the car. The doors were still open. She slammed the passenger door, then rushed around to the driver's side, climbed in, started the car, and drove off, gravel spitting behind the tires.

It happened so fast, I couldn't move. I didn't think she would leave, but she was pulling out of the parking strip. I ran after the car, screaming as loud as I could. "Abbey! Stop! Don't leave me here!"

The screaming made my throat raw. It was a complete waste of energy. She couldn't hear me. I started crying and went back to the porch of the diner and tried to look inside again, even pressing my face against the grubby windows, which was also a waste of energy. I already knew it was deserted. I'd known that when I pulled off the road, noticing its sad, tired appearance, the windows so horribly filthy they couldn't truly be called windows.

I stepped off the porch, trying to stop my crying. It wouldn't help. Emmett always told me not to cry, it doesn't help anything. It was irritating to hear him say that, as if he were of the superior male species that rarely cries, and never in fear or frustration. Still, he was right, and although I never told him that, of course any rational person knows it doesn't help. But sometimes it does make you feel better. You can think more clearly after a good cry.

There was a small, tired-looking house about fifty yards from the diner. Pots of herbs stood on the porch railing. The paint on the siding was old, but it wasn't peeling. It looked safe, but I didn't want to put myself in an out-of-the-frying-pan-into-the-fire situation, as my mother always reminds me.

First, I called Abbey. The phone rang a few times and went to voicemail. If she was out of range, a text might still go through. I sent one, telling her I was sorry. I didn't mention I was also terrified, since that seemed to irritate her so much. There was no answer. Not even the swimming dots suggesting she was working to compose a reply.

I walked slowly toward the house, blinking the tears away so I didn't look like a crazy person showing up at their door right at the time most people are eating dinner. The other buildings looked as abandoned as the diner. I guessed no one had knocked on the door of this house since the diner shut down.

The steps felt solid as I climbed to the porch, which made me feel more comfortable. I knocked.

The door opened right away. A woman about sixty years old with dyed chestnut brown hair and dark brown eyes smiled at me. "Hi, sweetie. What can I do for you?"

I hadn't thought about this part. She might not want to get into the middle of a fight between two strangers. And now that I was looking at her, I wondered what I expected her to do. Maybe she could call Abbey's number, and Abbey would pick up because it wasn't me. But most people didn't pick up calls from unfamiliar numbers.

"What's wrong, sweetie?" The woman peered up at me, smiling. Her teeth were sharp and very tiny, which made me shiver. I knew that was superstitious and foolish, to believe that her teeth said anything about her character, but it was a reaction I couldn't control. "My friend dropped me here because I wanted to stretch my legs, but I think she was annoyed about it. She's anxious to get to our destination and left me here. Now she won't answer her phone. I thought if you called..." I laughed nervously, almost hysterically.

She gave me a strange look but opened the door wider. "I guess I could do that. It's a little strange, but easy enough." She flashed her tiny teeth at me again.

With the door open wide, I could see into the entryway. At the far end of the foyer was a table. I recognized it immediately from the house where I grew up. Not the table, but the things on it—the candles, the chalice, the bundles of herbs. Of course, she had well-cared for herbs on her porch.

It wasn't that I'd become bigoted toward witches as an adult. I appreciated that my mother believed wholeheartedly, but I did not appreciate that I was raised in such a weird environment. My mother said it made me unique. I knew it made me strange.

I also knew from experiences with my mother and her witchy friends that this woman was likely to be far more helpful than I wanted. She would offer me tea, probably want to give me dinner. She'd urge me to tell my story, and she would try to offer advice. She'd want to find out about difficult areas in my life and offer to help in those areas as well.

I backed up to the edge of the porch. I laughed in a fake way, knowing she would pick up on it, and hating myself for doing it. "It is kind of silly. I'll just text her again. She gets in little fits. She'll be back any minute."

"You can wait inside," she said.

I shook my head. "No. No, thanks."

I turned and hurried down the steps. I was terrified Abbey wasn't coming back, and scared that the guy stalking me *was* coming back. Adding this creature to the mix was too much. I texted Abbey again, making the message light and breezy—*Okay. Sufficiently terrified. Let's get to Ashland. I see a bottle of champagne in our future.* I added hearts and champagne emojis, then walked slowly back to the diner.

I sat on the low porch, which was uncomfortable, forcing my knees up to my chin. I hugged my legs, feeling lost and pathetic. There was no way Abbey, or any woman, would leave her friend stranded on the side of the road. And definitely not in the dark, hundreds of miles from home, and miles from civilization. Abbey was the only person on earth who knew where I was.

Tears spilled out of my eyes again. I sobbed, trying to soothe myself. *She won't leave me. She cares about me. We're best friends. We were best friends. She invited me on this trip...*

Then I started to think about the fact that I didn't really know her anymore. I was assuming she was the same person I'd shared a room with, but it had been twelve years since we'd spoken to each other. Abbey herself, the Abbey I knew, might not exist anymore. I'd taken a trip with a total stranger, lied about it to my husband and friends, and now I was exposed, completely isolated. The woman in the house, no matter that she appeared to subscribe to similar beliefs to my mother's, was not guaranteed to be a good person or even vaguely decent.

I'd never felt so alone or so afraid.

I texted Abbey again, putting laughing faces that were the opposite of the expression on my own face. Maybe if she thought I was laughing, she would see that I wasn't going to be a downer for her trip.

The sound of a car made me look up so fast I almost dropped my phone. Headlights swam through the near darkness that had fallen while I was knocking on doors and crying. But they didn't belong to our sports car. They were the lights of the small bright blue car and its sole occupant—that man. I screamed. It was the worst thing I could have done, but it just came out.

I jumped up and started running. I skidded around the corner of the diner, knowing I had a clear shot at the front porch of the house before he would have time to pull onto the gravel and approach me. The car moved so slowly, I felt like I stood there for an hour, half-hidden, watching it drift past.

Finally, it was out of sight.

Once it was gone, I still didn't want to go sit in that woman's house. Anyone who believes they have powers to alter the natural world, even if they don't actually have those powers, is terrifying to me. Living with my mother should have made all those things familiar and not at all frightening. But for whatever reason, my childhood had the opposite effect. It had made me superstitious and slightly jumpy and more fearful than I liked.

The location service on my phone was turned off. I hadn't wanted Emmett to see where I was. I stared at the preferences, trying to decide if I should ask him to come get me. In the center of my fear was my absolute love for Abbey. I wanted to believe in her. Inviting me on this trip had given me so much hope. I felt like allowing myself to believe she was abandoning me would be throwing that all away.

I sent a text to Emmett, just to feel the connection to another human being. I told him I was having a good time, doing lots of shopping with my mom, and she was buying me all kinds of new clothes. He didn't answer.

11

ABBEY

I'd been driving for twenty minutes, with no idea where I was going, although it wasn't back to the main highway, so on a subconscious level, I knew I was going to return and pick up Raven. It wasn't that I left her stranded because I wanted to be rid of her for good. I was so shaken at what she'd said, I had to have time to think, time away from her voice.

But winding through trees and past small family farms, not a single car in sight, hadn't helped me think at all. I couldn't shake the numbness as her words echoed in my head. I couldn't absorb the meaning of what she'd said.

Finding Lily's leg on top of my coat had been sickening. Her legs in her cowboy boots had been bare. Her bloodless skin had rested on my clothing. My fingers had touched a dead foot; I'd stared into a dead face.

I should have had more compassion, maybe. But I was a teenager. That I might one day touch a corpse had never entered my mind. And there I was, my hand on her flesh, trying to wake her, something feeling not quite right as her body shifted under my touch. Then, seeing her eyes, I knew.

It had taken years for that image to fade out of my mind, to stop making its way into every single dream—two eyes, as if they belonged to two different people, staring without a glimmer of light.

It was creepy and disturbing and sickening, and at the same time, it felt oddly intimate.

I'd never told a single person. I'd never mentioned I'd found my coat under her leg, that I'd touched her body, that I'd yanked the coat free. All I'd done was scream and wait for someone to come, which took a while, because it was a party. Some amount of screaming was part of the background noise. The music was loud. People shouted to be heard above it. There was lots of laughter.

I couldn't remember who came into the room first. I did remember paramedics after a while. And that despite the obvious circumstances, the paramedics tended to her as if they might be able to help her. I couldn't remember much about what the police asked me, or whom else they talked to. I didn't remember where we were when they took her away.

The house was filled with teenagers. We didn't think about death, at least not death among people we knew. Everyone was horrified to the point of not really believing it was true. How could she be *dead*? It didn't seem real. Except to me, who had touched her and looked into her eyes. It was the most real thing I'd ever experienced.

Raven thought she was *helping* me by telling everyone that it was so awful for me because I'd found my coat trapped under Lily's corpse. All she'd done was make it sound like I really had been there when Lily died, that I'd done something wrong. That maybe I hadn't liked her lying on my coat and I'd smothered her. I didn't know. They didn't even believe the autopsy report that got posted online—aspiration of alcohol-induced vomit, irrevocable damage to her lungs, aided by a significant rise in her blood pressure and heart rate from taking Ecstasy.

Raven was right about one thing—people believe what they want, no matter what facts or reality are staring them in the face. So the accusations started, then grew like a living plant, tendrils creeping everywhere and taking root.

She should have called for help sooner.

She just stood there screaming, and then it was too late.

The music was loud; why did she just scream her head off instead of DOING something?

No one came right out and said I killed her, so I guess they believed that aspect of the autopsy report. But they believed Lily would have been alive if I hadn't just *stood by watching,* an event they'd conjured in their collective imagination.

Yanking my thoughts back to the present, I pulled into a turnout and headed back the way I'd come. I considered Raven. She'd been in that room that night, and she'd never mentioned it. If she knew Lily's leg was on the coat, she'd seen it herself. I'd pulled my jacket away from Lily's body. Not a single person who entered that room to take care of her remains, or tried to sneak in for a bit of gawking, saw my coat on the bed.

Raven had never said a word about being in that room. Why had she allowed me to be treated the way I was? What happened that night? I felt disoriented. I felt as if the experience I'd lived, and relived a thousand times, was entirely different from what I'd thought, and all the things I remembered were just slightly off.

About half a mile from the diner where I'd left Raven, I pulled off and raised the roof on the car. It was too cold, and I was too upset to enjoy the wind in my hair anymore. I wasn't sure what was going to happen next, but I certainly didn't plan to make Raven aware of her unintended exposure. If she'd hidden it all these years, she would lie her head off to make her slip sound like something it wasn't. She would try to make me believe I'd told her, that I'd gotten drunk, forgotten, and shared my secret. Maybe she would suggest I'd talked in my sleep.

There was a reason she'd never told me.

Now, our trip was absolutely for reconnecting, like she kept cooing about. I was going to get so tight with her, I was going to find out everything she'd done back then. I wasn't sure how, but I'd figure it out as I went along. I'd gotten pretty good at that.

When I pulled into the parking strip in front of the diner, Raven was sitting on the porch. She looked bereft. Maybe now she knew what it felt like to be abandoned. It wasn't as if that was why I drove off, but it was a nice side benefit. Shock and a tiny explosion of white noise in my head were what made me jump into the car and tear out of there. I couldn't process the words she'd said. I'd needed to be alone.

I stopped the car and unlocked the doors.

Raven stood and walked slowly toward me. She opened the passenger door and got into the car, curling up in the seat, hugging herself. "That was horrible. He drove past me. I thought he was going to—"

"But he didn't."

"I sent you all those messages, and you just ignored me."

"Yeah, well..." I sighed. "I shouldn't have driven away."

Her voice shook. "Why did you?"

I took a quiet breath and spoke calmly. "Those are painful memories for me. I still don't think you understand what I lived through."

"I'm sorry."

Was she?

"I know now I should have done more to be there for you."

I'd started the trip wanting an apology from her. But now? She simply wanted to make sure she didn't get dumped by the side of the road again. The apology was calculated to get what she wanted. That was all. She wasn't sorry, and in some ways, I wasn't sure she could be. I wasn't sure anyone could be sorry because they couldn't possibly know what shunning felt like unless they'd lived through it. Everyone thinks it's just cliquishness, but it's not. It's so much deeper and more profound. It shakes your soul. It's trauma, in my opinion.

"Water under the bridge, I guess." I turned onto the frontage road and headed back toward the freeway.

"You were pretty upset," she said. "I don't think you believe it's water under the bridge."

"I had some time to clear my head. I don't want to keep reliving something that happened a long time ago, something I can't ever change."

"That's healthy."

I almost laughed. Every time she opened her mouth, she was proving she didn't understand at all.

"I feel like we've cleared the air," she said. "Maybe it was good that you left me."

"I'm glad you see it that way."

"We can't let the past fester between us, or we'll never move forward," Raven said.

"That's pithy."

"I'm not just saying words. I really believe that. And I think you do too."

"I do."

"So we're good?"

I laughed. "I'm always good."

She shoved my shoulder playfully. "No, you're not. That's how this all started—hooking up with a guy you met in a bar."

"Don't push me. I'm driving."

"What do you want to listen to?" she asked.

"You choose." I pressed hard on the accelerator, and the car sped along the highway, headed toward the Oregon border. I was very curious about what lay ahead for us.

"Are you sure you're okay?" Raven asked.

"Yes."

"You seem different."

I laughed. "Different from what?"

"How you were before, obviously."

"I'm anxious to get to Ashland; maybe that's what you're sensing."

"No. It's..." She was quiet for a minute or two. I was about to ask her to start the playlist when she spoke. "I think it will be therapeutic for us to visit the frat house. We can be there together under happier circumstances, with more personal power. We can celebrate that we overcame it all and know that everything will be better going forward."

"That's a lot to expect from an open house."

"Buildings have memories. The smells, the feel of the furniture and the light, the shape of the space. It affects you."

"If you say so."

"I'm sure you've felt it. Anyway, I think it will help."

I laughed harder, finding it difficult to stop. "I don't need help from a house."

"Don't laugh at me."

"Okay. But then you need to stop saying funny things."

When she laughed, it sounded pained. She chose a playlist and started the music.

Visiting the frat house would be therapeutic alright. Maybe by the time she and I reached that point, I would find out what had happened back then. Maybe I couldn't fix it or change it, but it would be nice to know if this woman sitting beside me was my estranged BFF or my worst enemy.

12

RAVEN

By the time Emmett had responded to my text message—a lie sent looking for comfort—I felt guilty for sending him a message at all, because now I had to lie to him yet again.

Abbey kept insisting everything between us was good, but it felt as if she'd pulled away ever so slightly. I was trying not to read into every gesture and tone, trying not to assume the worst, but the feeling wouldn't leave me. It was my anxiety taking hold, that was all. This trip was good for me. It was taking my focus off my empty arms and my too-quiet dinners with Emmett. Abbey was helping me relax, and I needed to keep my focus on her good qualities.

It was slowly coming back to me that she'd always been the wilder of the two of us. It was also becoming clear that both of us had grown into stronger versions of the girls we were in college. I was more superstitious, even though I tried not to be, and she was more eager to take risks. Maybe she was trying as hard as I was, it just didn't show on the outside.

When we arrived at the Ashland Springs Hotel, it was eight forty, but the sky was still a soft gray now that we were farther north. The hotel's nine stories towered over the rest of the quaint town, home to an annual Shakespeare Festival. The building was a blend of Romanesque and Neo-classical Revival, constructed in the 1920s, and the lobby captured the flair of that era, decorated with ceiling fans, potted palm trees, and comfortable furniture upholstered in pastels.

The most recent owners had gone all out in trying to hold on to the feel of 1925. Clutching the past with both hands is a human drive. We retell our stories to everyone we meet. We relive the past in our minds and conversations and dreams. We worship the past with statues and monuments, books and historical buildings. I didn't think that was necessarily a bad thing. If you don't pay attention to the past, then you have no idea who you are or where you are right now.

This wasn't a popular opinion among my friends and co-workers. They never wanted to hear you say *that didn't work in the past* or *that was popular in the past.* For many of my colleagues, the past barely existed.

There was no bellman, so after checking in, we loaded our luggage onto a large cart and pushed it across the parking lot, through the back entrance to the elevator.

We rode in silence to the third floor and went to our room. It, too, had the feel of the twenties, featuring updated bathrooms with period-looking faucets and soap dishes. The beds were high with a heavenly garden of sheets and pillows and thick comforters.

"I'm starving," Abbey said.

"Me too."

"Let's not shower. I'm just going to throw on some boots and nice earrings. Brush my hair and teeth, obviously."

Thirty minutes later we were being shown to a table at a nearby Italian restaurant. There was a narrow second-floor patio overlooking the street and a larger, more secluded brick patio in the back. We chose the back patio.

We ordered an antipasto tray because it seemed like something that would be served quickly. First, they brought a basket of rolls and a dish of butter. We both took a poppy seed roll and began spreading butter.

I ordered a bottle of champagne, and Abbey didn't ask what we were celebrating. I was celebrating that she hadn't left me forever in front of that diner, that we still had a chance. It was fun having a girlfriend again. It shocked me how that year and a half I'd known Abbey remained such a significant part of my life. Part of me had been missing for all these years, and it felt good to look at her face across the table and remember all the good times during those months we'd slept a few feet from each other, breathing the same air.

The champagne was sitting in an ice bucket, and we were about to click our flutes together when the server returned. She was carrying two purple drinks. She placed them on the table.

"What are those?" I asked.

"Concord grape royals—champagne, bitters, and concord grapes. The message is 'Cheers, enjoy.'" She started to walk away.

"Who sent them?" I asked.

"Anonymous."

"I want to know," I said.

"I'm sorry. I was asked not to tell you."

"We can't drink them if—"

"I don't want to get in the middle of this." The server turned and hurried away even though I was calling after her that we had a right to know.

"Let's just enjoy them," Abbey said.

"No way."

"That's kind of rude," Abbey said.

"Why is it rude not to drink something you didn't ask for? It's rude to force drinks on people you don't know."

She took a sip of her drink. "It's tasty."

"We ordered champagne."

"We can have both. We're not in a rush. Now that we have food." She grinned at me and took another sip of her drink.

"It's a little upsetting, don't you think?"

"Why?"

"You don't remember?"

"Remember what?"

"It's the same color as the Jell-O shots."

"What?"

"At all the frat parties. For the UW colors. We always had purple Jell-O shots. Always. Every single party. How can you not remember?"

She shrugged. "Okay." She took another sip of the drink.

"It feels creepy. Like someone knows who we are." I turned and scanned the people seated behind me on the patio. I turned back, pushed my chair away from the table, and stood. "I'm going to check the bar."

"For what?"

"To see if I recognize anyone."

"Sit down. It was a friendly gesture, and I seriously doubt it has anything to do with Jell-O shots from a decade ago." She laughed and took another sip. "You should try it."

"Even if it's not about the Jell-O shots, it's dangerous to drink something when you don't know the source." I sat down and pulled her glass to my side of the table, nudging both drinks to the corner. "There could be drugs in it."

"No one even knows we're here. We only passed by the bar for thirty seconds. There are families and couples all around us. How would they even have time to put something in it? The drink went from the bartender to the server to us. Besides, why on *earth* would someone put roofies in our drinks? When it took effect, we'd just crash on the table. It's not like we're isolated where some guy could have his way with us."

"I don't know. I just think it's dangerous. I'm not drinking it."

"So you said, and you don't have to." She reached across and reclaimed her glass from my side of the table. She took a long swallow. "These could be dangerous in another way." She laughed. "It would be easy to drink a lot of them."

I picked up my gaudy drink and wriggled sideways out of my chair, trying not to splash purple liquid on my clothes. "I'm going to return this. And I'm going to find out who sent it."

"Please don't make a scene."

"I won't make a scene. But we have a right to know."

"I don't think we do, but I'll be curious if you find out."

I carried the drink to the bar, holding it away from me as if it were toxic. I placed it on the bar and waited for one of the bartenders to notice me. After a few minutes, a woman with short, curly red hair asked me what I wanted. I pushed the drink toward her. "Someone sent this to our table. I don't want it."

She laughed. "You don't want a free drink?"

"Not from a stranger."

"This is Ashland, sweetie, not Portland."

"Do you know who sent it?"

"No idea." She took the drink and poured it into the little sink behind the bar.

"How can I find out?"

She shrugged. "I don't know. Ask everyone at the bar? Then visit every table?" She laughed.

I didn't like that she was mocking me. "I'd really like to know."

She stopped laughing. "You seem a little upset."

"It's very unnerving."

She stared at me. "Do you have an abusive ex stalking you or something?"

"Can you ask the other bartenders?"

"Your server is the most likely one to know."

I nodded. "Thanks." I turned and saw our server headed toward the back patio, carrying nothing but someone's bill. I hurried after her. This was good. I wouldn't be disturbing her when she was juggling a tray of food. "Excuse me." I tapped her arm gently.

She stopped. "Is something wrong?"

"I need to know who sent the drinks to our table."

"He asked me not to say."

He. I wasn't surprised the sender was male. At least I had a little information. "Please tell me. I just got out of a bad marriage, and it's creeping me out that someone did this. I..."

She looked at my eyes, and her devotion to secrecy folded. "It's the guy at the end of the bar with the gray beard and the black T-shirt."

I turned to look. Half the guys at the bar wore black T-shirts, but only one had a gray beard.

"Please don't tell him," she said. "I got a nice tip for it."

I nodded. "Thanks." I followed her toward the patio, walking slowly so she could get ahead of me, trying to decide what I wanted to do. The guy was too old to have gone to school with us, and it wasn't the guy who was following us. This man had a woman with him, and she looked nice enough. They both did. Maybe we reminded him of his daughters or something. It still bothered me that the drinks were purple. There aren't a lot of purple drinks out there. Of course, the Jell-O shots had vodka, so this really wasn't the same at all. Maybe that guy following us had shaken me so deeply I was imagining ghosts.

The minute I stepped onto the patio and saw Abbey blissfully sipping that drink, I doubted my easy dismissal of the guy at the bar simply because he was older. Maybe the stalker was here, and this guy had met him. Just because the blue SUV drove past me on that frontage road didn't mean he hadn't waited on the highway and followed more discreetly, less conspicuous at night. He could have easily followed us all the way here because Abbey hadn't checked for anyone following, and I'd been so relieved she came back for me, I'd honestly forgotten about it for the rest of the drive.

I couldn't tell Abbey. She would dismiss me or, worse, laugh at me. I was starting to worry about her. It's one thing to want to go a little crazy and another to dismiss your sense of caution entirely. Gut instinct in the face of a threat is a gift that human beings possess, and we shouldn't treat it as something unimportant. Abbey was treating it as irrelevant.

I settled myself across from her. As if she'd been waiting for me to return before she finished the alarming purple liquid, she picked up the glass and gulped down what was left. She smiled at me, purple staining her lips and outlining her teeth, making her look ill. I ignored her dramatic gesture and took a few sips of champagne before adding more cold bubbles.

As she talked about the hotel and how fascinated she was by the 1920s and what we might do over the next few days, a separate part of my mind whirred in the background. I didn't believe that bearded man had randomly picked us out and decided to send us purple drinks. A Concord grape royal? How many people had heard of that drink? I certainly never had. My gut told me someone had worked overtime to find a drink that echoed the Jell-O shots.

Our food came, and as I picked my way through an enormous serving of lasagna, the thoughts continued to spin. We hadn't gotten rid of the stalker. And now this.

I wanted to relax. I wanted those thoughts to fade, but they refused. I wanted a lot. Among other things, I desperately wanted to forget about the pain of not having a child, but sitting in a restaurant filled with families, their tables bursting with babies and children, had stirred up those feelings again. Emmett hated it when I said this, but I truly believed I was cursed. The stalker filling me with fear and now these drinks echoing a part of my life I wanted to forget were making that feeling more intense.

It wasn't a very positive way to look at the world, to view yourself as destined for heartbreak, but I honestly did feel there was a curse on me—on my womb. Other women conceived children and gave birth as easily as if they were picking up cups of coffee for the office. They got pregnant by accident. They complained about pregnancy as if it were a burden. They delivered children and never paused to consider the miraculous nature of what had transpired. They appeared not to think at all. Pregnancy just happened. They didn't endure embarrassing, invasive tests. They didn't fight with their husbands about making love. They didn't cry their hearts out every single month when they saw the first spots of blood.

It was a private hell that most people didn't comprehend. I'd thought Abbey did, but now, I wasn't sure. For her, it was one thing in a list of many things she wanted, and not necessarily at the top of that list.

And that was why I thought I was cursed. Because I only wanted one thing in all the world, a thing that's given to billions of people on this planet, to all the creatures in the forest and the ocean, insects and even plants. They all reproduce because it's a biological imperative. And I could not.

I was a freak of nature.

13

LILY'S JOURNAL
SEPTEMBER 30, 2010

Maybe I've been giving off some unusual vibe, but another guy popped into our dorm room yesterday. Just like the first time, no one had invited him. This guy often comes to see the Roaches, but like the Predators, he showed up when the Roaches weren't there. He told me he'd seen them go out. He dropped by because he wanted to get to know me.

Is this normal guy behavior? Wanting to get to know a girl as a person? It doesn't feel like it based on most of the mini parties that take place in our dorm room. It got me back to thinking the Roaches are putting them up to it, creating a situation to mess with my head. The only confusing part is that the guys feel like they're being real. This guy, the Prince, I'll call him, is a prince in every way.

He sat on the floor with his back against Roach One's bed, stretching out his legs in front of him, and put his phone on the floor, facedown. That was impressive. He didn't want text messages distracting him.

After we talked for a while about what we liked about college, he leaned forward, staring into my eyes. "Why did you decide to study entomology?" he asked. "It seems like a weird choice for a girl."

"Why?"

"Because girls don't usually like crawly things."

"I'm different."

"Obviously. It's still unusual. You have to admit that, right?"

"Yes."

He was right, I do have to admit it's unusual. The class of entomology students at UW is small—a fraction of the number of people studying engineering or marketing, for sure, and even a fraction of those studying archeology or economics.

I love knowing how the world works. I love thinking about the hundreds of thousands of species of insects and how they all have unique characteristics and how they live such complex lives, completely outside the awareness of most human beings. They eat and create societies and reproduce. They have an inner knowledge of their role in the world, and they fulfill it. Each ant has a tiny brain, but all the ants of a colony combined can solve problems as a group, as if they're a single brain. Humans should take a lesson from that.

Even roaches have their place. They provide food for birds and lizards and geckos. They consume decaying plants, which controls the level of nitrogen in forests and enables plant growth. There are over 4,000 species of roaches, and they've been around for more than 300 million years!! I've found most people aren't interested in that fact. I wondered if the Prince might be interested, but it didn't seem the right time to bring it up.

"So why?" he said. "A lot of people probably don't even know what entomology is. And *forensic* entomology?" He laughed, but in a nice way. "You have some explaining to do."

I spoke softly, but he was actually paying attention, so I

knew he would hear me. "My uncle was murdered. They didn't find his body until four years after he died."

"That blows."

"Yeah." I felt my eyes fill with tears. I didn't want to cry in front of him, no matter how nice he seemed. I don't like crying in front of anyone, which is why I love my journal. I can write about my feelings and examine them from all different sides. I can inspect them like a scientist studies cells on a slide under a microscope. It keeps me from crying about things that hurt me.

I rolled onto my back and stared at the ceiling while the tears sank back into my head. Then I closed them.

"Am I boring you?" he asked.

"No."

"Sorry about your uncle."

"Yeah. Anyway, there was a forensic entomologist who helped determine when he'd been killed. That helped the detectives build a timeline from when he'd gone missing."

"Did they catch the guy who did it?"

I sighed, feeling a little scared that he could see inside me more than I wanted. I don't like people psychoanalyzing my career goals, but I guess it's obvious that there are some layers to my choice. It's not just about thinking insects are absolutely, mind-blowingly amazing. It's also about Uncle Bruce. My dad has barely come to terms with losing his baby brother, even now. Maybe you never get over someone you love getting murdered. Maybe you always feel like part of you is missing if your brother or sister dies.

"They haven't caught him. But we're still hoping. Trying to be optimistic."

"How long has it been?"

"Seven years since he died."

"Wow."

"Anyway. That's not the only reason, although it's the

reason for the forensic part. I do think insects are so interesting, not just pests. They're critical to life."

He nodded.

"Now I'm boring *you*?"

He laughed. "Nope. But it's hard talking to you when I can't see your face. You should sit on the floor so we can talk."

"My eyes or my face?"

"What?"

"You just want to look at my eyes and see how weird I am?"

"No. Why would you think that?"

"It happens."

"Your eyes are cool, but that's not it. I've noticed you when everyone is hanging out here, and you always look like you wish you were a million miles away. I never see you at parties...so I thought I'd find out more about you."

I sat up and slid off my bed, landing harder on the floor than I thought I would, which made my tailbone ache, but it was worth it.

Sitting across from him, my legs stretched out just as his were, with only a few inches between my right leg and his left, was exciting in a way that made me feel ridiculous and also very content. It was a strange feeling.

We talked about his classes—he's studying forestry. He wants to work for a national park because he loves being outdoors. He wants to make sure people realize how amazing it is to be in nature. "The only thing is, people who are at national parks already know it's amazing, and people who don't visit them aren't ever going to cross my path." He gave me a frustrated look, but it also seemed funny.

I laughed and so did he.

Then we talked about music and films we liked.

We talked nonstop for more than two hours, and after a while, I noticed his leg was a little closer to mine. It was so close I could feel the heat coming off his body. Or maybe it was the heat of my own body.

There's still a massive suspicious part of me that's wondering if he was up to something, but that can't be right because I had such good feelings. If he wants to trick me into liking him, then he'll turn on me and make fun of me for being so stupid to think he likes me, he didn't need to sit there for two whole hours.

Since the first and only boyfriend I ever had dumped me right before high school graduation, I haven't even gone out for ice cream or pizza with a guy. And in college, it seems like almost all of them want to party. I'm sure that's not true, but I haven't met any I like who don't, so it feels like it's everyone.

We were talking about a comic series he likes when the door slammed open. The Roaches were back.

"Oh my goodness, Lily. Another boy?" They smiled at me like they were my twin mothers.

The Prince laughed. Then he stood up, and I wanted to cry from not feeling his leg close to mine anymore. For half a second, I thought about moving to where he'd been sitting so I could feel the heat that was left in the carpet, but of course they would say all kinds of stupid things about that.

"I should head out," he said.

One of them said, "Lily is not into boys. Didn't you know that?"

He moved toward the door, staring at me as if he was trying to figure out if this was true. Which of course it wasn't, and I hoped he could tell by the past two hours that it wasn't true.

"Bye." I flopped on my bed.

"It was fun talking," he said.

This made the Roaches laugh. *Fun? Talking about bugs? How fun can that be?* They gave him flirty smiles. *She's kind of boring. All about disgusting insects.*

"I gotta go." He grabbed the doorknob and disappeared like he was afraid they were going to start in on him next.

I was sad that he didn't stand up for me. It was fun talking, and I thought he could at least say that again instead of letting them have the last word.

After he was gone, the chattering went on. Sometimes it seems like they don't even care if I'm listening. They just talk to hear themselves make rude comments, as if that's their primary entertainment.

She loves bugs, which is so boring and also very weird and a little scary.

She never talks because she's so boring.

I've never heard her laugh, have you?

It went on like this. Mostly one of them, but the other one never argues or pushes back.

I'm starting to hate them both, even though I know that hating people just makes you unhappy, it doesn't affect them one bit. But it's hard not to hate them. I don't understand what they want from me.

14

RAVEN

The next day, Abbey and I ate lunch at a deli before setting out to explore the shops in downtown Ashland. She wanted to take our food to a park, but I said we should just eat there because they had a nice patio. Why carry our food in a paper bag to a park and then eat sandwiches that were soggy because the juice from the tomatoes and pickles had soaked into the bread? She probably thought I was stifling her fun, again, but soggy bread is disgusting.

We finished lunch and decided to start with a bookstore two doors down from the deli. Inside, we quickly drifted away from each other, each of us following the breadcrumbs in her own mind. I hated myself for being weak, but without thinking, I went immediately to the section on pregnancy, birth, and parenthood. It was always a bad idea to visit this section in a physical bookstore. In an online store, I could look for the specific topic I wanted. Here, I had to look at all these books on breastfeeding and facilitating calm for babies and sleep issues and natural birth to find books on infertility.

It was an obsession with me. Always looking for the secret

that would tell me what I was doing wrong. Always hoping I wasn't really cursed, that it truly was a silly superstition and any day I would find myself slightly bloated and then my breasts tender and then the miraculous confirmation that I was pregnant.

My throat spasmed when I envisioned this scenario, as I had countless times before.

I studied the labels on the shelves, glad that Abbey had wandered off to the travel section. It was good to have a few minutes alone. Once again, things between us had taken a step back. I felt like she was simply being polite to me. No matter what I tried to talk about, she responded with comments that made me feel I were interviewing her, or that we were passing the time as we sat in an airport, waiting for flights to different vacation destinations. Strangers meeting for an hour and then we'd never see each other again.

A book caught my eye—it was advertised as being fun and filled with blunt, straight talk about infertility. I pulled it off the shelf and read the back—the eternal hope of something new. I opened it to the chapter on stress and started reading.

After a while, my legs got tired, and I realized I'd been reading for almost fifteen minutes. I'd finished the chapter and learned nothing new. I shoved the book back onto the shelf, not caring if it was in the spot where I'd found it, and walked toward the back of the store. The travel section was only two rows wide. Abbey wasn't there. I walked slowly around the rest of the store, still not finding her.

After a second pass around, thinking she'd been moving while I was looking, I went to the checkout counter.

"Can I help you?" The clerk kept her attention on the books she was scanning into inventory.

"Have you seen a woman with brown hair in a messy

topknot? She's wearing a bright pink shirt and black shorts and pink flip-flops."

The clerk stared at me. "I don't know."

"You saw us come in. You said *hi*. She had her sunglasses on her head. Also pink."

She looked blank as if she couldn't remember what she'd done four minutes ago. "Oh, right. Yeah."

"Did you see her leave?" I couldn't believe Abbey would do that to me again, but she wasn't in the store.

"Maybe."

"Maybe?"

"I don't watch everyone who goes in or out."

I pulled out my phone and sent Abbey a text. There was no response. I walked through the store again, speaking her name as loudly as I could without shouting, making the other shoppers shrink away from me as if I were a madwoman. I didn't see her, and she didn't answer, and my phone screen remained dark.

Walking out the front door, I looked up and down the street. Nothing. Her top was so bright, she wouldn't blend in easily. She also had a way of walking that attracted attention. I sent another text. When there was no response, I called her number. It went directly to voicemail.

Why would she walk out of the store without telling me she was finished looking? Why would she send her calls to voicemail? Had she dumped me for good this time?

I didn't know which way to turn. I decided to check the deli. Maybe she'd dropped something and gone back to look for it. I moved among the people strolling and stopping to look into windows, frustrated by the human obstacles.

The deli was crowded, even though it was almost three o'clock. Abbey wasn't there. I went to the counter, planning to ask if they'd seen her, then realized they would have even less recall than the clerk at the bookstore because they were numb from streams of hungry tourists.

I went outside and looked up and down the street again, feeling helpless. Standing there whipping my head back and forth wasn't going to make her appear. I opened my phone and found the contact info for our hotel. I called the main number. Maybe she'd gone back to our room. It was their job to notice their guests; surely they were paying attention.

The phone went to a centralized location and offered a voicemail menu for making reservations, confirming existing bookings, or learning about the history of the hotel. I hung up.

I started walking toward the Italian restaurant where we'd eaten dinner, simply because I had to take some kind of action, and the familiar seemed the most logical. Was she just being inconsiderate, expecting me to walk up and down every single street in the business section of town trying to catch up with her? Should I go back to the hotel myself and check our room? I turned and started in that direction instead.

It was hot, and I was irritated, which made walking unpleasant. The hot weather was unusual for Oregon, the last days of a heat wave that was sweeping through the Pacific Northwest. No one here expected hundred-degree temps for days on end, and you could see the heat dragging everyone down to the speed of a caterpillar inching along a fence.

A few people were seated in the lobby of the Ashland Springs, reading, talking, and looking at their phones. One guy was curled up in an off-white armchair, napping with his shoes shoved against the arm of the chair.

I wondered what the housekeeping staff thought about that.

I rode the elevator up and went to our room. The beds were made, and the room smelled clean, the air cool from the

AC turned on low. I kicked off my flip-flops and climbed onto my bed, curling into a fetal position. My only comfort was the cool air and the soft comforter and solid mattress beneath me. My purse was lying beside me. I pulled out my phone and checked. Still no messages.

I sat up as if I'd had a jolt of electricity, suddenly scared. She hadn't dumped me again because her things were still in the room. I jumped up, grabbed my purse, and slid into my flip-flops. I took the elevator down to the second floor, where a hallway led to the parking lot in the back. I ran out to the lot, my flip-flops slapping hot pavement. The car Abbey had rented was in the spot where we'd left it.

Where the hell was she?

She never worried about anything. She hardly even believed me that the guy who was staring at me near the river had followed us all the way to the California-Oregon border. That guy was still out there, whether Abbey admitted it or not. What if he'd grabbed her? That didn't seem possible from inside a bookstore, but I had no idea how long she'd even been inside. Maybe she'd spent two minutes in the travel section and gone outside looking to buy a bottle of water. Maybe he'd grabbed her then. Maybe she'd come back to the hotel, and he'd been waiting for her.

My shoulders began shaking as I tried to figure out what to do. I could report it to the police, but would they care? I imagined myself telling a police officer my friend and I were shopping, and I couldn't find her. Telling them she'd been gone for an hour. They would laugh me out of there.

I had no idea where to go and no one to ask for help. But that was the wrong attitude. I needed to ask everyone I saw. It was possible some random person noticed that hot pink top and easy, mesmerizing walk. I ran back into the hotel and went to the front desk.

"Have you seen my traveling companion? Abbey? She's wearing a hot pink top and—"

The woman chuckled. "Half our guests are dressed in pink."

I doubted that, but I wasn't going to argue. I needed answers. "She was wearing black shorts and pink flip-flops. She's about two inches taller than me. Guys consider her hot." I felt my face burn as I said this. It sounded kind of slimy, but I had to puncture the memory of the woman staring at me as if I were wasting her time.

The stare remained even, as if she was waiting for me to tell her something useful. "Did you text her?"

"She's not answering."

"Did you check your room? Maybe she's napping."

"She's not in the room."

"I don't know what to tell you. I haven't seen her. If I do, should I give her a message?"

I sighed. What were the chances Abbey would go to the desk and ask for messages when she was ignoring all the messages I'd sent directly to her? Still. No stone unturned, that was how I needed to think. "Yes. Tell her to text Raven right away."

"Is it urgent?"

"Yes."

"Is there anything we can help you with?"

"No. Thanks." I turned and walked toward the main doors and out into the oppressive heat. It felt even worse now because my body was so stressed it couldn't handle any more.

With no other ideas, I started walking again, looking down side streets, stepping into every shop for a moment or two for a quick look. I went to the counter in a wine shop where they sold bottled water and asked if she'd been in. She hadn't. Or if she had, the guy didn't remember.

I wanted to go back to our room, crawl under the covers,

and cry. I wanted to sleep, then wake to find she'd returned and was asking where I wanted to eat dinner.

That man who was stalking us had gone to the trouble of pulling off the highway solely to terrorize. Whatever he was after, it hadn't changed. I should return to the hotel and check the parking lot for his car.

It took me fifteen minutes to get there and another ten to walk up and down the rows of cars. There were several small blue SUVs, but I'd never been close enough to read his license plate or the make of the car, so I couldn't be sure any of them were his. Two had California plates, and I figured he was more likely from California than Oregon.

Knowing I was asking for trouble, I peered into the driver's window of the first car. There was a dark blue sweatshirt on the passenger seat. A small cooler sat on the floor in the back. The rear windows were tinted, so I couldn't see the cargo area.

"What are you doing?"

I jumped back, almost falling at the sudden force of movement.

"I was looking for..." I felt my face get hot as a simple explanation eluded me.

"Yes?" The woman had folded her arms across her ribs, ready for a fight. She wore dark glasses that covered her cheekbones. The kind of dark glasses that don't give the slightest glimpse of the eyes they're shielding.

"I thought this car belonged to someone I know. Sorry." I backed away.

"I'm going to report you to hotel management."

"Why? I was looking for my friend's car."

She gave a short laugh. "No, that's the lie you made up after you started to tell me what you were looking for, then changed your mind."

"I'm really sorry. Please don't. It was stupid of me. I didn't mean to upset you. I honestly thought it belonged to someone I know. They have the same car and JFQ in the license."

"I still think it's worth letting them know they should be patrolling this lot. Or install cameras." She turned and walked toward the back entrance.

I was pretty sure she wasn't going to mention me, because she hadn't asked my name, but it was still one more thing to make me feel like I was coming apart, one small, barely noticeable thread at a time.

I walked across the parking lot to the dead-end street that ran parallel, glancing at a café on the opposite side. I considered whether I should stop in for a glass of wine. I really didn't know what else to do. My phone had remained silent, and walking up and down the streets was a waste of time and miserable in the heat. She could be anywhere. Maybe a glass of wine would clear my head. If nothing else, time would pass, and I could contact the police. Or she'd return. Or she'd text me that I could have the room, she was heading on without me.

Crossing the street, I checked my phone again. Still no messages. I went into the café. There was a couple seated in the back. Otherwise, it was empty—too late for lunch, too early for the cocktail hour. I ordered a glass of white wine. I sipped it, trying to limit myself to checking my phone every five minutes instead of every five seconds. I was scared she'd been badly hurt. I didn't want to think about worse. I felt awful that I wasn't doing anything. But there was nothing I could think of.

When my wine was gone, I walked down the street toward the front of the hotel and began strolling in the direction of the bookstore, thinking I could work harder to get the clerk to remember if Abbey had left alone or with someone else.

I glanced at the street sign, trying to remember where it was. When I looked again at the people walking toward me, there was Abbey. Smiling, her sunglasses reflecting the colors around her. Instead of the stylishly messy hair twist she'd had when we ate lunch, her hair was down around her shoulders and arms. The heat didn't seem to bother her. She waved at me.

My first instinct was a desire to punch her. She was *waving* at me? She'd disappeared for over two hours, and now she was waving as if we'd planned all along to meet here at this time. Had we? Her behavior was so disorienting, I tried to think if maybe we'd said in the bookstore that we would shop alone and meet here later? No. Definitely not.

When Abbey was a few feet away from me, she stopped. She lifted her sunglasses to the top of her head, pushing her hair to the sides. "Did you find any fun shoe stores?" she asked.

"*Shoe stores?* I've been worried to death."

She laughed.

"You think it's funny? Where did you go?"

She shrugged. "I got bored, and you were so into your book, I just went outside to move around a bit."

"I texted and called you. Why didn't you answer? I was scared."

"Sorry." She pulled her phone out of her purse and turned it on, which was surprising and a little strange. "Oops. Lots of messages. All from you." She shoved it back into her pocket.

"What were you doing all that time?"

"Just having a little fun." She gave me a knowing smile.

"I thought you and I were having fun?"

"Looking at pregnancy books?"

I felt a pinch in my throat. I'd been right. She didn't feel the same way as me at all. That connection I'd felt had been an illusion, simply because I wanted so desperately to have her share that part of my life.

"Let's have a drink in the hotel lounge and figure out where we want to go for dinner. I want to see if there are any bars with dancing."

I nodded and followed her back to the hotel, angry and upset, but helpless. I was not giving up on our friendship, so following was my only choice.

15

ABBEY

There was no way I was going to tell Raven where I disappeared to while she immersed herself in sadness at the bookstore. The first part was true. I went outside to walk around because I was tired of standing in one spot. What I didn't tell her was I decided to go for a glass of wine. I wasn't going to tell her I met a very good-looking guy who swept me off my feet just a little bit. Of course, I wasn't so naïve to be easily and blindly swept off my feet. I remained wary of him, as if Raven's voice were playing in my mind.

Still, his charm overcame her voice, and I went to his hotel room. We had an awesome afternoon together. We clicked so well we even exchanged numbers, at his suggestion, which was nice.

If I wasn't set on finding out what Raven had lied about in college, I would have suggested we end the trip, or at least end her part of it. My curiosity and probably my long-buried desire to be proven right, even though it was far too late, kept me tolerating her fears. She was so anxious about everything.

And there was all that nonsense over the purple drinks. I had no idea why that was so upsetting. Purple is a common color. It's not as if it were unique to UW. I couldn't understand how she imagined they might be connected. The odds against that were astronomical. Not that I was a mathematician, but I did know odds for football games and the lottery, so I thought I was close enough.

After a fun night meeting a bunch of people at a sushi place where we were all seated at the bar, Raven faded to the periphery of my thoughts. We didn't find a place that advertised dancing, but we went with the same group to a bar and danced anyway. Raven hardly spoke to me the whole time, and she looked like she was going to cry.

Finding out her secrets was going to be difficult if we were in a fight, so I decided I would need to apologize further. The next morning, I suggested a hike, and she agreed. It would feel good to do something outdoors. It was summer, and we'd spent most of our time in the car and restaurants and bars.

We put on shorts and sturdy shoes, sunscreen and hats. I packed insect repellent in the small backpack I carried.

The trail wasn't difficult, which made talking easier.

"I'm sorry I scared you yesterday," I said.

"Yeah."

"I love being spontaneous. I dreamt about this trip for seven or eight months, imagining how freeing it would be. I realize I keep doing things that were part of that daydream and not thinking much about you."

"Okay," she said.

"Anyway, hopefully we can get past it."

"We seem to do that, most of the time." She glanced at me with a tiny, nervous smile.

As the trail narrowed, I walked ahead, and she followed. We'd been walking for about twenty minutes, not talking much, when Raven grabbed the strap of my backpack, yanking me toward her.

"What are you doing?"

"Someone's following us."

I laughed. "Are you okay, mentally? Because you're starting to sound a little crazy. Other people are out hiking. No one is following us."

"Look."

I peered through the trees where she was pointing. "I don't see anyone."

"He has on khaki shorts and a tan hoodie, so he blends in. Look more carefully. And don't look away; you'll miss seeing him move."

"I'm not going to peek through the trees looking for stalkers. Come on." I started walking. After seven or eight steps, I could feel that she wasn't behind me. I turned. She hadn't moved. "Raven, let's go. If he is following us, standing there isn't going to get rid of him or keep you safe."

She hurried to catch up to me. "I know he's following us, Abbey. It's not like I'm seeing stalkers everywhere, because I'm pretty sure it's the same guy who followed us from California."

"How can you tell if his head is covered?"

"Just a feeling. The way he moves. His build."

I laughed. "The way he moves?"

"It's not funny. I don't understand what he wants."

I shrugged. "Maybe we should chase him down and ask him."

"I'm not going near him."

"That's one way to take your power back. Because right now, he owns you. He's all you think about."

She didn't reply. I increased my pace, hoping she would get tired and be too focused on the terrain beneath her feet to check out the surrounding area.

"Abbey."

"What?" I walked faster, knowing from her stage whisper what it was.

"He's there again."

I kept walking.

"Please stop. I'm not crazy, and I think you should take this more seriously."

I stopped and returned to where she stood. I'd vowed just moments earlier to let things settle between us, but she was so easy to gaslight. It seemed mean to torment my long-lost friend like that, but she'd sort of asked for it. Because she'd lied to me all those years ago, she deserved it.

I'd seen the guy. I'd seen him the first time, but I wasn't going to tell her. I preferred, for now, to make her feel like she was going crazy, because she was absolutely driving *me* insane. "I don't see anyone. Your imagination is playing tricks."

"You're not looking. He's right there."

I shook my head. "Nope."

"Are you blind? He's so obvious."

"Maybe you should shout, and he'll move, and then I'll see him."

"No. You need to open your eyes and look harder."

I hunched my back and cupped my hand over the brim of my hat. "I don't see a single person out there. Let's go."

This sighting by Raven and my *failure* to *see* repeated itself three more times until I was ready to push her down the hillside, leaving her to find her way back to the hotel on her own. I'd thought the hike would be refreshing and fun, that we could be normal. It was looking like normal was not an option for Raven. Not since we'd met for champagne and agreed on this trip. She must have had her anxiety well under wraps that night.

She continued to whimper about him until it was difficult to control the laughter bubbling inside my chest. The guy did look familiar. I'd seen a flash of his shoes and realized it was the guy I'd met the day before. I'd told him we were planning to go hiking. He was just having a bit of fun. Silently flirting with me. But if I told Raven, she would get wildly upset. Everything was a threat in that girl's mind. I would enjoy his fun game by myself.

When we returned to our room, I wanted nothing more than to take a nap. Raven said she was going back to the bookstore, which suited me perfectly. I slept like a little baby, free from the weight of her anxiety. She got so hysterical I was compelled to overemphasize my calm. It wasn't hard because no one was going to hurt us. If the guy physically bothered us, we would call the police. We could defend ourselves. There were two of us.

I got up from the bed, smoothed the covers, and looked for something to wear to dinner. I was going to suggest casual because I wasn't in the mood for high heels. Not that I couldn't wear sandals to a nice place, but I hoped for a noisy restaurant filled with distractions. In the shower, I thought again about Raven's inaccurate memories and outright lies. The idea that she was hiding something had transformed itself into an even bigger lie in my mind. Hiding something important is lying. Making it seem like something else is more lying. I wanted to know why.

Having seen Lily after she died and not telling me was an enormous lie.

I probably needed to push her a little to get her talking. Asking wouldn't work, she was so good at her lies. Maybe scaring her might do it. If she thought I already knew, whatever there was to know... As water gushed through my hair, it came to me. I would tell her I'd dreamt about Lily trying to tell me something. Raven would believe that in a heartbeat; she was all about the supernatural and people having powers and dreams and all of that.

I dried myself off and got ready for dinner, imagining my fabricated dream as I did.

16

RAVEN

While I changed my clothes and brushed my hair, Abbey sat on the edge of the tub, watching me. Hanging out while I got ready seemed like something a close friend would do, which made me feel like maybe I hadn't been patient enough with her. Finally, she seemed as if she wanted to talk.

"I guess being with you is stirring up the past for me," she said.

"Me too." I stabbed the bar for a gold chain earring through the hole in my earlobe.

"I fell into a really deep sleep while you were gone," she said.

"I guess you were tired. It's stressful—"

"I had a dream about Lily."

"That's weird." I stabbed the other earring at my right earlobe but missed the hole.

"It was incredibly vivid." She paused, holding my gaze in the mirror until I looked away. "She was standing in the rain at UW. Remember that little circle area outside our dorm with the benches surrounding that maple tree?"

I nodded.

"It was pouring rain."

"You said that."

"I mean really pouring. Literal buckets. There was more rain than I've ever seen in my life. An atmospheric river, epic rain."

"Okay."

"I was standing just outside the doors to our dorm, and Lily was gesturing at me to go out in the rain. She was frantic about it, waving her arms at me. And you know how in dreams you kind of know things that you can't know in real life?"

"Not really." I wondered what she was trying to say. I wondered why she would be dreaming about a dead person instead of her own life.

"I knew, I just *knew*, she wanted to tell me something really important."

"What did she tell you?"

"I don't know. I couldn't get out from under the overhang. I think I was afraid the rain would hurt me."

"Maybe you thought *she* would hurt you."

Abbey shook her head so hard, she almost slipped backwards into the bathtub. "No. I wanted to go out there. I knew I had to get close to her. I knew I couldn't leave her standing there all alone."

"Were her eyes two colors?"

"What?"

"Were her eyes two different colors? Otherwise, how do you know for sure it was her?"

She laughed. "I just knew. I didn't notice her eyes. Her eyes didn't matter."

"That's pretty important."

"It was more about the feeling, that she desperately had

to tell me a secret and she couldn't rest until she did. Anyway..." She stood. She ran her fingers through her hair and looked in the mirror over my shoulder, arranging her hair around her face. "I think pathways in my mind are opening up because of spending time with you. Maybe the dream will continue another time."

"Maybe." I put on lip gloss. "Ready?"

In the elevator, she started up again about the dream. "It was really important to her. I can't stop thinking about it. Or her."

"Maybe it's your guilty conscience," I said.

"For what? My conscience is absolutely clear. I got blamed for something that didn't even happen, and it ruined my life. Getting a good job without a degree is almost impossible. I did nothing wrong, and you know that."

"It wasn't my fault. You wanted to drop out of school. I tried to get you to stay."

"How do you stay in school when every single person you know decides you're a killer?"

"I told you I tried to help, I tried to be there for you, but you gave up too fast." I punched the button to hold the doors open because she was taking so long to step out of the elevator. "I was going through a horrible time, breaking up with Carter after..." I stepped out of the elevator, not wanting to talk about this at all, hoping that we could switch our attention to making our way through the crowded lobby and out onto the street swarming with people walking to restaurants.

"After what?" she asked.

"You know. After Lily died... Everyone was messed up. Of course, they blamed you for not helping her because no one could believe she just OD'd. It was incomprehensible. Blaming you wasn't fair; it was totally not fair, I agree. But since you were the one who found her, you have to see why they thought that. We were all so upset. You weren't the only one. And I was in a lot of pain over my decision to end things with Carter; it was hard to focus on your stuff all the time."

I felt like I couldn't move. Abbey was staring at me. She was looking right into my eyes but didn't seem to be focusing on them.

"What's wrong?" I asked. "Did you forget something in the room?"

She shook her head, still staring, still not seeming to notice I was there.

I laughed. "You look like you're in shock."

"I'm just...you were so upset when he dumped you. So upset, it was a little scary. Why are you acting like you ended it?"

I wasn't sure why I'd said that. I remembered now how I'd carried on about our breakup. Of course Abbey remembered that part. I'd acted like I was out of control. "We had a huge fight, so at the time, it felt like he was dumping me. But then I didn't want to be with him after that. Now, I remember that part of it more than the other."

"You cried all the time about him dumping you. What was the fight about?"

I laughed. "This is ancient history. I haven't thought about him in years. Why are we even talking about it? Let's go." I started walking, and she followed, although she was lagging.

I really wanted a glass of wine. I needed to calm down. I felt like Abbey knew something she wasn't telling me. Wondering what she was thinking started the paranoid thoughts swimming through my head. Why had she really invited me on this trip? She'd hated me back then, when she dropped out. Had she really gotten past all of that? Her dream freaked me out. I wondered if Lily had spoken to her in that dream. Maybe Lily had shared a secret, and Abbey wasn't telling me that part.

I didn't like believing the dead could speak to us, but I couldn't help it. My mother was always saying the membrane between this life and the next was very thin. She said most people were blind to the subtle, intangible elements of life. She believed in visits from people in her dreams—the living and the dead. She believed she could heal people with her herbs and tinctures, and that there really were powers in the universe that anyone who was open could tap into.

I didn't want to tap in. Sometimes, it seemed as if children were almost brainwashed by their parents. It was difficult to stop thinking the thoughts you grew up with and believing the things you were told. I didn't like believing in the super-natural, but I couldn't help it. Any time I tried to tell myself it was all fantasy, I felt I was betraying her. I saw the sadness in her eyes, the hurt and disappointment. Emmett didn't under-stand why I still struggled with this. I supposed that was why he got so upset when I said I was cursed.

My mother had taught me that without a spiritual core, without knowing the universe was with me and that I had power over my life and my body, I would be lost in the world. Maybe that was why I felt a little lost. Instead of giving me guidance, maybe her words had cast a spell on me and doomed me to being lost.

I loved my mother, and I hated having these thoughts. She was a wonderful, loving, caring woman who made me feel safe every day of my life. But she did have this thing. This witch thing.

Abbey had finally caught up to me.

"I saw a high-end pub advertised in that brochure in our room. They have gourmet burgers and hand-cut fries. A full bar. Do you want to try that?"

"Sure."

We walked along the street, both of us in a daze, I thought. Abbey was obsessed with her dream, and I couldn't stop worrying that Lily was haunting me. Going to that fraternity house again after all these years would be good for both of us. If my mother was right about these things, we could confront Lily's ghost once and for all.

17

LILY'S JOURNAL
OCTOBER 6, 2010

I've never cried so hard in my life. I feel like my brain has been ripped out of my head. My midterm paper for my genetics class is gone.

Vanished.

I searched every single folder on my laptop. More than once. I asked a guy I know who's studying computer science to search for it. The paper was finished, footnotes and all. It was really good. I know that. I put an amazing amount of research into it. I used more sources than the teacher required. I worked on it for three weeks. Every single night. The only thing left to do was spellcheck. And now it's gone.

When the Roaches came home, they wanted to know why I was crying.

Papers don't vanish into thin air. I know I should have backed it up, but my computer is only a year old. Everyone says you should always, always back things up, but I've never known a single person who had a brand-new computer die. And it's not dead! Everything is fine. No other documents are missing. Just that paper. Maybe I should blame myself for being stupid enough to go to the bathroom sometimes and leave my laptop open on my bed. I know they're roaches, but I never thought they would jump on my bed and mess with my computer.

I was so upset, the words spewed out of me like vomit. "Who deleted my paper? Please, please tell me you're just trying to scare me. Please tell me you printed a copy. You wouldn't actually destroy it completely, would you?"

"I never touch your laptop," Roach Two said.

"Neither do I," said Roach One. "Unless it's on the floor; then I always put it on your bed for you."

That was a lie and almost funny because she knows that I know it was a lie. I didn't call her on it. Finding out where my paper was mattered a lot more than proving she was a liar.

"My paper is gone!" I stared at them, trying to force them to look at my eyes. Neither one met my gaze, but that isn't unusual. They never look at my eyes. Their eyes skip across my forehead, brush my eyebrows, settle on the place where my hair parting meets my forehead.

"You should be more careful," Roach Two said.

"I am careful." I was almost screaming, but I couldn't help it.

"Didn't you back it up?" Roach One asked.

"I know how to use a computer," I said.

"But did you back it up?"

I slammed the laptop closed. "I know one of you deleted it. I'm begging you...please, please, *please* tell me you printed a copy." I told them I didn't care if they thought I was stupid. I assured them they'd won whatever game they were playing. I even admitted I was terrified. Half my grade depends on that paper. They stared at the top of my forehead with little smiles on their faces—smiles of pity.

"I'm really sorry," Roach Two said. "It sounds like a catastrophe. *Half* your grade?"

"Me too," Roach One said.

I started crying. Right in front of them. I hated myself for doing that, but I couldn't believe it was gone. I still can't. If they weren't going to admit they'd deleted it, they probably hadn't printed a copy. It was a fantasy to believe even for a single second that they had.

They want me to fail. They don't just want to make me feel left out and embarrass me in front of guys. They want to sabotage my education. Maybe they think I'll flunk out, and they can have the room to themselves.

Tears poured out of my eyes, and my face twisted into ugly shapes, as it does when you cry. I hate showing that to anyone—that complete exposure of your heart. My nose started running. I was so embarrassed and so angry I couldn't even figure out which I felt more. I don't even know right now while I'm writing this. Despite them vowing on their lives they didn't do it, there's no doubt in my mind that one of them deleted it, or that both were in on it.

I get that I'm not like them. I get that I come across as superior and probably judgmental, but this is a whole new level of bullying. I don't think I'm being dramatic to use that word.

There's no way I can rewrite that paper. I'm sure I would remember parts of it, but it was a twenty-page paper! I can't remember every single point I made. I can reconstruct parts of it from my notes and my memory, but it's due in two days. If I'm beyond lucky, I *might* get a B-, but a C is honestly the best I can hope for now.

All afternoon and again after they came back from dinner, I begged them to tell me it wasn't completely gone. I totally humiliated myself, and they just looked at me like I was the biggest loser they've ever known.

Part of me wants to do something awful to them, but I'm not that kind of person. I just want them to stop. I want to have friends and enjoy college. I'm not here just to study, even though I love learning, love classes, love the lab work. I'm a normal person. They don't seem to believe that.

All I want is someone who likes me. A friend outside my study partners. I want to be in a room where I feel safe and welcome. They, especially Roach One, makes me feel like I'm illegitimately occupying space that belongs to her. She *wants* me to feel that way. It's not just me overreacting and not compromising or not being friendly or not trying to fit in. She wants me to know that she doesn't like me and that she thinks I'm a freak.

They talk about me when I'm sitting right there, pretending they don't realize I can hear them. It's not always absolute bullying, sometimes they just say things like—*it smells disgusting in here*, then go back and forth sniffing at each other and assuring themselves it's neither one of them. Sometimes they talk about parties and how everyone just loves each other and they're all a team and a gang and they'll be friends for life.

"That's a big part of the college experience," Roach One says. And not just once or twice. It's a favorite theme of hers. Making rock-solid friendships that last the rest of your life. Friendships that turn into professional contacts, but also friendships where you go to each other's weddings and become godparents for your friends' children.

It's quite clear they don't mean me.

18

ABBEY

As we walked to dinner, I clawed into my pit of memories, digging around for the smallest flicker that would help me figure out why Raven was insisting she had broken up with Carter a month before I dropped out of college. It hardly mattered. They were only together for seven or eight months, from the end of our freshman year. She insisted she didn't think about him anymore, and that made sense. No healthy person broods for twelve years about a college boyfriend when she's got a husband who adores her. No one thinks about college much at all after they've been out for a few years. Unless they're dissatisfied with the way life turned out and view those four short years as the best years of their life, everything since a bit of a letdown.

But I was certain Carter had broken up with Raven. She'd cried herself to sleep every night for weeks. She sent him faux-cheery, I'm-chill messages to stay in touch, as if that would bring him back. I know because she consulted with me on the wording and *tone* of these messages. And there were a lot of them. That was the main thing I remembered.

She wanted him back. If she'd ended it, why would she be strategizing about how to get him back? She would simply tell him she'd made a mistake.

It was strange to me that she wouldn't tell me what their fight had been about. It was years ago. She tried to brush it off as unimportant, but if it wasn't important, was no longer a secret between the two of them, why not tell me?

She'd either lied then or was lying now. Why? It was impossible to believe she'd forgotten what happened. If she was trying to protect her ego, to make it look like he hadn't tossed her aside, why did she care? It made no sense to me, and I couldn't stop thinking about it.

The burger place was crowded. We had to wait fifteen minutes for a table, which was actually not that bad since we didn't have a reservation. I suggested sitting at the bar while we waited. Raven trudged behind me to an open space between two stools. Her body said she didn't want to be there, but I wanted a drink to settle my spinning thoughts. I ordered a martini, and she ordered a glass of champagne. Less calories than wine, she said. I was not on a road trip to count calories, but I didn't criticize her.

Once we were seated at our table, food ordered, a second round of drinks in front of us, Raven pushed her champagne glass away from her. "I actually shouldn't be drinking at all."

"Why not? We're not driving."

"When you're trying to get pregnant, you shouldn't drink. You never know when you might conceive, and those first weeks are so critical to development."

"I think one or two drinks aren't a huge issue."

She picked up her glass and took a tiny sip, acting as if I'd forced her into it.

Our food arrived—a cheeseburger with fries for me and a grilled chicken breast and steamed vegetables for Raven. I was fully aware beef and cheese were not the best choice, but it was a road trip. Why was she so strict with herself? What had she thought this was going to be about? A week of infertility discussions with daily weigh-ins? It depressed me. At the same time, what she wanted or expected no longer mattered, if it ever had. I wanted information. I wanted secrets. I wanted lies confessed to, not the gluing together of a friendship that had been dead for more than five times the number of years it had existed to begin with.

I was also still determined to have fun. How many times did I have to tell her that? This was my victory lap, my chance to realize how very free I was, and to consider what was coming next in my life. Instead, I had petty arguments with a woman who was doing everything she could to spoil that fun. I took a bite of my burger, then a sip of the beer I'd ordered because it seemed to go better than a martini.

"I know you just got divorced, but once you meet someone new, there's still plenty of time for you to have children," Raven said.

"I know."

"Hopefully you'll meet someone soon."

"I'm not in a rush."

"It's definitely good to take your time. But it's hard when the biological clock is ticking so loud you feel like there's a hammer in your head, pounding out the days and years."

I took another sip of beer. Her champagne glass remained in the center of the table, the bubbles streaming to the top, as if they were saying *please let us make you happy*. But they were ignored. After a while, they would give up.

"Oh my God!" Raven's face was so white I thought she might pass out.

I felt a sharp stab of irritation in my chest. Not again. I swallowed some beer and shoved two fries into my mouth.

"He's here," she said in a loud whisper.

I didn't have to ask who *he* was.

"He isn't giving up. Oh my God, Abbey. What should we do?"

"Eat your dinner. Drink some champagne."

"He's staring right at me."

"Either stare back or quit thinking about him. Come on, Raven. There are forty or fifty people in here. He's not going to do anything to you."

"Why aren't you concerned? I don't get it."

"Because I know he can't hurt us. Yes, it's annoying, but it's nothing to get so worked up about."

"Oh my God. Oh my *God*."

"What?"

"He's walking toward us. I think he's coming to our table."

I smirked.

"It's not funny."

"It sort of is. Maybe now we'll get an explanation. And then you can relax."

A moment later, he was standing beside our table. He looked at me, not Raven. He gave me a teasing smile. "You look familiar."

"Do I?" The lilt in my voice was obvious to me. I wondered if Raven heard it.

"Leave us alone," Raven said. "I don't know what you want, but you need to stop."

"I wonder where I've seen you before." He stared at me and ran his hand over his smooth, glossy scalp. He rubbed it slightly, as if he was actually trying to figure it out.

"I have one of those faces," I said.

"A stunning face," he said.

Raven glared at me, making angry noises that sounded a bit like a snorting pig.

I picked up my beer and took a sip. "Why are you following us?"

"Who wouldn't?"

"It's unacceptable," Raven said.

I put my beer on the table and gave her a sympathetic look. "He's nice enough."

"That's all you can say about me?" he asked. "Nice *enough*?"

"I have insufficient information to say more," I said.

He laughed. "We'll have to fix that."

"Stop it," Raven said. "Leave us alone."

He took a few steps back. "Your friend seems very upset, so I'll let you enjoy your dinner."

"Bye," I said.

When he was gone, Raven grabbed my beer and placed it out of my reach. "Are you drunk?"

I laughed. "I only had one martini and a few sips of beer."

"You were flirting with him!"

"So?"

"That's the guy who followed me by the river! Who followed us all the way here. And you're flirting with him? You have no idea what he wants."

I laughed again. "I think I have an idea what he wants."

She gave me a stern look, as if I were a child, a very naïve child. "You need to do a better job trusting your gut. I wonder if your ex-husband weakened your instincts."

"I trust my gut. Always. And my gut says he's fine."

"That doesn't mean anything."

"He's just an aggressive flirt."

"You're delusional. That guy stalked us for two hundred miles. That's not an *aggressive flirt*, whatever that means."

I took a bite of my burger. As I ate, I sipped water since Raven was still holding my beer captive. We didn't speak for several minutes, eating and chewing and sipping in silence, avoiding the other's gaze.

I pushed my chair away from the table. "I'm going to the restroom."

"Be careful."

"He's gone. You chased him away."

"For now, maybe."

I wove past the table toward the restrooms, hoping he hadn't left. I knew I was probably more messed up than Raven realized, having sex with the guy who had followed us, but he was very hot—he worked out, and he had a perfect skull to pull off that shaved look nicely, and the sweetest dark blue eyes.

The afternoon that I'd bailed on Raven in the bookstore, I'd met Lee while I was enjoying a cold glass of wine. I'd known immediately he was the guy Raven had described, but he was so nice. Easy to talk to. After we chatted for a while, I asked him if he'd been following us. He just laughed, but it didn't seem important, so I didn't push it. My instinct told me he was a decent guy. Except for the following thing, he wasn't at all aggressive. He was a good listener. He was funny. We talked and drank wine and marveled that we felt an immediate connection. He asked if I wanted to go to his hotel room.

I said yes.

Raven would kill me. What I was doing was definitely weird, over the line, risky, but it was fun. How often in my life had I stepped over a line? Never. Flirting with a near-stranger, a man Raven was irrationally afraid of, was entertaining. Not to mention—very good sex.

Being with him made me feel more in control of the situation with her, knowing that I'd not only proven her anxiety was irrational, but that I had a secret she would want to know as badly as I wanted to know hers.

I turned the corner to the alcove that housed the restrooms. There he was. He stood right beside the door to the women's, arms folded across his chest, a grin on his face.

"I knew you looked familiar," he said.

I laughed.

"How about a repeat?"

"Now?"

"Not right this minute. You look like you're busy."

"Yup."

"You could come to my room later." He moved closer. "After she goes to sleep." He was standing so we were almost touching, but not quite. I felt a charge rush through me— desire mixed with a tiny shiver of fear, which surprised me. Had Raven twisted my instincts, or was that pulse of fear genuine? He was tall, almost six two. But it was mostly those muscles. They looked, and truly were, I'd learned, as hard as steel rods. The guy had the potential to squash me like a bug when he meant to be holding me close and kissing me.

"I could do that," I said.

"See you then." He moved as if he meant to kiss me, then backed away, leaving me slightly confused. He winked, turned, and disappeared back into the restaurant.

I spent longer than I should have in the restroom, but I needed to steady my breathing and wait until the blood throbbing beneath my skin receded.

19

LILY'S JOURNAL
OCTOBER 30, 2010

I don't know why these Roaches are even at college. They live to party. School is what they do while they're waiting for the next party, or the next football game, or the next trip to the mall. Tonight, Roach One kicked it up a notch.

While they were getting into their costumes and putting on elaborate makeup so they could go to their Halloween party as twin vampires, which I thought was appropriate, Roach Two asked what I was dressing up as. I said I wasn't going, which they knew, because I never go to parties. She looked sad. For half a second, I thought it was real, that she was honestly disappointed I wasn't going. A moment later, I recognized the fake sympathy in the almost invisible curl of her lip. I reminded myself to wake up and remember that roaches don't transform into butterflies.

Once their faces were covered with thick white paint, their lips blood red, and their plastic fangs installed, Roach One suddenly yanked the fangs out of her mouth and let out this almost hysterical giggle. It was the kind of laugh I would imagine a vampire having. "Go find Carter and the others. I'll be there in a minute."

Roach Two told her to hurry up; then she left.

"I almost forgot," Roach One said. She almost sounded like she was purring. "I definitely want to feel the love tonight." She winked at me as if I were her new best friend. She opened the side pocket in her backpack and pulled out a plastic bag of red tablets. She plucked a tablet out of the bag.

"Heaven, here I come!" She popped it into her mouth and swallowed without water. Then she looked right at me, meeting my gaze for once. "You know who should really take it..." She held out the bag to me.

I said no thanks. I turned onto my stomach and moved the book I had open on my pillow, shifting around on the bed until I couldn't see her.

"Don't turn your back on me." She deepened her voice, trying to make herself sound more serious. "You need this, Lily. You are the most rigid, anxious, unloving person I know."

I told her I wasn't interested, but of course that didn't stop her. She grabbed my arm and started shaking me. "I just now realized this explains your problem. You don't know how to relax. You make everyone around you nervous and insecure. With E, you'll feel ecstatic, I promise. You'll love *everyone*."

I asked her if she loved everyone and reminded her that it was clear that she hated me.

"If you took some, you'd feel better about yourself and the world. You would *want* to be around other people instead of locking yourself up in a pathetic dorm room. And maybe I would love you if you were more fun."

I told her to leave me alone, but she kept going. She sounded like a street preacher—getting herself wound up as she went on and on about the *magic* in those red tablets with the sightly crooked hearts stamped on them.

Finally, she dropped the plastic bag of tablets onto my textbook. "Think about it. I'm happy to share. I'm a very generous person."

The minute the door closed behind her, I tossed the plastic bag onto her bed. I closed my book and started writing in here.

While I'm writing, I feel a microscopic bit of sadness for the Roach. How horribly unhappy she must be if she needs chemicals to make her like people. It sounds like she's a prisoner inside a cage made of her own angry, hateful feelings. How can anyone live knowing there's nothing about the world they really like? My sad feeling for her was there for as long as it took me to write those words. Now, it's gone.

Roach One talks a lot about witchcraft and ghosts. I guess her mother is really into that stuff, and she has this weird blend of believing in those things but laughing about it and saying it has nothing to do with her life. Despite the supposed *best friend* status of the Roaches, only one of them actually likes the other. It sounds like Roach One doesn't like anyone, not even her boyfriend. Otherwise, why does she need to take a pill to make her feel love?

I feel so lonely. It feels as if every single person living in our dorm is at a Halloween party. More than anything I wish the Prince would stop by, but I know he's celebrating, along with ninety percent of the college. It's too late to try to figure out who else might be sitting it out to see if we can find something to do.

It bothers me that the Prince is sort of in control of me. I never know when he's coming by. He comes over at least once a week, but the not-knowing kills me. Every day I'm lying on my bed studying, looking at the clock, trying to decide if it's past the time he might visit. Of course, maybe he doesn't know when he's coming either. He has to wait until he sees the Roaches go out. If they're in the room, they take up all the airspace. He feels that too. I didn't have to tell him.

But even knowing that he can't always know, it would be nice if he at least told me when he's thinking about it. I asked for his cell phone number, but he said he'd give it to me later, and then he forgot about it, I guess. I hope he forgot, and it's not that he doesn't want me to have it. Maybe he thinks I'm the type who would message him seventy-five times a day.

I don't like that he's in charge of how I feel. I don't like that my life now feels a tiny bit dull when he hasn't come by for a few days. I feel completely helpless in his hands, and that is a very scary feeling that I wish would go away.

Last week, he came over and only stayed for about twenty minutes because he happened to look out our window and see the Roaches coming back from the library much earlier than they'd said. I was more upset than usual that they were coming back because I thought, right before he looked out the window, that he was going to kiss me.

Instead of sitting on the floor as usual, he'd been walking around the room, looking at our posters up close, asking which ones belonged to which one of us. I think it's fairly obvious because they're all on the wall beside our beds. It was strange, since he knows we aren't cozy enough to share wall space. Then I wondered if he was just using it as an excuse to walk around the room, getting up his nerve.

He moved to my nightstand. I was sitting on my bed close to the nightstand, so the side of his leg bumped my knee. I moved a few inches, but it seemed like he must have also moved because we were still touching. He picked up a carved wooden bird, the only thing I keep on my nightstand besides the lamp.

He said the bird was really cool and kept running his finger over the smooth wood, stroking the feathers. It's made from olive wood, so it's incredibly smooth, almost like the feeling of silk under your fingertips. He put the bird down but stayed where he was, then turned so he was looking down at me. Laughing, he held out his hand. "I pinned you in. Do you need a hand?"

I took hold of his hand and let him pull me up to my feet. We were standing very close. I smelled cinnamon gum on his breath. He was looking into my eyes, and at first it felt warm and lovely, and then I was overcome by the thought that he was thinking about how weird my eyes are, wondering if it was going to drive him crazy if he had to look at them one more second.

Then he moved away, and I knew he wasn't going to kiss me. I couldn't figure out if he really had planned to, or if he'd even thought about it. Or if I imagined the whole thing.

20

ABBEY

It had taken forever to disentangle myself from Raven after our encounter with Lee at the burger restaurant. I felt I was wrestling an octopus. Or maybe it just felt sticky and prolonged because I had someplace else I'd rather be. Something else I'd much rather be doing.

Finally, I was walking along East Main Street, headed toward the inn where Lee was staying. All the rooms faced outdoors, making it easy to go directly to his.

He opened the door and pulled me inside, starting to kiss me while he kicked the door closed, which was quite thrilling. I almost asked him to do it again. We kissed for a long time until we were so utterly absorbed by each other I felt I was literally melting into his body. It was nearly midnight when we were lying naked beside each other, pleasantly drained, my head resting on his shoulder, my hand on the solid muscles of his belly.

He shifted my body away from his, put his face close to my ear, and whispered, "Do you want to know why you look familiar?"

I poked his hip, laughing.

"We know each other," he said.

I giggled. "Yes, we do."

"We knew each other a long time ago."

"Please don't tell me you believe in previous lives."

"I'm Lance Mitchell."

I felt my breath catch for a moment; then I laughed. "You're funny." I sat up. "How do you know him?"

He rested his head on his hand and gave me a cold stare. "Losing your twin sister splits you apart. Half your brain and half your heart are amputated. It feels like you're dead yourself. Finally, after college, I decided drinking wasn't working to numb the pain. I got into rock climbing and mountain biking. I backpack, sometimes for two months. I go alone into pretty rugged country. With all of that, your body changes. I figured you wouldn't recognize me. We didn't really even know each other that well."

I stared at the shaved head. I looked into his eyes, so blue, almost like one of Lily's. I had no idea if her twin brother had blue eyes. I'd never been that close to him. We'd been introduced once, and then all I knew of him were the vicious lies he told about me, the way he got everyone to believe I could have saved his sister's life, but simply walked away and left her to die. Since I hadn't called for help in time, I was her murderer.

How would I really know if this guy was Lance? But my gut whispered that he was telling the truth. The ice in his eyes...

I slithered to the side of the bed. The way he'd so easily and completely charmed me made it instantly clear how he'd managed to persuade so many people to go along with his version of Lily's death during the most devastating months of my life.

I got out of bed, grabbed my clothes, and began dressing,

struggling to shove my legs into my tight jeans. "Why would you...this is sick. You're really Lance? Prove it."

He turned to the nightstand and opened the top drawer. He pulled out an orange notebook covered with insect stickers. I'd seen that notebook before. Dinner and beer swam in my stomach. I took a deep breath and held it for a moment, then let it out carefully. "That doesn't prove you aren't just someone who knew Lily."

"You don't really need to believe me. All I need is what's in this." He waved the notebook in the space between us. I was fully dressed now, digging in my purse to make sure my phone was there.

"You and your friend bullied her to death."

"We did not."

"She called you roaches in here."

"I don't know what you're talking about."

He waved the notebook again. "The only problem is—I can't figure out who was worse. One was definitely worse."

I stared at him. "What do you want?"

"And I figured out some guy who was visiting Lily in her dorm room is the guy she had sex with before she died. The police never figured that out. Not that they tried—*No evidence of assault. It was consensual.*" He made a sound of disgust. "She went to that party to meet that guy."

I stared. Could it be Carter? I closed my eyes as memories from college rushed into my mind. I saw myself walking into our room, Carter sitting on the floor, his back against Raven's bed, gushing over how he and Lily had such a great time talking. Raven's fury...

"You know Lily took Ecstasy that night? It contributed to her death," he said.

I nodded, feeling my lips tremble.

"In here, she said one of the so-called roaches told her she *needed* to take Ecstasy. That it would help her be more friendly. Disgusting. Was it you? Or her?"

"I didn't." My head ached, trying to make sense of what was going on. I still only half-believed this guy was Lance, but I couldn't say with certainty that he wasn't. He was the right age. He was extremely upset, a vein in his neck pulsing. That was the most compelling proof. I could almost feel the grief in his voice. Even after all this time. And the hatred. But I had some of that as well.

"I thought your lazy, selfish, stupid behavior killed her," he said. "But I think it was both of you. And now I think it wasn't so accidental."

I shook my head furiously, as if the rapid movement and my flying hair would distract him. "I didn't hurt her. I should have stood up for her. I know that now. But Raven could be funny, and I laughed when I shouldn't have, and I didn't tell her to stop...not very often. I'm so sorry. But Lily was dead when I found her. And I think you know that." My mind continued racing. I should leave. He might hurt me. He very well might kill me. In a terrifying life-passing-before-your-eyes-as-you-face-death sensation, the things Raven had said over the past few days began to play in my mind. Raven had seen Lily dead or dying. Raven had lied about her breakup with Carter, which made no sense as a subject for lying, except now maybe it did. Raven had pretended she adored Lily's eyes when in reality she'd been absurdly terrified of their unusual nature. And now the Ecstasy. Raven loved that stuff.

"I think Raven knows something about the night Lily died," I said.

"Tossing your friend under the bus?"

"No. But the Ecstasy..."

"What about it?"

"She was really into it."

"I don't need you to confirm." He got up and pulled on pants and a shirt. "Lily wrote about it in painful detail. I just wasn't sure if it was you or her."

I needed him to focus on Raven. Maybe he could help me to get her to spill her guts. "Raven was in the room where Lily died."

"Lots of people were."

"She was there either before she died or right after. Before I found her. And she never said a word about it."

"So?"

"So she knows more than I do."

"How do you know she was there?"

I explained about my coat being under Lily's leg and how I'd felt about moving part of her body. Tears seeped into his eyes as I told him. He didn't wipe them away and he didn't say anything.

He opened the journal and thumbed the pages. He paused on one, reading words that I imagined he'd memorized by now.

"How did you find me?" I asked.

"Your helpful picture of the Benbow Inn announcing a road trip." He gave me a slightly nasty grin.

My desire to be open to anything that came my way, to share my dreams on social media, had instead picked up my past and shoved it into the center of my celebratory road trip. "I've tried gaslighting Raven to get her to tell me when she found Lily," I said. "She lies about everything. She even lied to her husband about going on this road trip, so asking her straight out is useless. Maybe we should...you could... together we could..."

He laughed. "You want me to help gaslight her into confessing to Lily's murder?"

I felt like he'd punched me in the throat. "I don't think she *killed* her! Not on purpose. I think she..." What did I think?

Ecstasy was mostly safe. People didn't OD from it on a regular basis. You couldn't say that Raven had committed murder. She'd done awful things, but not that.

We left that hanging between us. The police hadn't done anything back then and probably wouldn't care much now because any discrepancies that might undermine their theory of just another OD were still as thin as cobwebs.

"Maybe gaslighting could work," he said. "If there's enough pressure, anyone will tell you anything."

"Nothing violent," I said.

"No, sure. Just mental pressure."

He sounded agreeable, but I felt a little unsure. Was he really helping me? Or did he want to hurt Raven now that his focus was shifted off me? "You shouldn't have blamed me for her death. All I did was walk into that room. The things you said destroyed my life. I know you were hurting, but you shouldn't have. You knew it wasn't true."

"I didn't know that. I heard you screaming, and it sounded completely fake."

"How many women have you heard scream because they found their roommate dead?"

"What else could I think? The police wouldn't do anything." His voice rose. "They wrote her off as another dumb college kid drinking too much and doing drugs. They didn't believe that she would never do that, and they didn't want to hear about it. They said all kids drink. She had a lot of alcohol in her system; therefore, not liking drinking was just an opinion and it meant nothing. It wasn't evidence."

"They talked to me."

He gave a short laugh. "*Talked?*"

"They asked me questions about how I found her, why I was in the room..."

"Irrelevant questions," he said.

"Probably. But all I did was find her. So there wasn't much to say."

Lance and I did not kiss each other goodbye. I was glad he didn't try. The thought that he'd played with my mind by charming and seducing me was frightening. I shivered, thinking about how gullible I'd been.

All the way back, my head spun, trying to make sense of what had just happened. It felt slimy to be making plans with the guy who had ruined my life. I felt like I wasn't giving myself any respect. At the same time, I hadn't been able to upset Raven enough to get her to tell me what had happened, and his help might be what I needed. Every time she saw him, she got upset. Eventually it would be too much.

When I walked into our hotel room, I was greeted by a hysterical Raven.

"Where were you this time?" She was almost screaming.

"Shh. You're going to wake other guests."

"You keep disappearing! And you don't answer my texts. That's so rude. It's cruel."

"I don't look at my phone every five minutes. When it's in my purse, I don't always feel it vibrate." I was making excuses, but I owed her absolutely no excuses.

"Where were you?"

"I went for a walk. To be honest, after that thing in the restaurant, I feel a little oppressed by your fears and superstitions. I needed some air."

"You were gone an awfully long time for getting air. What else?"

"I told you I needed some space."

"I don't believe you."

"Believe what you want. I'm going to bed."

After the lights were turned off, I lay awake for a long time, wondering where I was headed.

21

LILY'S JOURNAL
NOVEMBER 1, 2010

The Roaches are trying to destroy me. I knew people could be cruel, but it never happened to me until now. I can hardly write this. The ink is smearing because my tears are dripping all over the page.

My necklace is gone. The only time I don't wear my necklace is at night and when I'm in the shower. They must have taken it while I was dead asleep.

It's not valuable, but it means everything to me. My mom gave me that necklace. The ring is her mom's wedding band —sterling silver. It's hanging on a camel-colored braided leather strap. I love it so much. Feeling the leather on my neck, fingering the ring whenever I'm trying to think about something difficult, is almost like saying a prayer or a mantra. That necklace makes me feel connected to my past, to the people who love me the most. Besides all that, it's a cool piece of jewelry—simple and unusual.

I can't stop crying. Every time I think I don't have any more tears and think I'm forgetting, I reach for the ring hanging from soft, aged leather, and the tears start pouring out of me again. I keep remembering the awful sick feeling when I went to my top drawer after my shower, to the little wood box where I keep it when I'm asleep. The box was empty. I let out a cry that was probably unbearably loud in our not very large room, but they acted as if I sounded like the siren on an emergency vehicle.

"What are you *screeching* about? It's seven thirty in the morning," Roach One said.

I faced her, telling myself this time I would make her confess. I wouldn't back down like I did with the term paper. "Where's my necklace?"

She turned on her side and readjusted her pillow. "Thanks for ruining my last five minutes of sleep. I haven't seen your necklace. I don't even know what you're talking about."

"My silver ring."

"Never noticed."

"That's a lie." I looked at Roach Two.

She shrugged. "Maybe I've seen you wear it. I forget."

I crossed the room and yanked the covers off Roach One. "Where is it?"

"Hey!" She grabbed at the comforter and sheet, but I had a tight grip. "Give me back my blankets. I'm freezing."

"Where is it?"

"I have no idea what you're talking about. I'm reporting you to the RA if you don't give me my blankets right now."

I threw her covers on the floor. "I want it back."

"I don't have it. You can look in my dresser if you don't believe me."

I yanked open her top drawer. I grabbed her bras and thongs and tossed them on the floor, shaking the camisoles to see if the necklace was hidden in one of them. I was sure it was in her dresser because she didn't think I would really go through her things. She wanted to make me look stupid, digging through her clothes in such pathetic desperation.

"Pick up my things," Roach One said.

"Let's calm down." Roach Two stood and moved over next to me, trying to close the drawer, but my hand was still inside. "You don't need to throw her stuff all over the floor."

"She stole my necklace."

"I'm pretty sure she didn't. She doesn't even know what it looks like. And she wouldn't go in your drawer."

I yanked open the second drawer and tossed T-shirts and sweaters onto the floor.

Then, without a sound or any kind of warning, Roach One was on me. She rushed out of bed and jumped onto my back. The force of her body against mine pulled us both onto the floor. She grabbed a fistful of my hair and yanked it. I managed not to scream, even though it hurt like hell. Instead, I squirmed around and sank my teeth into her thumb.

"You little bitch," she screamed. She yanked her hand away and looked at her thumb. A moment later, she went for my hair again. I shoved her off me and scrambled onto my bed.

"Stop," Roach Two said. "Stop it. We'll all be in trouble if the RA hears you."

"I know you stole it. Tell me where it is. Your stupid little *joke* is over."

"You can't accuse me of something based on nothing but the fact you hate me," Roach One said. "You have no proof. People come into our room all the time. Anyone could have taken it. Anyone."

"I wear it every day."

"You don't have it on now."

"Because I was taking a shower."

She shrugged. "You could have been in the shower and we were out at early classes."

"When has that ever happened? And I wore it yesterday.

This happened after I went to sleep last night. No one else was in here."

"You don't know that," Roach One said.

"We could search for it," Roach Two said.

Roach One scooped up her lingerie and shoved it back in the drawer. She started refolding her shirts and sweaters. "I don't have time to search. I have to clean up the mess she made. I'll be late to class."

"You were already late. You were sleeping." It was a stupid thing to say. I wanted my necklace, but I was so tired of her always making it seem like things were not what I saw right in front of me.

I grabbed my backpack, shoes, and jacket and walked out. I left the door open and put my shoes on in the hallway.

Now, I'm going to sleep with my journal under my pillow. I'm going to carry it to class in my backpack. If Roach One, or both, are looking through my things, I can't have them find this. They would cut me into tiny pieces and watch me bleed with smirks on their faces.

22

ABBEY

There was a polite but very firm knocking on our door. It shattered my dream into a million pieces. I opened my eyes, yawning, trying to recall the dream, then squinting because the light was intense. Even though we'd pulled the drapes, sunlight was pouring in through the bathroom window, hitting the white tile floor, and splashing into the rest of the suite.

I turned on my side, knowing something was very different in my life, trying to recall what it was that had shocked me to the core.

The knocking resumed. It hadn't been part of my elusive dream. "Raven, can you get that? I'm not awake."

"It sounds like you are."

I sighed, and with the next inhalation of breath, the events of the previous day flooded my mind. Lance. I sat up suddenly.

"Thank you," Raven said.

I slithered out of bed, pulled on the thick terrycloth robe the hotel provided, and went to the door.

"Check the peephole before you open it." Raven's voice was loud and commanding.

I laughed.

"And open it with the chain attached."

I very much wanted to look through the peephole, but after that I would avoid it at all costs. The remaining pieces of the previous night clicked into place—Raven might have directly caused Lily's death, even if she hadn't intended it. I felt my stomach twist into a thick mass of confusion—Raven. Lance. Sex with a guy who ruined my life...I hoped whoever was knocking was bringing complimentary bottles of sparkling water to settle my stomach. I opened the door.

A guy wearing a staff jacket and holding a small box was standing a few feet away from the door. The box was wrapped in pale brownish-green paper with a blue bow. "This was left at the front desk for you." He handed it to me.

"Is there a tag? There are two of us staying here."

He shook his head. "Just the room number."

"What is it?" Raven was suddenly behind me, her breath warm and sour on the side of my face.

I moved away. "A gift."

"From who?" Raven asked.

The guy shrugged. "I don't know."

"Find out," Raven said.

"You can ask a manager," he said. "They won't tell me, probably."

Raven grabbed the box out of my hand. She shook it hard. There was the sound of something sliding around and a soft tapping of something hard against the inside of the box. "It's light," she said.

The guy backed away from the door. "'K, bye."

Raven turned toward the door. "What's your name?"

"Ben." He pointed to his name tag.

"Thanks, Ben."

I closed the door.

"Do you think it's safe to open it?"

"Of course." I knew who had sent it, but not what it contained. He hadn't wasted any time starting his assault on Raven. And it hadn't taken much to get her rattled. The mere existence of the beautifully wrapped box made her words jittery and rushed. Her pupils had expanded to large black disks, blotting out her eye color almost entirely, like pools of oil in the centers of her eyes.

"What if it's..."

I laughed. "What? A bomb? A scorpion poised to sting us?"

"Stop making it sound like I'm hysterical. I know what you're doing, trying to make me look unbalanced. Scary stuff is happening to us, and people who ignore the small warning signs and red flags in situations like this are the ones who end up dead. You need to take this more seriously."

I undid the bow.

"I don't have a good feeling about this," Raven said.

I tore the paper and lifted the lid off the box. Tissue paper was folded carefully around the object inside. I pulled it away. In the bottom of the box was a light brown braided leather cord with a clasp, looped through a thick silver ring. "Lily's necklace."

Raven screamed. She batted at the box, knocking it out of my hands. The necklace flew out of the box and landed on the carpet.

I bent to pick it up. "Why did you do that?"

"Are you serious? Someone from college knows we're here! I assumed that guy was stalking us because he's a creep, but maybe someone hired him. That would make a lot of sense. It would explain why he doesn't seem to do anything to hurt us, just tries to scare us. Like this is some game."

"Why on earth would anyone from college hire a man to follow us?"

"It's her necklace."

"Yeah." I laughed. "I thought you never noticed it."

She grabbed it out of my hand and wrapped the strap around her fingers, then stared at the ring swaying gently a few inches below her fingertips.

"What does it mean?" she asked. "It can't be good."

"I don't know. You tell me."

"How would I know?" She picked up the box and dropped the necklace back inside. Most of the leather hung over the side.

I scooped up the strap, coiled it back into the box, and put the lid on. "What should we do with it?"

"What we do with it isn't the problem," she said. "Wake up, Abbey! Someone knows we're here—"

"Clearly."

"What are we going to do?"

"Nothing."

"Someone's trying to scare us. They want...I don't know what they want, but it's not good." She started crying softly.

"I don't understand why you think that. For what reason?"

She looked at me, not blinking, then turned away. "I need coffee. Do you want some?"

"Sure."

She went to the little pot on the counter over the fridge, which was concealed inside a wood cabinet. Water gushed out of the faucet, preventing either of us from talking as it pounded against the metal sink and then the glass of the coffee pot. When the machine began its task, she turned back to me. "Who would have her necklace? After all this time?"

I shrugged.

"Maybe her brother, since he picked up her things from the dorm. Probably they were stored at her parents' house..."

"Why does that matter?"

"Because, Abbey, I'm trying to figure out who might have had the necklace, and that will help us figure out why they want to freak us out."

"You're the only one who's freaked out. Why is it bothering you so much?"

"Because we didn't put anything on social media after the Benbow Inn. No one on the entire planet knows we're here unless you told a bunch of people what our route was."

"I didn't."

"If you're telling the truth—"

"Of course I am."

"Then the most logical thing is that this guy following us was put up to it. I've never seen him before. Have you?"

I shrugged. "How can you say for sure you've never seen someone?"

She glared at me. "Did you know him before or not?"

"Not."

The coffee finished brewing with a loud burp. Raven returned to the counter and filled two mugs. She carried them to the sitting area—two armchairs facing each other across a low table. "We have to figure out what's going on, and decide what we're going to do."

"Why do we need to do anything? Is there something you're not telling me?"

"No. Why do you think I'm not telling you something?"

"I don't know. If you're not telling me, I can't know."

"Don't be cute. You know me better than anyone."

"I used to know you better than anyone. Maybe. I sure don't anymore."

"In a lot of ways, you still do."

We sipped our coffee and stared at each other. I wondered if I looked as wary and hostile as she did. When the coffee was gone, Raven went into the bathroom and shut the door. A moment later I heard the shower running. I rinsed the mugs and left them in the sink. I looked through my purse to assure myself once again that nothing had fallen out when I was in Lance's room, although it was too late now. The souvenir from the guy's suitcase on my first night at the Benbow Inn was still nestled in the bottom of my purse.

The bathroom door crashed open, and Raven made a full run at me, wearing nothing but a towel around her torso and another wrapping up her hair. "You need to understand how terrifying this is. I don't understand why you aren't afraid."

"Stop screaming at me."

She grabbed my arm, shaking it.

"Let go of me."

She loosened her grip but didn't release it. "Please tell me you understand how scary this is. Someone we knew years ago is stalking us, and we don't really know why, but it clearly has something to do with Lily."

"Someone had her necklace and knows we're here. A guy followed us from California. Those are two different things. They seem like they're related, but that doesn't mean they are."

She squeezed my arm again. Her shoulders began to shake as she sobbed, tears oozing across her face. With my other hand, I patted her back. I tried to pry her fingers off my arm where she was cutting off the flow of blood. Still, she kept crying. It was fascinating and embarrassing. But despite all her sobbing and the obvious terror I saw every time I looked into her eyes, she refused to tell me exactly why she was so terrified.

All she was doing was proving to me that she had an awful lot of guilt from what had happened to Lily. Otherwise, what was there to be afraid of? She knew exactly what that necklace meant.

23

RAVEN

While Abbey was in the shower, I stood by the window, gazing at the street below, watching people strolling by, probably trying to decide where they would eat breakfast. When I touched it with my fingertips, the glass was warmer than I expected, promising another hot day, but I felt unnaturally cold.

Seeing that necklace terrified me. It seemed as if it had risen out of Lily's grave, coming to wrap itself around my throat, cutting off my oxygen. It was so in your face. Clearly someone knew I'd stolen it all those years ago, and they wanted to let me know that. But who could possibly know? Despite what Abbey said, it had to be connected to the guy following us. A guy who had the raw nerve to come right up to our table and act like we were friends, pretending he wasn't terrorizing us every minute of the day.

It was sickening to watch Abbey flirt with him. She was putting us both in danger, and I was getting concerned for her. It seemed as if she didn't have any boundaries, no sense of self-preservation. Maybe I should have known that years ago. Didn't dropping out of school and cutting your career plans off at the knees show a lack of self-preservation? Sure, it was hard being shunned, but she could have changed schools. She could have changed dorms and found a group that wasn't connected to the fraternity culture. But she just quit, like she thought it would punish everyone. The only one she hurt was herself. And me.

The most likely people who would have that necklace in their possession were Lily's parents or her twin brother—the guy who started all the rumors and whipped everyone into a hateful mob. Abbey didn't want to believe this could have been orchestrated by him. If she didn't wake up, she would put us in a very dangerous situation, if she hadn't already. But she didn't seem to care.

Going clothes shopping, which was our plan for the day, was like dancing on the deck of the *Titanic*. We were pretending the trip was still a normal vacation. Abbey said shopping was a good distraction. She said I shouldn't give in to irrational fear. She said this was what the trip was about. I called it ignoring an obvious threat.

Unless...I hated when these thoughts came to mind, but in some ways, it made more sense than imagining Lily's brother managing to find us on a road trip. When I was lying awake the night before, wondering if Abbey was okay, wondering if she was coming back, a voice began to whisper deep inside me. Again, when I was standing in the shower, seeing that silver ring in every drop of water that streamed past my face, I heard the whisper grow louder—the voice of my mother. Her tone was always gentle and soft. She never tried to force me into thinking a certain way. She just stated her views. They were usually so clear and kind that I believed them. They felt comforting. They sounded true.

And they'd stayed in my head. No matter how hard I tried, they were always ready to speak up. Her voice whispered that Lily's ghost was haunting me. She'd cursed my body, poisoning my eggs, and now she was trying to scare me until I died of fright. My heart was racing and beating so loud I couldn't think. It felt like my blood vessels couldn't take it anymore. She was well on her way to destroying my body.

There was no one I could talk to about these thoughts. To my mother, her beliefs were truth. She thought it was smart to consider supernatural explanations for every troubling situation. It was almost impossible to fight something that had become part of me.

I couldn't talk to anyone else. When I'd tried, people treated me like I was crazy. Growing up, most kids stayed away from me. Whether they thought I was weird or their parents told them so, I never knew.

It's hard to be treated as if there's something wrong with you. It tears you down. At first, I couldn't understand why they thought that. My mother never seemed crazy to me. There wasn't a moment when I thought she couldn't be trusted or that there was something off about her. When she talked about ghosts and spells, messages in the stars and anyone who possessed *powers*, it felt utterly real. More real than the world other people lived in. It felt normal.

If this was Lily's ghost trying to destroy me, I needed to make sure Abbey and I made it safely to the fraternity house where we could confront her. If my mother was right, some part of Lily would have lingered in that room where she died. If this vaporous form of Lily expected an apology from me, I could make myself do that. I definitely didn't owe her one, just the opposite, but if that was what I needed to do to break this curse, I would.

It was almost eleven by the time Abbey and I finished breakfast and started walking toward the shops where we planned to try on clothes. During breakfast, I managed to push the necklace out of my head. I forgot about the creep following us. I forgot about Lily.

With Abbey chattering about how she had always dressed to please her husband, and how she would now be dressing for herself, it was easy to get caught up in trivia. I knew she was trying to distract me, but it didn't matter. I started to feel better. I was looking forward to buying new clothes. New things always made me feel better. Maybe putting on a new outfit makes you feel like you've added something fresh to your personality, your life. You feel good, and it makes you believe that your life will magically improve as a result.

I loved shopping in unique stores where it was almost guaranteed the clothes you bought wouldn't show up on another woman's body. Clothes that made people ask where you bought it.

"Let's try this." Abbey stopped in front of a shop that displayed vintage clothing in a bay window with pale blue trim framing the glass.

"I was looking for clothes I can wear to work," I said.

"We can do that, too. But let's try this first. It could be fun, right, girlfriend?"

I felt a surge of warmth. After everything we'd been through the past few days, she still thought of me as a good friend. A girlfriend. I'd spent so much time upset with her, I hadn't worked consistently to deepen our connection. But without me even trying, she was feeling close to me. Maybe it was the bond that grew out of facing danger together.

We went inside the shop and split apart—Abbey to the shoes and me to the dresses. I had a moment of panic that she might slip away again, this time for good. Maybe she would keep disappearing on me and lull me into believing she would return, then, in a moment when I least expected it, she'd be gone forever. I pushed the thought away. Her disappearances were one-offs. It wouldn't happen again. She hadn't invited me on the trip just to abandon me.

I pulled a soft cotton dress off the rack—pink with tiny

yellow dots. It had a lace collar and sleeves that were designed to flow like gently moving butterfly wings around your upper arms. I pulled two other dresses off the rack and walked to where Abbey was looking at shoes.

I showed her the dresses.

"Cute," she said.

"Come wait outside the fitting room while I try them on. I want your opinion. Maybe it would be interesting to wear something unusual to work. So be honest."

"Absolutely."

We walked to the back of the store, and I stepped into one of the changing rooms, unhooking the strap that held the velvet curtain open. It fell into place, leaving me in a tiny room that barely gave me space to lift a shirt over my head without my elbows bumping the mirror or stroking the inside of the curtain.

The pink dress settled over me. I pulled up my hair and held it on top of my head. With a few tendrils clinging to my neck, I looked like someone from another era. Fragile and delicate. I turned and strained my neck, trying to see the back of it. There was only one mirror, so I couldn't get a sense of how it looked from other angles.

I pulled open the curtain and stepped out of the room, my feet bare, which I thought made me look a bit like a farm girl. "I'm not sure when I'd wear it. But I really like it."

"Oh my God."

"What? Does it look ridiculous? The wrong color for me?" I stared at her face. "What's wrong?" She looked shocked and upset, almost scared. It was gratifying to see she was capable of fear, but what had caused it? I looked past her into the shop, wondering if she was frightened because the stalker had shown up again. The only person visible to me was the shop owner, but that didn't mean he wasn't hiding just out of sight, showing himself to Abbey but not me. "Abbey! What's wrong?"

"You look so...thin. Like a skeleton."

"Oh." I laughed. "You looked scared for a minute. Being thin is a good thing." I smiled and turned, looking toward the end of the short hallway where another mirror was hung for those who ventured out of the changing rooms.

"Not in your case." She stood and came close to me. She placed her hand on my back. "I can feel your spine."

I laughed. "That's normal."

"I think you've lost almost ten pounds since our road trip started."

"I doubt that."

She shook her head. "You must be a lot more upset than I realized."

"I'm upset, but I haven't lost any weight." I walked away from her until I was standing a few feet from the mirror. I didn't see any difference in my body. The cut of the neckline exposed more of my collarbones. And now that I looked, the sleeves were an awkward length, making my elbows appear large and bony. I took a step back. My legs were the same as always. You could almost see my hip bones because the cotton was thin and the dress clung to me. I wasn't any skinnier. Was I?

"I'm sorry I haven't realized how awful this is for you. How frightened you are."

"You could fix that easily by showing some concern."

She gave me a condescending smile. I guess she wasn't truly worried about me.

"Now that I think about it," she said, "you hardly eat."

"That's not true. I do try to choose healthy foods instead of filling up with fatty fries and appetizers, but I haven't lost any weight."

"I think you aren't very objective about this. It's hard to

assess changes in your own appearance. I'm telling you, you're dangerously thin."

Maybe she was jealous. She looked thicker around the waist, and I'd seen her struggle to pull on her jeans. I laughed. "I'm perfectly healthy. Except for not being able to have a baby..." My throat closed over those words as if they regretted being let out into the open.

"It's more difficult to get pregnant when you're underweight. Did you know that?"

"Yes, I know that. But I'm not underweight. Stop acting like there's something wrong with me."

"I'm not saying it's your fault. You can't help how you feel. You've been so anxious and so worried, I can see it's affecting you more than I realized."

I turned away from the mirror. I stepped into the changing room and closed the curtain. I didn't want to hear any more. I took off the dress and placed it on the hanger. I didn't want it. She'd spoiled it for me. Now I felt like it hung on me like a sack. I was definitely not too thin, but as the words passed through my mind, I glanced at myself in the mirror. In my bra and underwear, I looked like a scrawny thirteen-year-old girl. My breasts were small and didn't swell much over the top of my bra. I looked bony. My skin was unusually pale, and not in a delicate, beautiful way. Abbey was right. I looked ill.

I shoved my bony arms and legs into my clothes and pulled my phone out of my purse.

"You're taking a long time." Abbey's voice was right on the other side of the curtain, as if she wanted to whisper directly into my ear. I could almost feel her standing there, breathing into the thick curtain.

"I changed my mind about trying on the others," I said.

"Okay. Well, I'm going back to the shoes."

I held my phone, waiting to hear her walk away. Not that

she would hear me texting. The phone was in silent mode. The space around me was equally silent, nothing but the distant click of hangers as the owner rearranged the clothes on their metal racks. I waited for over a minute before I unlocked my phone. I sent a text to Emmett.

> *Having a great time. Really relaxed. I'm feeling calmer about nature taking its course.*

I added a smiling face with the flushed cheeks of contentment.

He answered right away.

> *That's great! Thanks for the text. Please don't think you need to check in. Relax and enjoy yourself. You deserve it.*

He added a kissing emoji, which made me feel really happy. Ridiculously happy. It was just a sticker used by billions of people every day, but it meant he loved me and wanted me to be happy. My eyes blurred, and I blinked back tears.

My message to my husband was a lie. I was not having a great time. I was the most unrelaxed I'd ever been. I was terrified I would never have a baby now that I knew my body wasn't soft and welcoming. But I was trapped on this trip. I had to stay with Abbey. I had to get to that fraternity house. I had to find a way to communicate with a girl who had been dead for twelve years. A girl who was trying to ruin me.

And I was not crazy for thinking this was a good plan. Although I was feeling like I was crumbling, and there would soon be nothing solid left of me.

24

ABBEY

W e didn't get very far with our shopping. We stepped out the door of the vintage clothing store and onto the sidewalk, but before I could even open my mouth, Raven let out a little shriek.

"There he is." She turned quickly, as if that meant he couldn't see her. "He's watching us again. Oh my God, Abbey. We have to do something."

"Please stop. You're exhausting me. He's just a guy, and he seems nice enough. And yes, it's a little weird, but he hasn't done a single thing to hurt us or even threaten us."

She stepped in front of me, glaring at me. "Stalking two women is threatening by itself. What the hell is wrong with you? Do you really believe the things you keep saying? There isn't a woman on earth who would think this was okay or consider it nothing to worry about. Except you."

"No serial killer is going to keep showing himself to his intended victims, if that's what you're worried about. A serial killer is not going to chat to us in a restaurant."

"That's not true. They can be very friendly to women, trying to get them to let down their guard."

"It's broad daylight. There are hundreds of people all around us."

"It was the same for quite a lot of women who ended up brutally murdered."

"He's not a serial killer."

She looked at me as if those were the stupidest words she'd ever heard. "I'm going back to the hotel." She turned and began walking quickly, almost running by the time she reached the corner. She hugged her purse close to her hip and plowed forward, not looking back to see if I was following, or if the man was pursuing her.

"Raven!" My voice carried down the street. "Wait."

She slowed but kept walking. A moment later I caught up to her. She was breathing hard, her lips trembling, making her look like a small child.

"Is everything okay with you?" I asked. "I know you're upset about not getting pregnant...but you seem a little..."

She stopped and yanked her purse strap higher on her shoulder, closer to her neck, as if that would keep it safer. "A little what?"

"Are you on some kind of medication? Are you seeing a therapist?"

"No. There's nothing wrong with me."

"You're insanely afraid. It's not normal," I said.

"I'm going back to the room. I don't feel safe out here. He's following us everywhere."

I walked beside her but didn't say any more.

In the room, she put the security lock on the door as well as the chain lock.

"Please don't be so upset." I put my arm around her shoulders and gave her a gentle squeeze. "He's just playing with us. He's flirting. Maybe he's being a bit stupid about it, but that's all it is. You saw how nice he was when he came to our table."

She put her purse on the floor and flopped onto the bed. She was holding her phone close to her face, staring at the screen. "I'm calling the police."

"What for?"

She tapped the phone.

"You can't call the police."

"He's stalking us, and I want them to know, even if they can't do anything about it right now. Maybe they'll talk to him. Even if they won't, they need to be aware."

"Please don't."

"I'm not going to let him terrorize us without fighting back." She sat up and unlocked her phone. "I don't know if they'll like this reported to 911, so I guess I need to figure out the nonemergency number. Although this situation is close to meeting 911 criteria, in my opinion."

"You can't call the police, Raven. If they talk to him, you and I will look like we're trying to cause trouble."

She ignored me, tapping her phone, hunting for the number for the Ashland police.

"Stop." I went to the bed and pushed the phone to the side. It fell out of her hand onto the comforter. "You can't call the police. I hooked up with him."

She covered the phone with her hand and turned her head to look at me. "You hooked up? As in, you...in the restaurant? What are you talking about?"

"When I left you in the bookstore the other day. He came into the bar where I was having a glass of wine. He was really nice, and we got talking and—"

"You had a drink with the guy who's *stalking* us? And you never bothered to tell me?" She sat up. "That is so seriously messed up, I don't know what to say." Her voice rose. "Why didn't you tell me?"

"Because I went to his room, after. And you seem a little judgmental about sex. I didn't want a lecture."

"You had *sex* with the guy stalking us. I don't believe..." She laughed. "Are you saying crazy stuff to upset me? You didn't really go to his room, did you?" She laughed harder, the giggle turning to hysteria.

"It wasn't about you. I did it because he's nice. And we clicked."

"You *clicked*? You put us in terrible danger. You lied to me. Sex with two strangers in one week?"

"Well, technically he isn't..."

"He isn't what? A stranger? Do you *know* this guy?" She got off the bed, shoving her face close to mine. "Is that what dropping out of school did to you? Turned you into a liar and a manipulator? If you hated me this much, why did you subject me to the torture of a road trip? Or is that the whole purpose, to make me miserable so you can punish me for whatever you think I did wrong?"

"I'm not trying to punish you." I pushed her shoulders slightly to get her to move away.

"Don't push me."

"I didn't push you."

She put her hand on my shoulder and pushed. Hard. I started to fall. I grabbed the nightstand to keep myself from losing my balance and moved away from her. It wasn't going to help anything if we got violent with each other. I just needed to make sure she didn't call the police.

She raised her voice. "Do you know him? Is he some guy you already started an affair with, and you invited him to follow you, playing some weird little sex game with you?"

"No."

"You know this guy, and you let him terrorize me like this?"

"No, I didn't know him until..."

"Then what are you talking about?"

"You're not going to like this."

"I don't like very much about this trip at all, at least not the things you're doing. It feels like you might be more upset over losing your husband than you're saying. Because you're incredibly self-destructive."

"I didn't lose my husband. I stopped putting up with his emotional abuse."

As if she hadn't heard me, she kept talking. "You're feeling insecure and alone. You need to do all these risky things to make yourself feel noticed."

"That's not even close." There might have been a sliver of truth in what she said, but she was turning it into something neurotic, and it wasn't.

She folded her arms across her chest.

"I didn't recognize him. All he did was sit next to me and order a glass of wine. We started talking, and it just flowed."

"I don't understand why you would talk to a guy who wants to hurt us, much less—"

"You have no evidence he wants to hurt us."

"Oh, you're sure of that now? He said so, and you believe him?"

"I got a good vibe from him. Although—"

"And you went to his room? He could have killed you."

"It turns out that he's...there's no easy way to say this without shocking you...he looks so different because he does extreme outdoor sports. And he shaved his head, of course. And it's been so long...I truly didn't recognize him. Thinking back, there was something familiar about him...maybe?"

"What are you talking about?"

"He's Lance. Lance Mitchell."

She stared at me, her lips slightly parted, her eyes glassy.

"Lily's twin brother."

"I know who Lance Mitchell is. You don't have to tell me."

"You looked like you didn't get it."

"I definitely get it. I get everything. You're recovering from a disappointing marriage by sleeping with any man who will have you. It doesn't matter if he's a total stranger, and it doesn't matter if he might be violent. And now, you don't care if it's someone who you claim ruined your life."

"I didn't know it was him."

"Then how do you know it is?"

"He knew enough about Lily and her rooming with us. He was obviously either telling the truth or he'd been given a dossier on Lance and Lily. When he came to our table, there was something that made me feel as if I might know him. When we were in his bed last night—"

"You did it again? You didn't need a break from me, you needed sex. Nice lie...mislead me and make me feel shitty at the same time. Well done."

I wondered if I was pushing her too far. It was interesting to watch her freak out, but if none of this nudged her to telling me everything that had happened the night Lily died, it was a waste of time. She was so upset about my behavior, but she didn't have any inclination to apologize for her own, far worse, behavior. "It was the truth. I did need a break. I've told you a hundred times, I came on this trip to have fun and go a little crazy and let things happen as they will. You're so anxious and upset, I feel like I can't breathe."

"Sorry for being cautious and looking out for you. Of course, how would I know there was nothing to worry about because he's someone we knew?"

"I only realized it last night."

"Yeah."

"It's the truth."

She narrowed her eyes, peering into mine as if she could somehow figure out from the size of my pupils if I was telling the truth. I was not, but no one can tell that by looking into your eyes.

"I guess we know where the necklace came from," she

said. "Do you think she told him I took it? She must have, or why else would he send it?"

"They were pretty close. What she probably told him was that *I* took it." I glared at her, but she didn't seem to notice.

She nodded, a distant look in her eyes, as if she were trying to recall the details of taking the necklace and Lily finding it, wondering how the events had been presented to her brother. "I guess he must have seen your post about the Benbow Inn and tracked us down."

I nodded.

"What does he want?"

"Nothing."

She let out a staccato laugh. After a moment, she said, "What does he *want*?"

"He said he—"

"He wants something. He didn't send that necklace because he thought she'd want one of us to have it. He was trying to upset us." She closed her eyes for a moment, then opened them with a look of pure hatred. "You knew it was him when the necklace arrived. But you didn't say a word about it."

"You get so wound up about my sex life." I laughed and tried to make a face at her.

"That's irrelevant. You should have told me."

"I'm telling you now."

"Don't be stupid. He wants something." She looked more terrified than ever, as if Lance were standing in the room, holding a gun, and moving toward her, aiming at her throat, ready to stop the flow of lies with a bullet. "Why are you still so scared? We know him. Wasn't that what you were worried about? A stranger who might hurt us? He's a former class-mate. We're absolutely fine."

"You sure are cheery about it. What happened to *he ruined my life*?"

"He apologized."

"And that's all it took?"

"Yes."

"It's not that easy. You didn't ask any questions about why he was following us? Did you know he had her necklace?"

"We made love—"

"It's not making love when you don't know the person. It's just sex."

"We had *sex*, and then he told me who he is, and I left."

"I don't understand you. Were you this clueless and trusting in college? I don't remember you that way."

I moved away from her and grabbed my hairbrush off the nightstand by my bed. I started toward the bathroom.

"That's it? A guy who hated us in college is stalking us, and you had sex with him, and now you're going to brush your hair?" She was almost screaming. I wondered if someone would report us.

"I thought you'd be happy. There's nothing to be so afraid of now that we know."

"He isn't following us and seducing you, or whatever he did, and sending her stuff to us because he's flirting. This is even more frightening than when I thought he was a stranger." She whimpered. "He wants to punish us, don't you realize that?"

"If he's punishing anyone, it's me, not you. I'm the one he blamed."

"But now all is forgiven? For both of you."

"He seemed sincere."

"Stop trusting everyone without thinking," Raven said. "He knew who you were, he followed you, he came onto you, and then had sex with you and never told you who he was. He lied about his name, I assume."

I nodded.

"The way he calculated it is so messed up and very scary. If you can't see that, there's something broken inside you."

"I get that it's messed up."

"Then we should call the police."

"Don't you see that we'll look like part of the problem?"

"Well, you are part of the problem. Because you *have* to have sex whenever some random guy smiles at you."

"I think he's much more stable now. He seems centered. You can't carry that level of grief and blame for all those years without it eating you from the inside out. And all his outdoor stuff, pushing his body to the extreme, I think it was cleansing."

"He's not over it. He would not have sent *her* necklace to us anonymously if he was *over* it." She pushed past me and went into the bathroom. She slammed the door and locked it.

I'd thought the shock of knowing he was looking for us might scare her enough to want to be on the same side with me. I thought she might feel the need to tell me everything so we could come up with a plan for getting him to leave us alone. But she didn't. The longer she held out, the worse I imagined her sins were.

25

RAVEN

I poured scented bath salts into the steaming water filling the tub and stayed in the bathroom for an hour. The water was as hot as I could bear so I wouldn't be forced out before I was ready. I needed to think without Abbey buzzing in my ear. The almost too-hot water would numb my body and shut me off from the world.

I closed my eyes and rested the base of my skull on the porcelain. Each time something new and disturbing had taken place on our journey, I'd felt slightly more trapped. Most people would consider my willingness to continue the trip with Abbey to be the choice of a woman who's part of an abusive relationship. The surprising and certain fact was that I still wanted to be friends with her. I wanted to get back what we had. I wanted a girlfriend. It didn't feel abusive, but I could see that it might look that way. My mother would call it abusive, and I suspected Emmett would as well.

The water cooled, and I still had no idea what I should do. Part of me wanted to call the police despite Abbey's prediction of looking like troublemakers. I was terrified of what Lance might do next. The other part of me knew that calling the police would mean explaining a lot of things that had happened years ago, things that were difficult to explain to someone who hadn't been there. What police officer cares about the complicated relationships of college kids?

As I climbed out of the tub, a new thought pricked my mind. I pulled the plug and watched the opening suck water into the pipes. It was clear that Abbey didn't respect me. If I drew a line in the sand, maybe that would change. I could force her to look at me differently. She might realize she had to work harder to keep our friendship because she would suddenly recognize what she had to lose. She would give up her slutty behavior, and we'd figure out what to do. Together.

I dried off and went into the bedroom. Abbey was sitting in one of the armchairs, drinking a bottle of water.

"I think I should fly home," I said. "Today."

She screwed the cap onto her bottle. "That's a little extreme."

"If we leave soon, we can get to Portland by afternoon, and I'll book a flight for this evening or go standby."

"If that's what you want."

"It is. I'm sorry to abandon you."

She gave me a wicked, probing smile. "Are you abandoning me?"

"I hate seeing you driving all alone, but you haven't given me a choice."

"Whatever. Maybe I'll ask Lance if he wants to travel together. That could be interesting." She stood and went to the closet, opening the door and running her hand over the clothes hanging there.

I felt like we were playing a video game and she'd just leaped one thousand points ahead of me. I couldn't leave her with Lance! I'd thought she would beg me to stay, I thought she would tell me she'd change her behavior. I couldn't figure out if she didn't care about me at all or if she was trying to force me into accepting her version of reality.

"That seems like a really bad idea," I said.

"Not really. I never knew him in college, and from what I've seen, he's a pretty nice guy."

"He hated your guts. What are you trying to prove?"

"He understands now what really happened."

"What is that?"

"I found her dead. He's finally able to face that. He doesn't need to blame someone for a tragic accident."

I nodded. Traveling with Lance could get her killed. With one simple, risky suggestion, she'd trapped me again. My determination to command her respect dissolved. She needed me to keep her safe. And as it dissolved, I remembered I still had a date with Lily's spirit in that fraternity house. Even if Abbey didn't want to renew our friendship, I still longed for a child to love. And for that, it looked like I would be required to give Lily the apology she demanded but didn't deserve. "Okay. You win."

"Were we playing a game?" Abbey asked.

"I'll stay, but you need to realize he has not gotten over his sister's death. He hung on to that cheap necklace all this time."

"I don't think it's cheap. The ring is sterling silver."

"That's not the point. He's using it to stir up our memories of her. We need to lose him. I think we should check out now and head to Portland before he realizes we're gone."

"That doesn't make sense. We only have two more nights. We wanted to go hiking. And we still haven't eaten at that seafood place..."

I knew I was being stupid. Maybe Lily wasn't the only person who had me in her power. I couldn't leave. I was either weak or the most loyal friend every. I wanted to cry, because I was pretty sure I was mostly weak. "Okay." My voice trembled, showing the tears were close. I took a breath to steady it. "Then we're changing rooms." I grabbed my purse and walked to the door. "I'll tell them there's a guy bothering us. Or something."

"The room is in my name. I'll do it." Abbey picked up the receiver on the hotel phone and called the front desk, asking for the manager. She had to do a bit of pleading, but she finally convinced them to move us up one floor and to the back of the building. Our new room overlooked the parking lot instead of East Main Street, but I didn't care. It was much safer now that he had no idea if we were still there. Slightly. Maybe he couldn't find our room, but he would check the parking lot for our conspicuous convertible.

It was a headache to pack everything and get a cart to wheel our things to the elevator and up one floor, but so worth it.

"Originally, I was thinking we would go kayaking this afternoon," Abbey said. "I assumed we would go together, but if you don't want to..." She stripped off her T-shirt and bra, dropping them onto the floor. She grabbed her bathing suit top off the bed and put it on. "I don't know about you, but I need to get rid of some of this adrenaline. It's tempting to douse it with alcohol, but not a good idea. And this will be more fun. I've heard the kayaking at Emigrant Lake is divine. I don't want to miss it."

"Sounds fun. I'll go."

"Are you sure?"

"Why not?"

"You're so jumpy, it might be hard to control your paddle..." She eyed me, letting her gaze travel up and down my body. "And you look so frail."

"I'm not frail." I yanked my swimsuit out of my bag.

Abbey dug into her suitcase and pulled out a San Francisco Giants baseball hat and a white hoodie. Along with her phone, she stuffed her ID, a credit card, our new room card, and lip balm into a small waterproof bag and zipped it closed. When we were dressed, we walked silently down the hall and waited for the elevator without speaking.

While I buckled myself into the passenger seat, Abbey lowered the roof of the car. She opened the driver side door, then closed it. "I forgot sunscreen."

"How did you forget that?"

She shrugged. "I'll be right back."

The sun burned my head while I waited for her to run back to the hotel. By the time she returned, I'd taken off my hat and was using it to fan myself.

It was a fifteen-minute drive to Emigrant Lake. We parked and found a place with kayaks and paddleboats for rent.

"Solo or tandem?" Abbey asked.

"I'd rather go with you. I've only done it once, and—"

"It will be a lot more fun if we each have our own." Abbey turned to the guy behind the counter and ordered two single-occupant kayaks. I felt weak, listening to her shove me off to my own kayak, clearly wanting to put all that water between us. My arms seemed to grow heavy as I wondered if I had the strength to paddle on my own. If we had shared, I would also have to paddle, but the work wouldn't all be on my shoulders.

In the end, I was glad she insisted we go alone. Paddling the boat across the quiet water calmed me. I felt connected to the earth. It made me feel strong because I had no choice but to take care of my own safety. And that made me feel more in control of my entire life, if that wasn't making too much of a simple outing in a kayak. I was choosing to do this. I was going to burn away all the bad things in the past and win back my best friend. And now, I had the chance to protect her from herself. She'd paid for the trip and chosen the stopping points, and most of the restaurants and activities. I'd finally made a choice. She was raw and wounded from her horrible marriage and wasn't thinking clearly. For all her bravado, she was scared and feeling very alone.

The more I entertained these thoughts, the better I felt. It seemed as if the grip Lily's ghost had on me was weakened slightly. There's strength in friendship, in the presence of another person. As much as I loved Emmett, I needed another woman. I had my co-workers, and Emmett and I had our couple friends, but there was no one who belonged solely to me. That person was, and always had been, Abbey.

We paddled around the northeast area of the lake for nearly two hours. My arms ached. My shirt was soaked from water dripping along the paddle each time I raised it to plunge the opposite end into the lake. But the air was hot, and it felt good.

During the short drive back to the Ashland Springs Hotel, I rubbed my arms, massaging the underused muscles. The next day I would be sore, but it would be a great reminder of how strong I was. I hadn't thought I could do it alone, and Abbey had forced me into it. That's the kind of thing good friends did for each other.

We went back to the burger place for dinner. We only drank one beer each, but lingered for a few hours over several cups of tea. It felt real. The closeness filled me with so much hope I thought I might float up to the ceiling like a helium balloon.

When we returned to the hotel, we took the elevator to our floor. We were halfway down the corridor before we remembered. We giggled and ran back to the elevator, impatient for it to return and take us up one more level. At our door, I stuck the key card into the slot and pressed the handle.

The room was dark, which surprised me because usually we left a light on so we could find our way around when we returned. "Did you turn off the light?" I asked.

"No. We must have forgotten to leave one on. Since it was light when we left."

"I was sure I checked."

I felt along the wall to the switches and pressed them both. The entryway lit up. The rest of the room was so bright, I squinted. Then I screamed and started to cry.

Our suitcases were open as if they'd been split with a cleaver. Clothes were all over the floor and beds, some of my lingerie ripped in half. The pristine white sheets were smeared with what looked at first like blood, but then I realized was some kind of dark red jam. As we walked farther into the room, I noticed the air had the faint, sour odor of weed.

"Oh my God!" Abbey said.

"He found us. He's upping the stakes."

"What stakes?"

"I don't know. You're the one who talked to him, yet you have no idea what he wants. I know that whatever it is, it's not good."

I went to the bed and saw that my favorite white T-shirt was also stained with jam, including the seeds and bits of pulverized fruit. I knelt and began digging through my things, searching the pockets of my suitcase. I had jewelry in there. Nothing wildly expensive, but a few pairs of earrings and necklaces that were important to me.

With tears stinging my eyes, and the ache in my shoulders and arms no longer feeling quite so victorious, I went into the bathroom. It was obvious from the damaged pencil lying in the sink that he had used my eyeliner to scrawl a message on the mirror.

Cockroaches are the lowest form of life.

I screamed, louder and longer this time. I had no idea what it meant, but it sounded ominous. Repulsive. I rubbed my arms and thighs, feeling as if the hideous insects were creeping across my skin.

"What's wrong?" Abbey came running into the bathroom.

"Cockroaches? What's that supposed to mean?"

Abbey didn't look directly at the words. Her attention was on me. "That's..."

"Is he calling us cockroaches?"

"We don't know for sure that he..."

She must have realized how stupid she sounded because she stopped talking.

I was shaking, my thoughts wobbly and unclear. I felt violated. I felt like he could see into my mind. How did he know we'd changed rooms? How did he know we were in *this* room? How did he even know we were still at the hotel? If he'd checked the parking lot while we were kayaking, he should have considered the possibility that we'd left. He should have tried to follow us up Interstate 5.

"Assuming it was him—" Abbey said.

"It was him. Don't play games. We're past that."

"Then how did he get in?"

"He seduced one of the staff members. That kid who brought the necklace was clueless about how threatening it felt to get an anonymous gift in a hotel room. He would be easy to enlist, with a little cash. And I'm sure he's not the only one."

"Maybe," Abbey said.

"Definitely." I pulled my phone out of my pocket and took

a picture of the mirror. "You need to call them to come see the room. This is unacceptable. They're supposed to keep us safe."

Abbey went into the other room, and a moment later I heard her talking on the phone. I stared into the mirror, those words crawling across my face like insects, my face a white, bony backdrop with eyes like deep holes in my skull.

26

ABBEY

Carla, the hotel manager on duty, had blond hair slicked back to form a shell covering her scalp. Her eyes were blue but didn't look all that attractive despite her nice makeup, because her lower eyelids were red from overwork or irritation. It made it difficult to look her in the eye, but that wasn't stopping Raven from staring her down with a look of rage. Raven seemed to believe she could transfer her feeling of violation to this woman by the sheer force of her anger. Instead, Carla looked back at her with a blank, noncommittal expression.

"Your commitment to your guests is that they're safe in their rooms," Raven said.

"We aren't responsible for loss. It states that clearly on the—"

"This isn't simple theft. Someone entered our room intending to hurt us! He wrote a threatening message on the mirror. He destroyed some of my clothes. Worst of all, he destroyed my sense of security. You need to make that right."

"I'm sorry for that, but we can't—"

"He didn't break in. Someone *unlocked* our door for him!

You need to do an internal investigation—all the staff, not just people working tonight. You need to set up a reward system so everyone is motivated to report what they know."

"We can't—"

"All you're talking about is what you seem to think you *can't* do. How about showing some concern for your guests and an attitude of making things right?"

Carla took a step away from her, back toward the enclosure surrounding the front desk. She glanced toward the counter, where a man was checking in, talking in a voice that was slightly louder than necessary. She turned back, looking over Raven's shoulder at me. "We can comp your room for one night. We're so sorry this happened. Just because we don't have the resources to investigate doesn't mean we aren't deeply concerned."

"Being concerned fixes nothing," Raven said.

I moved up beside Raven and put my hand on her arm, tugging her forearm down slightly as if it were a lever that might seal her lips. "That's so sweet of you," I said. "We appreciate it. We do feel violated, so I hope you'll do some staff training. But of course, we realize you personally can't do anything about it. And it already happened, right?" I shrugged.

Carla smiled at me. "Yes. We are deeply sorry. I also want to give you a gift certificate because we'd love to have you back here on your next visit to Oregon."

"That's so gracious," I said.

"Meanwhile," Raven said, "I'm afraid to get into bed and close my eyes."

"The break-in occurred when you were out," Carla said. "When you're in the room, there are additional security locks. That's why we have them."

"Because you expect your staff to open guest room doors for anyone who asks?"

"No."

Raven looked irritated that Carla didn't offer an explanation. "I want to talk to every single person working tonight."

"They report to me, and you've expressed your upset, which I absolutely understand. I don't know how else to say I'm so very sorry this happened. We'll implement training, and I think we've offered fair compensation."

"You can't buy peace of mind," Raven said.

Carla nodded. "That's true."

"Someone on your staff is a criminal. Doesn't that bother you?"

"We'll deal with it. Again, I'm so sorry. Please let me know if you need anything in the future." She turned quickly to be sure she had the final word. She stepped behind the partition and walked to the front desk, where she vigorously welcomed a group of college-age girls.

"Let's go," I said.

"Are you satisfied with this?"

"I think we got all we're going to get. And I think comping our room was pretty nice."

"She *had* to if she doesn't want the hotel sued."

"Calm down." I grabbed her forearm, squeezing hard. She winced. An image flashed across my mind of the bone snapping in two. I moved her almost forcefully toward the elevator. When we were locked inside, I leaned against the wall and closed my eyes.

"Someone on that staff took a bribe," Raven said. "That's serious. She acted as if this were a mild case of someone stealing the complimentary bathrobes."

"Hotel staff probably don't make much. I'm sure they're vulnerable to that kind of thing."

She glared at me. "Are you seriously excusing criminal behavior as vulnerability?" She laughed bitterly. "Our sense of safety, which is the entire reason for choosing a more expensive hotel, has been destroyed."

"We have the extra locks."

"Are you deliberately missing my point?"

"I just don't think we should accuse people of crimes when we have no proof."

"Sometimes, you don't need proof," Raven said. "It's the only logical answer. And you just know."

"That's true. But they're simply doing their jobs, so you need to be careful. You shouldn't think the worst about people."

"You're naïve," she said.

The elevator stopped, and we stepped out. Raven rushed ahead to our room as if she were being chased, shoved her card into the slot, and slammed the door open. I followed her and let it close gently behind me.

She turned to face me, her hands on her hips, her hair wild around her head as if she'd been running for her life. "Lance wants to punish us. You were so torn up about him blaming you for Lily's death, you quit school over it. Now, you act like you don't care what happens. Back then, it was just gossip and missing your social life. This is so much worse, and you're acting like it's nothing."

"You have no idea what you're talking about. What they did seriously damaged me."

"Yes!"

She sprang on this like a cat pouncing. "Lance destroyed you. It was bullying of the worst kind. He accused you of murdering his sister! Have you forgotten what that felt like?"

"I've put it behind me. And it seems I've done a much better job than you have. Why is that, I wonder?"

"I never think about that year. He's the one digging up all these memories."

"I'm tired. I'm going to sleep."

"How can you?"

"The door has *three* locks—"

"One of which is useless now that we know anyone who wants to can walk into our room and destroy our stuff and write things that we can't even understand but are clearly meant to scare us."

I went into the bathroom and started brushing my teeth. She followed me in and stood behind me, watching me in the mirror that had thankfully been cleaned before we'd returned to our room.

"What's going on with you?" she asked. "Do you have a death wish?"

I laughed, dribbling toothpaste down my chin. I spit and washed the paste and saliva off my face.

"Do you?"

"Of course not."

"Then what's going on? I don't understand why you're so apathetic about this."

"I'm willing to wait and see what happens. I think it's interesting he's so obsessed with me after all these years, when he's surely realized it was a horrible accident and I was just the unlucky one to find her. Maybe he feels guilty or something."

"What would he feel guilty about?"

I shrugged. "His fixation is interesting to me."

"You're nuts. That guy has brooded over his sister's death for twelve years. He stalked you on Instagram and wormed his way into your life the minute you mentioned you were traveling. You might as well have announced you were ready to be pursued—by good men and bad. But you didn't think about the bad ones."

"You make it sound sleazy," I said.

"It is. But most of all, it's naïve. You, of all people, should know that human beings do terrible things. Even when it has nothing to do with them. He's angry the police didn't treat her death like a crime. He's bitter and still grieving. If you think he's friendly and nice and wants to start an honest relationship with you, you have the savvy of a four-year-old."

I removed my makeup and brushed my hair. The whole time, she stared into the mirror so that every time I glanced up, I saw those frightened, desperate eyes. Despite the fact she was getting increasingly anxious, she was no closer to telling me what lay beneath her anxiety.

I went into the main room, changed into a nightshirt, and slithered into the cloudlike bed. I picked up my phone and began scrolling through it, trusting she would take this as a signal to leave me alone. She remained in the bathroom. I heard the door lock. Placing the phone beside me, I let my head sink into the pillow and closed my eyes.

She was right. I was naïve. I believed Lance had woken up to the truth because I wanted to believe that. Being so focused on what Raven was hiding, and so satisfied to get a few questions answered from what Lance had told me of Lily's journal, I'd willfully forgotten how horribly he'd treated me. He'd ruined my life. Maybe the endorphins had blurred my perception as well. I was relishing good feelings and forgetting everything else. He was a near-stranger. What little I knew about him now was a complete transformation from the guy I'd barely known then.

All that rage and blame, lashing out at whoever was the most convenient, had simmered inside him when he was single-handedly battling the wilderness. He was alone for days at a time, possibly weeks, hiking challenging trails, pushing his body to the limit. But his mind no doubt retold the same story over and over again.

He and I had agreed we would meet at an abandoned historic church he knew about, halfway between Ashland and Portland. It was situated off a two-lane highway, far from the interstate. He said we would force Raven to tell the truth. I foolishly believed that with a bit of gaslighting, Raven would confide everything to me. But she hadn't done that. She was tougher than I realized.

He and I might have agreed to a plan, but that didn't mean there weren't more pieces to his plan that he hadn't revealed to me. It was possible Raven was right. I needed to make sure I had an alternate plan of my own. I'd been so eager to have a man fall for me again, even if only for a short time, I'd been easy prey for a smile and a bit of easy charm. He knew I was divorced, and probably made some assumptions, a few of them unfortunately true.

I thought about the souvenir I'd taken from Dirk the first night of my road trip. In the innocence of that first day of my journey with Raven, I'd thought I would be having a fabulous time meeting new people, trying new restaurants, and marveling over new landscapes. Instead, I'd been babysitting my neurotic former roommate. But already, my gut must have known I needed more thrills than Raven was ever going to offer. That was what led me to manufacture my own thrilling moment.

When I had gone through Dirk's things that night, I stumbled upon a handgun. I took it because I could. The entire next day, I wondered if he would notice it missing before he checked out of the hotel. If he had noticed, maybe he hadn't been sure who to blame because he'd taken a different woman to his room every night. Maybe the gun wasn't registered, and he didn't want to be caught. For whatever reason, he never tracked me down to ask about it.

The gun had been in a zipped pocket inside another, larger zippered section. Maybe he didn't think he needed to check that it was still there. Maybe he thought the women he brought to his room weren't looking out for themselves, that all they wanted was him. Maybe he didn't think about it at all, if he was used to carrying a gun around with him everywhere he went, even to his sister's wedding.

Now, the gun was mine. I'd truly only taken it for the thrill of getting away with something. Such a dangerous theft, in several ways. But once I'd seen it, I knew I wouldn't be satisfied with something unimportant like a hairbrush or a T-shirt. Seeing the shining barrel, admiring the perfectly engineered bullets inside, I had to have it. I've never done anything like that in my life, but in that moment, I had no choice.

When I took that gun, I didn't know about Lance. I didn't know about Lily's journal. I didn't know Raven had lied to me —from the night of that party twelve years ago until the day I left school, and she'd started up again the moment we reconnected. Never in my wildest imaginings had I thought I'd need a gun. Now, I wondered if I might.

When I sat up to turn out the light, I heard Raven's voice coming from behind the closed bathroom door. I hadn't seen her take her phone in there, but it sounded like she was either talking to herself, praying, or on a phone call. I slid out of bed and walked to the bathroom door. I stood close, making my breath shallow and light.

"I love you so much," Raven said softly.

A moment later she breathed, "I miss you too."

I waited, listening to several murmured sounds of agreement. "Soon," she said. "This separation has been good for me. I've gotten so much perspective. I don't know why I forgot that you're the most important person in the world to me. I honestly could not live without you. A child only enhances what we have, but it's not required." She paused. "Mmhm. Yes. And I allowed the *idea* of a baby to come between us. We existed before a child, and if we have one, we'll still be us, and we'll continue on long after our children are gone from our home." She sighed.

After several minutes, she spoke again. "I'll see you in a day or two. I'll text you the details as soon as I decide for sure."

She continued murmuring so softly, I wasn't aware she'd moved toward the door. The lock clicked, and before I could move, the door was open. She was holding her phone, the call ended. She gave me a smug look and walked past me toward her bed.

"Are you calling in your husband to protect you?" I asked.

"No."

"I didn't hear you mention how terrified you are."

"I didn't want to worry him."

"You mean you didn't want to expose your lie."

"Don't think you know anything about my marriage."

"Why didn't you tell him?"

"I want to tell him face-to-face. I'm sorry to say this, it might be hurtful, but you have no clue how a healthy marriage works." She yanked back the covers, crawled into bed, and pulled the comforter over her head so all that was left of her was a long wavy strand of hair reaching across the pillow like a vine creeping up a wall, intent on consuming the entire structure.

I turned out the lights and got into bed. Would Raven be brave enough to tell her husband what was going on, knowing he would forgive her for anything? I didn't want her leaving me. It had been scary enough calling her bluff when she'd threatened to fly home. I needed to know the truth about Lily's death with a fervor I could hardly explain. I couldn't let her out of my sight until I got that. If it took meeting up with Lance to make that happen, I was ready. If he planned to destroy me as well as Raven, I was ready.

27

LILY'S JOURNAL
NOVEMBER 10, 2010

Every single day I've been thinking about my missing necklace. I adore that necklace. It's part of me. The back of my neck feels naked without it. My fingers don't know where to go when I want reassurance or confidence. Touching the ring calms me. I'm having an impossible time falling asleep because it's all I think about. I stare at the backs of my eyelids and wonder why I feel so lost without it. I think about the look on the Roaches' faces when I said it was missing, and I think about the impossibility of someone coming into our room without one of us there. So even if someone else took it, one, or both, of the Roaches knew about it. Which is the same thing—they stole it.

Today, I decided I have to prove it was one of them. I can't have them looking right at me as if I'm stupid enough to believe their lie. Of course, they're so disturbed, they might have thrown it in the dumpster, but I'm trying really hard not to imagine that. It's too awful. I shouldn't even write it here. I *have* to believe they're hiding it. Maybe they have other plans for it, some other way to hurt me. That's fine. I just want it back.

When they left for their usual Wednesday night trip to the mall, I started going through their things. I figured that by the time they came back, I would know some of their secrets. I started with Roach One's dresser because she's the worst. So much worse. Roach Two is just weak. She never speaks up for me, or for herself, which is really sad.

I looked through every drawer in Roach One's dresser and the center drawer in her desk. I slid my hand under her mattress and felt around for the leather strap, the hard circle of the ring. Instead, I found two condom packages and a hundred-dollar bill. Since I'm not like her, I left everything where it was.

I looked through her backpack, where I found that plastic bag with ten of those red tablets embossed with hearts, and a tiny gold cross in the tiniest wooden box I'd ever seen. Maybe there's more to her than I realize. I opened the small wooden boxes on the shelf over her bed. I searched the pockets of her clothes, her spare purses, and inside her shoes. Since I was in the closet, I turned to the pockets on Roach Two's outfits. Then I went through all of Roach Two's drawers and other things. The necklace was not there.

I collapsed on my bed and closed my eyes. They couldn't have thrown it away. They wouldn't. I would die if they had. I knew my necklace had to be in the room. I could feel it. I got up and poked my finger around the edges of the carpet to see if there were any loose spots, but there weren't any.

Then I went back to Roach Two's nightstand. Next to the jewelry box and jars of polished pebbles I'd already searched was a small cactus. The plastic nursery container was sitting inside a blue ceramic pot. I carefully lifted out the cactus, still managing to prick my finger. A drop of blood fell on her nightstand. I wiped it away with my fingertip and smiled that it left a very light smear that she probably won't notice for a long time. Beneath the plant was my necklace. I guess she figured since a cactus doesn't get watered much, the necklace would be okay there for a while.

I was so happy, I cried.

When they came back to the room, I thought about throwing the necklace at Roach Two, letting the strap hit her like a whip. I'd thought she wasn't as bad as the other Roach. I was wrong. But instead, I let the necklace dangle from my finger, wrapped around tightly in case one of them tried to grab it. "I guess you need to learn the definition of the word *stole*," I said.

"I didn't take it," Roach Two said.

"I found it in the pot with your cactus. Don't look right at me and lie. You act like I'm stupid, that I didn't lift out the cactus, stab my finger, and find my necklace."

"I didn't—"

"You know what she did, don't you?" Roach One asked. "This was an obvious plot to go through our things. She lost her ridiculous-looking necklace herself. She figured out that was a good excuse for looking through our things. So you'd better check to see if anything's missing." She glanced at her bed, and I wanted to laugh. She wasn't going to check under the mattress right in front of me, but I could see she was worried.

"That's not true," I said.

"You could get kicked out of the dorms if we tell them what you did. It's in the agreement we signed—that we'll respect each other's privacy. So you'd better watch out, or you could find yourself out on the street. Dorm-less." She laughed, and it sounded like a cackle.

"I wasn't disrespecting your privacy. I was looking for something that was stolen from me."

"What you did is a total violation. But you don't have any boundaries, do you?" She glared at me, and for a moment, I thought I saw the tip of her tongue, ready to slide out of her mouth, waggling at me.

"I went through your things because I knew one of you took this. And I was right. Are you going to apologize?"

"Not for something I didn't do," Roach One said. Roach Two nodded. She looked like she didn't even care that I'd caught her. Maybe they both knew about it. Maybe Roach One put her up to it. That wouldn't surprise me. But she's the one who had it. There wasn't an ounce of shame in her.

I'm a little worried that Roach One is trying to threaten me—telling me they'll say I violated their privacy and broke the dorm policy. Trying to destroy my grades wasn't enough. They want me out of their room. I wasn't imagining that. I tried to talk to Lance about it, but he acted like it was a bunch of petty catfighting. Maybe I didn't explain it clearly. I didn't want to sound pathetic, so I probably didn't make him understand how scared I am, how lonely I feel.

It's so *hard* living with them. It's as if I've camped out, uninvited, in someone else's house, and they're tolerating me, but not really.

The only good thing about this room is that the Prince has been coming by even more whenever I'm here alone!

He's driving me insane, but in a good way. The way he looks at me—OMG! We talk about everything, and he's actually interested in my thoughts. But I feel like he wants to torment my body. He always sits the same way, with his back against Roach One's bed, his legs stretched out, sometimes his ankles crossed over, sometimes not. I always sit the same way, leaning against my bed, except I put a pillow behind my back. He doesn't seem to mind the wood frame stabbing him in the spine.

Just like he has before, I feel like he's always moving closer to me, our legs almost touching by the time he gets up to leave. But I never see him move, and he never moves enough to *actually* touch me. He gets close enough that I feel like his leg is rubbing mine and my body is going absolutely insane. It's almost embarrassing how I feel when he's close. Who gets that worked up about *not* touching? It's not a kiss. Not even holding my hand. Just inching closer without ever letting me see him do it.

I wish he would do something or say something about what he wants. I guess he does because he says he really likes talking to me. But he acts like it's more than that. He acts like he's teasing me and inviting me and testing me, all at the same time.

28

ABBEY

The morning after our room was trashed, Raven woke me at six o'clock with the aroma of coffee brewing.

"I'm not ready for coffee," I mumbled.

"I've been up since three, so I need coffee. And I've made a decision."

I turned on my side, my back toward her. She pressed the switch that turned on all the lights in the room.

"Raven, turn them off. I'm tired."

"We need to check out and drive to Portland. This morning. The sooner the better. If we can get out of here by seven, he won't even know we're awake yet. We can get on a flight to Seattle, and then he won't be able to find us." She went to the window and yanked open the drapes.

I sat up, putting my hand over my face to protect my eyes from all the gleaming late summer sunrise. "We were going to hike—"

"It's the only way to be rid of him."

"He's not going to do anything. He's just messing with our heads. Isn't that obvious? Why do I have to keep telling you?"

She made a sound of frustration and stomped into the bathroom. When I heard the shower, I knew I wouldn't be getting more sleep, so I got up and poured a cup of coffee. I stood by the window looking over the parking lot. I couldn't let her follow through with her latest desire to flee. Lance had another plan to frighten her, and it meant going ahead with our planned hike. Hopefully, it would be enough to avoid the final stop he'd proposed.

It took an hour of conversation, but I managed to persuade her we were safe as a twosome, and it was daylight. I threatened again to finish my trip by sharing my experiences with him. She had a sour look on her face, but she yielded.

We went to brunch. We declined the complimentary champagne, thinking ahead to our hike. The weather was still hot, which wasn't ideal, but maybe a bit of sweat and physical discomfort would burn some of that anxiety out of Raven's system. Mine too.

As we nibbled our way through pastries and perfectly cooked eggs Benedict, I kept my eye on Raven's phone. She had it on the table beside her knife, which she'd been doing since we left California. The phone was her lifeline to her misled husband. Looking at it now, I wondered if she was expecting a call from him.

Like the other early arrivals to the restaurant, we'd been seated in the center of the room where the tables were arranged around a large pool of water. In the center of the pool was a structure of rocks with a stream of water flowing from the top. I knew what I had to do, and that was why this restaurant had come to mind when Raven asked where we should eat. I'd seen the photographs promoting it in the brochure in our room.

I hadn't been aware of Raven communicating with Emmett until the night before. As far as I knew, she'd sent a few text messages to assure him she was safe and doing well. That was the first phone call.

I worried now that she was planning to fly home when we got to Portland. She might be thinking she was saving me from Lance by doing this. She thought she would get me safely on a plane to Seattle, and then she would go in the opposite direction.

I refilled her water glass for the third time. "You need to drink more water. We should be well hydrated for the hike."

She sighed. It was obvious she wasn't thrilled about going hiking, but for whatever reason, she'd decided not to complain about it. Maybe she was hoping for a rescue phone call. Maybe she still believed she could convince me to drive to Portland in a breezy convertible instead of sweating in the forest, making our way along narrow trails. Maybe she was desperately hoping for an alert about a weather advisory, telling us outdoor activity wasn't safe due to wildfires in the eastern part of the state.

She took a few sips of water.

"Drink up," I said.

"I'm not thirsty."

"This is prep. It's not about being thirsty."

She took a few longer swallows of water. I immediately topped off her glass.

"Stop filling my glass."

"It's good for you. There's a lot of sodium in restaurant food."

"I know that, Abbey. But I'll bring a bottle of water on our hike."

"You need it now. Your cells need to process it."

"Fine." She picked up her glass and drained it. She placed it on the table with a slight thump, rattling the flatware against the plates. "Now I have to pee."

"It might be psychological."

"No, it's two huge glasses of water before this one." She pushed back her chair and got up. She walked rather quickly to the restroom, as I'd hoped. As I'd planned, actually.

The moment she disappeared around the corner, I reached across the table and moved her phone closer to the edge, adjusting her plate so her croissant was almost touching the phone. I waited a few minutes.

When I saw her heading back to our table, I partially rose out of my chair. I made a rough grab at her croissant, knocking it to the center of the table and flipping her phone into the pool of water in one wild gesture. The phone landed with a splash loud enough to turn the heads of the couple at the table next to ours.

"Oh no!" I pushed my chair out. "Oh, shit! No, no, no."

The woman looked at me. "What happened?"

"My friend's phone." I scrambled around the table, making myself clumsy, taking longer than necessary, and nearly bumping the woman's chair. She gave me a sympathetic smile.

Raven was a few feet away when I reached into the water. It was colder than I'd expected, and my hand immediately felt stiff. I pulled out the phone. Water ran down the screen, dripping onto my arm.

"What the hell?" Raven grabbed the phone out of my hand. "How did that happen?!" Her voice was loud and shrill. Now the woman beside us, and her partner, looked less sympathetic.

"Shh," I said.

"I won't *shh*. How did you manage to knock my phone into the water?"

"You said you weren't eating your croissant, and I just wanted a bite. Sorry. When I grabbed it, the phone—"

"It's probably dead!"

"Can't you put it in rice or something?"

"Do you have a pound of rice handy?"

"We can ask in the kitchen."

She looked at me with disdain that turned slowly to muted hope. She scanned the room, trying to locate the entrance to the kitchen. I followed her across the room, murmuring *sorry*, which she ignored.

The kitchen did have rice, but they were not inclined to use it to resurrect a phone. "It has to stay buried in rice for at least twenty-four hours," the chef said. "Probably longer. We can't be responsible for it."

Raven let out a quiet cry of despair.

"Maybe we can use a hair dryer." I'd looked up the various options for resurrecting a drowned phone. I needed to make sure it would stay dead. I didn't tell her about removing the sim card. I didn't tell her the hair dryer had to be on a cool setting.

Raven complained all the way back to our room. I tried to slow her as much as I could, knowing all solutions work best when they're immediate. In our room, she placed the phone on a towel and turned the hair dryer on the hottest setting, aiming it at the phone. The noise made talking difficult, which was just as well.

After a few minutes, she tried to turn the phone on. Nothing.

"Oh my God, what am I going to do?"

"You'll be okay for now. You can use my phone any time."

"Emmett doesn't know I'm with you. Did you honestly forget that? I can't call him from your phone."

"You could say—"

"No." She picked up the phone, carried it into the bedroom, and shoved it into her suitcase. "Maybe I'll buy a prepaid one."

"Good idea," I said. "Let's get ready for our hike. Being outdoors will help put it into perspective."

She gave me a disgusted look but started taking off the capri pants and top she'd worn to brunch.

I'd bought myself some time, but not much. The first chance she got, she would buy another phone. Or she'd figure out she could use mine and tell her ignorant husband it was a prepaid, that she'd dropped hers into the bathtub.

29

RAVEN

Hiking was the last thing I wanted to do. I've always loved it, but now, I just wanted to get to the fraternity house and offer the required apology to Lily's ghost. Then I wanted to get home to my beloved husband and feel his arms holding me close. I'd had three dreams about talking to Lily's ghost. In each one, her strength overpowered my will, as it always had. In my dream I groveled before her, which was not right. I had nothing to grovel about, but I didn't remember that until I woke.

The only good thing about hiking was that it would force me to concentrate on my surroundings, pushing the scraps of my dreams and memories out of the way. It was also possible we would be able to slip away from the hotel unobserved. If that happened, we were driving far enough that Lance wouldn't be able to easily find us. It was a slim hope, but I clung to it, and it inspired me to be agreeable.

The trail Abbey had chosen was a loop that covered three and a half miles. It was only noon, and already the temperature had climbed to eighty-one. By the time we finished, we'd be disgusting with sweat. Abbey was thrilled, acting as if this was her own approach to a cleansing ritual.

Within the first fifty yards of our hike, the trail narrowed to a thin ribbon, and we had to walk single file. Shortly after, we hit a somewhat steep incline.

I wore a baseball cap over my ponytail, but part of me wanted to dump the hat. It was shady where we were hiking, so I didn't need it for sun protection, and it made my scalp perspire relentlessly. Abbey was carrying her little backpack with our water bottles and two power bars.

Every few steps I whispered a reminder to myself—*Relax*. I wanted to enjoy being outdoors, to appreciate the shade and listen for the various birds who sang their hearts out. Of course, songbirds had predators too, so maybe they were singing in the face of their fear, not because they didn't have any threats to their well-being.

My skin felt swollen and hot, making my shirt stick. I plucked it away from my skin, but it grabbed me again without allowing me even a moment of relief. I was thirsty despite all the water Abbey had poured into my glass at brunch, but I didn't want to stop and drink water. That would provide too much time to think. I liked my thoughts wandering, diluted by the need to pay attention to the terrain and my footing.

"Isn't this perfect?" Abbey asked. "It's so peaceful. It makes me feel safe."

I ignored that. She'd said it to irritate me. She would feel safe if a man jumped out of the woods with a knife in his hand. Nothing bothered her except me, apparently.

"Are you feeling any better?" Abbey asked.

"No."

She stopped and turned to face me. "Please don't spoil this."

"I'm being truthful."

She laughed, which made me simultaneously nervous and offended. "Try to relax," she said. "Try not to see demons behind every tree."

"I don't."

"Tell me about your husband; that will distract you. You haven't talked about him much."

"It's hard to talk when I'm behind you. Let's just enjoy the silence."

She turned and started off at a much quicker pace. I hurried to catch up.

We were a little over a mile into our route when I heard a sharp sound, like a gunshot. I stopped, my heart thudding. I felt my lungs gasping for air. Then my mind cleared, and I realized it must have been a branch snapping. Someone close by, with shoes heavy enough to break a thick branch. I turned. The trail behind me was empty, stretching down toward the last curve we'd rounded. I couldn't see anything but tree trunks and vines, shrubs, fallen branches, and ancient downed trees covered with moss.

Sensing I was no longer directly behind her, Abbey turned and called back to me, "What's wrong now?"

I wasn't going to shout what I'd heard. He would hear me. He was out there. Very close, but not wanting to be seen, for now. The snapping of that branch was too loud to be a squirrel or rabbit. A large animal making a sound like that would have caused an accompanying rustle of branches or more snapping sounds. My breathing grew shallow, and I had to force myself to take in an adequate amount of air.

Abbey walked back to where I was standing. I held my upper arms, peering into the woods, unable to decide whether it was safer to keep going or to turn back. We were closer to the starting point, but for some reason my instinct told me to keep moving forward. As a result, I was frozen. Logic versus impulse.

"What's the problem?"

"I heard someone."

"You imagined it. You've gotten yourself so worked up, your brain is playing tricks on you. Let's go." She grabbed my arm and tugged gently.

"He's out there. Watching us."

"Possible, but unlikely. It was probably a wild animal, if it was even a real sound."

"It was real. It sounded like a gunshot it was so loud."

She laughed. "It wasn't a gunshot. Come on." She tugged on my arm again.

I stumbled after her, and she let go. I turned again and saw a flash of something gray, something out of place among all that vegetation. I stared at the spot, straining my eyes until my vision grew blurry. A moment later, I saw another flash of gray and dark blue. Without speaking to Abbey, or thinking about what I was doing, I plunged into the undergrowth. I climbed over a fallen tree, turning sideways to avoid one of the branches trying to scratch at my bare skin.

"Raven! Come back here!"

I didn't shout back; that would tell the stalker where I was. I moved as fast as I could, keeping my eyes on the ground to be sure I didn't echo his mistake and step on a brittle stick that caused an unnaturally loud sound. I wove my way through trees, glancing up every minute or so, hoping to catch sight of him again.

"Raven! Where are you? Are you insane? I'm not coming to get you!"

I didn't care. I was going to get him and...I stopped. I sat down abruptly on a fallen tree. I was breathing hard and unbearably hot. What would I do once I found him? I hadn't thought, I'd just thrown myself into the woods. What if he had a knife? Or a gun? What if he hit me or tried to strangle me? There was no way I could stand up to someone that big, someone so obviously strong.

I would have to figure out a way to sneak up on him. That was not going to be easy, but it was the only way to get an advantage. I settled myself more comfortably. If he was going to continue tracking Abbey, he would have to pass somewhere in the area where I was sitting. For now, I was nicely sheltered by short, slender new-growth pines.

Abbey was right about one thing. So far, the only thing he seemed to want was to frighten us. But I was sure that wasn't his final goal. His behavior would escalate eventually, as all obsessions do.

I heard a rustling that was so faint, I might not have heard if I wasn't at the end of a breath, no sound of air entering or leaving my body. I crouched lower, shifting in the direction where I thought I'd heard it. Locating the right spot was difficult because even though there wasn't an echo, sound spread out and filled the space around me until it felt like it was everywhere.

For several minutes I sat without moving, hearing nothing more. Abbey had stopped calling for me. I wondered if she was standing on the trail, waiting for me to return, or if she'd continued the hike without me. It seemed like she should want to make sure he didn't attack me. Alone, I was so much more vulnerable, and now that my head had cleared of my sudden mad desire to confront him, to make him tell me what he wanted from us, I realized this had been a terrible idea. Without my phone, I had no way to contact Abbey. Without my phone, I also wouldn't have any GPS help in finding my way back to the trail. Although I probably wouldn't be able to get a signal anyway.

Tears welled up and trickled down my cheeks. I'd been so stupid, so desperate to make him stop. Because that was the only thing I wanted. I wanted him to *stop*. I wanted him to leave us alone. I wanted him to forget all about us. I couldn't concentrate on anything but him and what he might do next.

I heard someone moving in the undergrowth. The adrenaline I'd felt when I first rushed off the trail rushed through my body once again. The realization I might be lost, and he'd caused that, filled me with rage. I was ready to attack him with my bare hands. I jumped up and began running toward the sound, rewarded by another glimpse of a dark blue ball cap.

I heard more branches breaking and rustling undergrowth as he began moving more quickly. Was he circling around behind me, or was he running *from* me? I didn't know why he would, but with that thought, something primal clicked in, and I stopped trying to figure things out. I simply looked for the smoothest path forward in the direction where I continued to see occasional flashes of blue and gray. Following the sound of him crashing through fallen branches, rocks and pine cones kicked to the side by heavy boots.

I was sweating so badly that I had to take off my hat. Hair was plastered across my forehead. I shoved the hat into my back pocket and wiped my forehead, moving as best I could toward someone I couldn't see for more than a few seconds at a time.

I followed more slowly now, pausing to wipe my face with my hands, which were wet enough that bits of bark and pine needles clung to them when I grabbed branches to move them out of my way. I was breathing harder and had no idea where I was going.

Then I saw him clearly. He wore a gray T-shirt stained dark with sweat and a blue ball cap, the bill pointing backwards. He was standing on a rock or a fallen tree, so I could see his entire body, including the strong, serious-looking hiking boots I'd heard disturbing everything in his path.

He could also see me scrambling over branches, clawing my way around vines, my face no doubt dark red, my hair drenched, and my shoulders heaving from breathing so hard. What was I thinking? He was a hundred times more likely to hurt me than to tell me what he wanted. He was loving this, knowing I was terrified, acting without thinking.

For now, he wanted to make me suffer. I knew that without speaking to him.

As I stood watching him looking at me, he started laughing. He reached into his backpack and pulled something out. He waved it in the air. An orange notebook with stickers all over the cover. He jumped down from where he was standing and took off. Even with those heavy boots, he was running. A few minutes later, the sounds of movement became harder to decipher.

Then it was silent. Finally, I heard a few brave birds announce a tentative all clear to their families and friends.

And now I was utterly lost. I looked up at the sun and tried to recall its position when I'd started running, but I hadn't bothered to pay attention earlier, so my effort was useless. I began walking, peering through the trees, trying to see if there was any evidence of the trail we'd been on or one of the other, longer trails through this area.

The sun had moved close to the treetops by the time I heard the trickle of a creek. I rushed toward it, grateful for the first good thing that had happened to me all day. I squatted beside the creek, then cupped my hands and splashed water onto my face and shoulders. I cupped them again and tried to drink a few sips before it ran through my fingers. It tasted so good. I didn't care if it might contain something tasteless and odorless but toxic. It seemed as if I could actually feel the water molecules replenishing my cells.

The creek had another benefit. It provided a fixed land-mark that I could now follow. I continued in the general direction I'd been going, but this time keeping the creek to my left.

Although the sky was still pale blue, the sun was no longer visible above the trees by the time I found a trail. I had no idea if it was the one we'd been hiking, but I followed it. Eventually, it would lead me to civilization. I was sure I'd been thrashing around in the forest for two hours, possibly more.

When I arrived at the parking lot, Abbey was standing by our car, talking to a park ranger. She saw me and ran toward me, sobbing. She wrapped her arms around me so tightly, I thought I might no longer be visible outside of her embrace.

"Okay," she said. "I get it now. Worrying about someone is scary, even if you know they're probably okay."

The ranger looked relieved. She asked if I needed water or first aid. Abbey held up my water bottle and handed it to me. The ranger told us to stick together next time. She returned to the SUV parked near the entrance to the parking area.

"Why did you run off like that? It's insane. You could have been out there overnight; you could have been lost for days."

"You could have come with me."

She pulled away slightly, still holding on to me. "That's not fair. You disappeared so fast, I couldn't even see you. And when I called, you didn't answer. I wasn't going to get myself lost as well. Then we'd really be in a mess."

"I was out there for hours. The ranger was just now talking to you?"

"It took a while for me to figure out how to contact them. And a while for her to get here."

I wriggled away from her arms. "I want a bath. I'm starving."

She opened the car door, and we climbed in. She didn't ask if I'd found him or if it was truly Lance. I didn't tell her about the orange book he'd waved at me. Either he was trying to give me a message of some kind, or he was seriously disturbed. He'd looked like a maniac, his face in a grimace as he waved that orange book.

30

ABBEY

Raven took a long bath after her ordeal in the forest. She needed to soak the grime out of her nails and off her skin, she said. But she spent over an hour in there. She didn't have her phone to entertain her, and she hadn't taken a book. I wondered if she was sulking because I hadn't asked whether she'd caught up with Lance and found a way to persuade him to leave us alone. I wondered if she was sitting in the tub reliving the past. I also wondered what was going to happen next. The plan I'd had to gaslight her to the edge of sanity, hoping to force a confession out of her, was not working. She was strong. I had to give her that.

But, pushed to the limit, she'd pursued Lance without any logical purpose. It was pure animal reaction to the fear consuming her. But why would she allow it to reach that level of desperation when she could have told me the truth about Lily and enlisted my help in getting rid of him? Even instinct should have told her it was hopeless to chase him—she was the guaranteed loser in a physical confrontation.

When she finally came out of the bathtub, I told her I'd

ordered room service for dinner. "I think we need to take it easy this evening. It's been a rough afternoon."

"For me. It wasn't so bad for you."

"I was worried about you."

"Thanks." She went to the sitting area and settled in the armchair closest to the window. She picked up the room service menu off the table and began flipping through it.

"I already ordered."

"I heard you."

"Then why are you looking?"

"Just checking what's available."

"We're having roast beef sandwiches, fries, and chocolate cake. And champagne."

"Champagne doesn't fit the situation or the food choices."

"Can't we celebrate that you're okay?"

She tossed the menu on the table, leaned her head back, and closed her eyes.

"Did you ever actually see him?" I asked.

"Why do you care?"

I sighed. "Don't sulk."

"I'm not. But I'm completely baffled by you."

"Same here."

She laughed. "Nice to know we still have one feeling in common."

"Did you see him?"

"Yes."

"Are you going to tell me what happened? Did you talk to him?"

She adjusted her position in the chair, sitting up straighter. "I didn't talk to him. To be honest, I'm not sure why I went after him. It was stupid, I know that. But I was so angry that he has all the power. I want him to stop! I didn't bother to think about how I would make that happen."

"It's frustrating to feel like other people have control over your life."

"Yes."

"So what happened?" I walked to the other chair and settled across from her. I rested the bottoms of my feet against the edge of the table, enjoying the pressure of the wood against my aching muscles, like a mini massage.

"He proved that he's dangerously off-balance."

I laughed. "What does that mean?"

"He's breaking down mentally. Maybe the breakdown happened a long time ago. It feels like he never stopped hating us and wanting to punish us."

"Why would he want to punish you?"

"For being mean to her. I told you that."

"Being mean is quite a bit different from believing it was my fault she died."

"Well, he's disturbed, so I'm sure he doesn't categorize things as precisely as you do."

There was a knock on our door. "It's the food." I went to the door and opened it even as Raven was ordering me to check the peephole. A woman wheeled in a cart with several covered plates, a bottle of champagne in an ice bucket, and two flutes. She spread a cloth over the table and arranged our food, leaving the covers in place.

When she was gone, I opened the champagne and poured some into our flutes. I lifted my glass. "To survival."

Raven clicked her glass against mine but didn't echo my toast. She placed her glass back on the table without taking a sip, then picked up half her sandwich and took a small bite. A moment later, she said, "I'm wondering if I should tell Emmett everything and ask him to come get me, or if—"

"What's *everything*?"

"About you...our road trip..."

I waited. She ate her sandwich, methodically biting and chewing, avoiding meeting my gaze.

"Where is this idea of ending our trip coming from?" I asked. "Did something happen you're not telling me?" I fully intended the innuendo in my question, curious if she would finally tell me everything instead of revealing her sins only to Emmett. At the same time, I was willing to settle for her telling me what else had happened when she chased Lance through the woods.

"He's mentally disturbed, I think."

"You can't know that."

"If you let grief and bitterness fester inside for years, it destroys you."

"True." Had it destroyed Raven? Maybe she couldn't get pregnant because she'd become a tormented knot of guilt and secrets and fear of being found out. "If you didn't talk to him, then what happened?"

"He climbed on a rock so I could see him. He just stood there, staring at me, kind of laughing, which made him look deranged. It was extremely frightening."

"I can imagine."

She laughed. "It sounds ridiculous saying it, because it was ridiculous, but he pulled a book out of his backpack. He started waving it at me." She laughed again. "He acted like it was a weapon, but it was just an ugly orange notebook with stuff glued on it."

"Oh," I said. "I wonder if he was trying to tell you he knows what she said about us."

"What?" She placed the remains of her sandwich half on the plate and took a sip of water from the bottle she'd been drinking from earlier. Fizz still danced across the surface of her untouched champagne.

"It sounds like her journal. He was waving it at you so you'd realize he knows things about you."

She stared at me. She picked up the metal cover and plunked it over her plate, leaving half the sandwich and most of the fries. "What journal?"

"Lily kept a journal when she lived with us. He showed it to me when he told me who he was."

"It's probably full of lies."

"Why do you think that? Who lies in their journal?"

"Lots of people. Did you ever read that Patricia Highsmith book *Edith's Diary*?"

"No."

"People lie in their journals. Just like they lie to themselves."

"The parts I read were all true—about her necklace being stolen, and how she went through our things and found it..."

"So that's the reason he's after both of us? Because we were mean to her?"

"We were."

"She asked for it."

"No, she didn't."

She stood and stretched her arms over her head. "I don't know why he thinks a diary would scare me." She picked up her champagne glass and took several large swallows, then placed it on the table. "She hardly knew anything about me, so I can't imagine she wrote anything important, or true."

"Then there's nothing to worry about, is there?"

She looked at me as if I'd asked her a trick question.

"What else did it say?"

"I didn't read the whole thing."

"Well, is there anything that would make him want to *kill* us?"

I laughed. "She certainly didn't write in it while she was lying in that room, drunk and blissing on Ecstasy."

"It's not funny. She could have said anything. She could

have made it sound like we wanted to kill her. Don't you realize that?"

For the first time, I faced the thoughts that had put down roots below the surface of my conscious mind. Roots that had spread and grown stronger, and now the seedling finally poked its head through the soil.

Maybe Lily's death hadn't been an accident at all. Maybe Raven had murdered her. I wasn't sure how. It wasn't as if she gave her an overdose or poured alcohol down her throat. And even then, Lily might have survived. Still, Raven had been absolutely terrified for days now. This was about more than being followed, and more than knowing a guy from our past had tracked us down. It was more than guilt over our bullying, which did not seem to be the source of her guilt. "You're so scared all the time. What's really bothering you?" I asked.

"He is!"

"But why? We didn't do anything but hurt her feelings. And all kids do stuff like that. We shouldn't have, and we know now it was awful, but he's not going to kill us over it."

"You don't know what she wrote. She could have written *anything*."

"I'm not going to live in fear of what she might have written, of what he might be thinking. It's not healthy, and all you're doing is imagining something that will probably never happen. Eighty percent of what people worry about never happens. You've heard that, right?"

"That means twenty percent *does* happen. And maybe I'm worried for you. He was so sure you could have saved her, and you didn't. Maybe he had sex with you and charmed you and showed you her diary, but he hates you as much as he always did. Even more. That kind of hatred doesn't just dissolve." She sat back down and topped off her champagne. She stared out the window and didn't talk again until I began stacking the dishes on the tray to leave outside the door.

I was absolutely convinced, and I wondered why it had taken me so long to recognize the truth—she had contributed to Lily's death in some way. That was why she didn't want to tell me what had happened that night. All the gaslighting in the world wouldn't force her to confess to murder.

31

ABBEY

The next morning, at Raven's insistence, we ate in our room again just as the sun was coming up. We shared an entire pot of coffee along with buttered English muffins and fruit. By eight, we were checked out of the hotel. It was already warm enough to put the top down, so I did, even though Raven looked very unhappy about it. She probably thought it increased our exposure to Lance, but the top up or down wouldn't matter if he truly wanted to hurt us.

Settling into the car took a few minutes as Raven arranged herself, trying to sit cross-legged on the bucket seat. She wriggled around for several minutes, convinced she could make this pose work.

"You can't sit like that," I said.

"I was going to try meditating while you're driving."

"Pull your knees in and close the door."

She slammed the door, and I started the car. I brought the map up on the GPS screen. "Since you're so worried about Lance, I thought we would avoid I-5." I pointed to the screen. "If we cut over to Highway 62 at Medford, we can keep going north, then turn east and come back around through the Umpqua National Forest. It looks like a really nice drive and only takes about an hour longer."

"Okay. But he's probably already waiting for us. I wouldn't be surprised if he was watching us load the car and he's ready to go."

"Maybe. But in Medford we can stop for cappuccinos and croissants or something. We'll keep an eye out for him, then head toward 62 when we're sure he's not around."

"We can try."

It wasn't the appreciative reaction I'd hoped for, but maybe that would change once we were on a less well-traveled highway and she wasn't jerking her head this way and that, frantic to catch sight of him.

Maybe she needed more pacifying. I still didn't want to alienate her entirely or I'd never learn the truth. "It is disturbing that he keeps following. I've probably been too casual about that. It might have been a mistake to sleep with him."

She didn't look at me. "You think?"

"I didn't know it was him, so I'm not sure how I would have avoided it, but maybe I should have picked up on something."

"You could just stop sleeping with every guy you meet."

"I said it was probably a mistake to sleep with *him*. Let's leave it."

We reached Medford half an hour later, and after driving around for fifteen or twenty minutes, we found a coffee shop with more pastries than I'd ever seen in a single display case. It took us forever to make up our minds. While we ate, Raven kept her gaze glued on the two-lane street outside our window. She picked at her pastry. I devoured mine.

"We should make this a sightseeing diversion," I said.

"What does that mean?"

"He's taken over this trip, and I don't like it."

"Neither do I."

"If we make plans to stop at a few places, it will feel more like fun than running away from someone we're scared of."

"You don't seem all that scared."

I pulled out my phone and opened the map. "There's an abandoned church I read about." I pointed to a spot that was a few miles up another, smaller highway right outside the National Forest. "It was built in the mid-1800s, but it was only used for two years, then the town collapsed. One large family owned the place, and they had a feud that erupted, and half of them killed the other half. There's a cemetery behind the church where the victims are buried. We could look at the gravestones, which is always kind of interesting."

"Is it?"

I laughed. "Well, you're into ghosts. Maybe we'll meet one."

"Let's hope not."

"There are also a lot of really amazing waterfalls in the national forest."

"That sounds nicer, but we can stop at the church if you want to."

I finished my coffee.

"You know he's still out there," she said.

"Have you seen him while we've been eating?" I stared pointedly at the cranberry scone on the plate in front of her, missing only two or three bites.

"No, but that doesn't matter. He's not going to park along the curb outside the window and wave at us."

"We'll drive around a bit before we get on Highway 62. You can keep an eye out for him to be sure he's not behind us before we turn off."

"I've already been doing that."

"Good. Let's go."

I drove casually up and down most of the streets in the downtown area. We stopped at a deli and bought sandwiches, potato salad, drinks, and homemade oatmeal cookies for later. We walked around a bit, stopping in two antique stores and a shoe store. Raven bought a disposable phone, which she dropped into her purse without setting it up. She never saw the small blue SUV. She finally admitted he might not have noticed us packing the car after all. Maybe we were finally free. I turned toward Highway 62, and we continued our journey north to Portland.

As the highway turned east, the towns became smaller and the roadside buildings sparse. Magnificent fir trees towered beside the highway, and I relaxed into the natural beauty of it. Despite not having seen him all day, Raven couldn't stop herself from turning to look, but there were so few cars on the road, it was easy to see the other vehicles around us, and for the past seven miles the sole car behind us had been a white luxury car.

I knew all about the church and cemetery because Lance had told me. He and I planned to meet there. Together, we would confront Raven and show her the journal. This no longer felt like the solid plan it had seemed when he proposed it. At the time, I'd been utterly caught up in the shock of discovering who he was, still half-drunk on sex and the alcohol I'd consumed that evening. I was so shocked by what he'd read to me from Lily's journal, fixated on exposing Raven's lies, and honestly, relieved he no longer blamed me, I hadn't questioned anything he suggested. I blindly swallowed his assurance that he'd come to understand I'd simply been the one to find Lily, that his blame and the attacks on me had been irrational and cruel.

Now, I no longer believed he'd forgiven me. He'd chosen a secluded, unpopulated area to meet us. When he'd described it, I hadn't fully realized how isolated it was, how it was hidden within a massive expanse of wilderness.

Lily's death was made more tragic because it was entirely preventable. She never drank. She shouldn't have been a statistic, another teenager who inadvertently killed herself with too much alcohol. She never took drugs, so that added complication wasn't fair either. I wondered if she'd even known she was taking Ecstasy. I couldn't believe she would have done it deliberately.

Lance had bided his time and brooded for twelve years, and now he was going to take his sweet time in delivering our punishment, and I'd been an unwitting and then a very willing participant in making both Raven and me incredibly vulnerable.

Of course, I didn't have to keep our appointment at the abandoned church, but that wouldn't remove him from my life. He would simply wait somewhere else, and if I evaded that, somewhere after that, and after that... If I was careful, the isolated nature of our meeting spot could be made to suit me as well. As a result of my own sluttiness and my own curiosity and lack of boundaries, I'd acquired protection and the means to take control of the situation. The thought of being in control was like a drug in my bloodstream. After years of losing control to my ex-husband, not to mention Lance and those bullying kids in college, this was an entirely new experience. I liked it. A lot.

I liked that Raven was riding silently beside me so I could indulge in these thoughts, but it made me wonder what direction hers were taking.

After I'd stared into Lily's vacant eyes that November night, I'd screamed for a long time. It felt like my cry went on forever. I couldn't grab ahold of a single thought. I was swallowed by overwhelming despair and revulsion. I wanted to leave the room, but my feet seemed to be welded to the floor.

Because I'd noticed those staring, dead eyes, I hadn't immediately noticed that her face and neck were covered with vomit.
But even with the stink of it, those blank, lifeless eyes inside
her motionless body, the lack of air moving into her lungs,
sickened me more.

I rushed to the door and into the hallway, where I was
sick again, spewing the remainder of what I'd eaten and
drunk that day all over the runner carpet and the polished
wood floor. As soon as the vomit was out, I screamed again,
crying for help. A moment later, the music downstairs
stopped abruptly. Feet pounded the stairs as people raced to
find out what had made someone scream in that awful,
inconsolable manner.

It was the worst night of my life. I never forgot a single
moment of it. I dreamt about it. The images of Lily, drunken
friends, paramedics, questioning police officers, passed
through my body when I least expected. They charged at me
from out of nowhere. Over the years, those memories
surfaced less often, but they were still there, lurking.

THAT NIGHT, I was forced to tell the story over and over. First
to the kids who raced up the stairs, recoiling at the sight of
my vomit. Then to the officers of the fraternity who marched
into the room like they had it all under control, but were as
horrified as I was, just less vocal about it. Then I repeated the
events to the police. As it turned out, the police were the only
ones who believed my story.

The police wanted to know what time I'd entered the
room and the last time I'd seen Lily. They wanted to know
whom she might have had sex with, and who might have
been there when she was in distress. I couldn't answer
either of those questions. No one at the party admitted to
having sex with her, although they asked every male who

was still there. They asked the females to report any rumors they'd heard. No one had any stories to tell. In the end, they didn't pursue it any more than that. The position of her body and, later, the alcohol and E in her blood made it obvious, in their view, that she'd simply partied too hard. End of story.

It seemed hours before I found Raven that night. Finally, I discovered her huddled in the corner of a large room on the first floor that featured a pool table and several old-fashioned arcade games. It was the room where everyone had been dancing, and was now silent, most of the lights turned off. It smelled like alcohol and sweat and, oddly, candied apples. I don't know why that struck me, but the aroma was very strong, and it remained in my memories of that night.

Raven was curled into a ball, hugging her legs, her face pressed into her knees. I went to her side and knelt. Her head snapped up. "Where were you?" Her eyes were red from crying, and her skin was horribly pale.

"Were you sick?" I asked.

She nodded.

"You heard what happened?"

"How could I not? You screamed long enough to wake the dead."

"Why didn't you come?"

She shook her head. "I couldn't."

I didn't ask what that meant. I should have. "Did the police talk to you?"

She nodded.

"Should we go home now?"

She nodded again. As I helped her to her feet, Lance came into the room. I'd never spoken to him before that night. Seeing his face contorted into an inhuman shape to keep more tears from flowing, I was overcome with a disturbing, unwarranted sense of guilt.

"What's wrong with you?" he shouted. "Why didn't you help her?"

I stared at him. "Help her?"

He rushed toward me. He grabbed my free arm and shook my body with such force, I heard my teeth click against each other. "You should have turned her on her side; you should have called 911. What the hell is the matter with you?" His voice rose, and I cowered under the force of his rage.

"She was d—"

"She was not!" His cry sounded like a bellowing rhinoceros.

"I'm sorry. I didn't...she was already dead." I was crying now. Raven shrank behind me, tugging on my sleeve, murmuring that she wanted to go home. It felt as if she were a toddler and I were her mother, failing to give her the comfort she needed.

Now I remembered, she'd said something I'd completely forgotten.

"Don't argue with him, Abbey."

Why had she said that? At the time, I thought she simply wanted to get out of there. Now, I wasn't sure. Was she desperate to leave because she couldn't face Lance? Or because she was afraid something might come out that could implicate her?

It was officially determined that Lily had had consensual sex, so no DNA was taken from any of the boys at the party. It was also confirmed that she'd died of an overdose. The implication—no one was at fault but Lily herself. This splashed lighter fluid on the helpless grief burning inside her twin brother. How dare they blame his sister! Girls didn't just die at fraternity parties. Especially girls who didn't drink and do drugs. Especially intelligent, clever, cautious girls like his twin sister.

He was convinced she could have been saved, and since I

was in that unfortunate position of finding her body, he chose to believe she wasn't truly dead when I walked into the room. In his mind, I'd wasted precious moments screaming and indulging my own discomfort. I'd done absolutely nothing to help her, and had failed to call the paramedics. Her blood was on my hands, which was what he wrote on our dorm room door.

It was only days before the slander started—the vicious notes left on my desk in every class and shoved under my door at night. The things they said about me on social media forced me to close my accounts. The more Lance talked, and the more people speculated about me, the more hateful and cruel it became.

Within a week, I was completely isolated. Raven kept insisting I'd given up too fast. Instead, I'd endured it far longer than most people would have. I hung in there for the rest of November and December, until the holiday break. I told Raven I didn't ever want to see any of those people ever again.

Raven assured me that after the new year, they would forget.

She was wrong. They became more intense—messages written in permanent marker on the wall of the lounge area on our floor. Soda poured onto the food on my lunch tray if I turned away for even a second. Gunk spilled on pathways as I was walking by, causing me to slip and sometimes fall with a painful jarring of my bones.

College students cannot believe that a smart, thoughtful girl could just die alone in a darkened bedroom at a party. It was against the laws of nature as we knew them. People our age didn't die.

32

RAVEN

We slowed as we neared the church Abbey was so eager to explore. At first, I didn't see the building because it was set back about two hundred feet from the road. Abbey pulled the car into an area with firmly packed dirt, driving slowly so the tires didn't kick up too much dust. When we stopped, she put the roof up to protect the car from the overhanging maple tree.

Shrubs grew in a tangled, wild mess at the right side of the church, some of them so large they covered the windows. Behind the building, partially visible from where we sat, was an iron fence forming a rectangle that enclosed the cemetery. It was filled with large stone monuments, statues of angels, and several sepulchers.

About a third of the church roof was missing, and there was an open slot beside the main doors that looked like it used to have a stained-glass window because some of the leading that had connected the pieces of colored glass still hung like petrified worms from the frame.

The whole landscape gave the feeling that the dead were in control. They'd been lowered into the earth and had taken the town and were in the process of taking their church building with them.

Abbey locked the car out of habit even though there wasn't the barest evidence of civilization anywhere within shouting distance.

We walked around the church, taking in the cracked windowpanes and the paint that had peeled off in large strips on some parts. We longed to see what was inside the building, but assumed it was locked. Besides, the state of the structure suggested one wrong step down the center aisle would send us crashing through to the concrete floor of the basement. On the side of the building farthest from the highway was a basement entrance that lifted up from the ground. It was secured with a latch and a broken padlock, presumably opening to steps that descended into utter darkness. Neither of us had the nerve to open it.

The gate to the cemetery stood partially ajar. One of the hinges was broken, so the gate was angled down, the outer edge embedded in the dirt. There was still enough room for us to squeeze through. Most of the graves were flat rectangular slabs of granite, settled in the earth, weeds encroaching and, in many cases, covering the inscriptions.

The sepulchers were in better condition, with brass plates bearing the names of the people whose bones rested inside. I tried not to think about what the interiors of those tiny but ominous structures looked like—stacked skulls and misplaced bones, with a smell that was unnatural, the source of the odor mostly imagined. Those bones had lain there for over one hundred years. There was no longer any actual smell of death.

Abbey and I drifted away from each other, reading names, trying to find people who had died at the same time, hoping to piece together the people whose passions had destroyed civilization in this remote patch of the northwest.

After a while, I needed to get out of there so badly I felt as if insects were crawling out of the ground, climbing my legs and creeping up my spine. I no longer cared about the history. It had only distracted me for a short time. Now, I was unsettled by the steady heat that felt out of place with the lengthening shadows. I went to where Abbey stood looking down at a gravestone. Carved in the stone was the name Amelia Langdon. Below her name it read—*Beloved daughter, a true angel, October 9, 1872 – November 11, 1873*. Not only was it chilling to read of this poor child's death, but the proximity to the date of Lily's death—November 12—shook me. "I'm hungry," I said, my voice much too loud in the silent graveyard.

Abbey jumped slightly, then laughed to cover her fright. "I suppose death stirs up our animalistic instinct for survival."

"Whatever. I'm going to get the food."

She followed me out of the cemetery.

We carried our picnic to the side of the church where we could see the cemetery, choosing a massive oak tree that somehow felt safer because we were hidden from the road. Abbey spread out a blanket she'd bought in Ashland, and I opened the cooler and placed sandwiches, utensils, and small bowls for the potato salad on the blanket.

As I pried the lid off the potato salad, I heard a sound that I couldn't identify. I whipped my head around, but I couldn't see the road. I jumped to my feet, knocking over the container of potato salad.

"Calm down," Abbey said.

I still couldn't see the road, but I was sure I'd heard something close by. "Did you hear that?"

"No, I'm too busy wiping up potato salad off my new blanket."

"It might have been a car door." I was suddenly cold

despite the heat. I shivered several times, then wrapped my hands around my upper arms. My fingers were hot on my skin, even though I felt ice just below the surface.

"If it was a car door, we would have heard a car pull off the road."

"We were talking; we might not—"

"Stop it, Raven. We came this way to put all that behind us. Right?"

"We're so isolated out here. I'm not sure this was a good idea."

"He wasn't behind us the whole way. You were watching."

"I know...I just have a bad feeling."

She laughed. I knew she would, but it was the truth, and I had to say it.

We ate our sandwiches, and I listened to Abbey speculate about the people who had died more than a century before we were born. I got caught up with her, wondering about the details of their lives and whether their thoughts followed the same pathways as ours, or if being born into the modern world had formed entirely different psyches.

"Even if he didn't follow us here, how are we going to be rid of him?" I asked. "He can easily find where we live."

"But he hasn't. Not for all these years."

"Doesn't that make you wonder even more what's going on now?"

"Maybe he read the note you put on my Instagram and realized we were getting in touch for the first time since I dropped out. Maybe he put the pieces together when I posted that I had a friend traveling with me. I don't know. It doesn't matter."

"It matters more than anything," I said. "I can't live the rest of my life knowing he's watching me."

"If he ever actually bothers either one of us, we can get restraining orders."

"Those don't work."

"They wouldn't exist if they didn't work. I'm sure most of the time, they do." She scooped more potato salad into the small bowl the deli had provided, and ate a forkful, then sipped from her water bottle.

She looked so calm, I actually hated her for a moment. I was completely trapped by my desire to rebuild our friendship and, now, by my need to look out for her, which she didn't seem to appreciate at all. I was trapped by Lily's journal and whatever Lance assumed had happened before Lily died. When I'd started out on the road trip, I felt free. I thought I could shove the things that caused me pain to the back of the closet for a while. Now, Abbey had flung open the doors of a closet that I'd almost forgotten existed. All the rotten, damaged memories that had been piled in up to the rafters were spilling out.

"Why do you think he was waving her journal at me the other day?"

Abbey took a bite of a cookie. She chewed it carefully, then looked up into the tree branches. I shifted my position, and she grabbed her purse, pulling it away from me.

"It wasn't in my way," I said.

She moved the purse closer to her hip. "He wanted you to understand that he knows about everything we did."

"She wrote down every single word we said? Every argument, every complaint she had about us? That's hard to believe."

"It looked that way. The book only had about five or six blank pages left. She'd started writing in it the day she moved into our room. So..."

"Tell me everything you read. How many entries?"

"I didn't count them."

"More than three?"

"Yes."

"Ten?"

"Probably."

"One every day for the entire quarter?"

"No, but I would guess there were several entries a week."

"Then tell me what else she wrote. All of it."

"I already told you what I read. The part about losing her necklace was in there. She wrote about you deleting the paper from her laptop, and how she knew you were afraid of her eyes. She was very philosophical."

"I don't care about that. What else?"

"It was a little stressful when I was reading it. He was standing right there, watching me. And I wasn't sure if he was going to hurt me, so I skipped over a lot of it. There wasn't time to read every page."

"So you are afraid of him. You just pretend you're not."

"When I was alone in his room and naked? Yes, I was afraid. Now, not really."

"I don't understand why he's so fixated on her journal. It's nothing but a college girl complaining about her roommates. There are thousands of diaries like that in every dorm room in the world."

"He said it was eye-opening. And then he apologized for what he did to me. So maybe she also wrote good things about us."

"I seriously doubt that."

"You probably don't need to worry about it. She called us Roach One and Two, and he wanted to know which of us was Roach One. I said I couldn't tell from what I read. She wrote a lot of conversations we had word for word, but she didn't always write who was talking."

"That's strange."

"She had a crush on some guy, but she didn't name him either."

"Could you figure out who he was from what she said about him?"

"No. All I know is that he came by our room all the time, but we were usually out. It sounded like he planned it that way."

"And you have *no idea* who it could be?" I knew she was lying. But I couldn't tell her how I knew.

"Nope. Do you?"

I shook my head. I heard a slight humming, rumbling sound. I wasn't sure if it was a car or maybe a low-flying plane far away from us. I turned my head. "Do you hear that?"

"No," Abbey said.

My stomach was tied in painful knots. I didn't like imagining what might be in that journal. She could have written anything at all. She could have written something that made me look like I had a reason to kill her. She could have written about the things she'd found when she went through all my drawers. What would Lance think about the Ecstasy I'd tried to get her to take? Had she written about that? Would he add two and two and get seven, like he had when he launched the slander attack on Abbey?

The only thing I could think was that I'd been incredibly stupid to let Abbey talk me into supposedly escaping him by driving to the middle of nowhere. I was more vulnerable than ever.

33

ABBEY

Raven was shaking. She looked like she'd developed an uncontrollable spasm—jerking her head toward the highway every few minutes, her hands trembling without her seeming to notice. We couldn't even see the highway from where we were. If a car happened to pass by, I wasn't sure we would hear it. But she was certain he was there, certain he was waiting for us or coming soon.

Maybe she did have a sixth sense of some kind. Maybe she knew he would find us in this remote location no matter how carefully we'd tried to elude him. Or maybe her guilt had grown to such monumental proportions she was fantasizing about the punishment Lance believed she deserved.

She began packing up the food, so frantic, she couldn't steady her hands enough to attach the lid to the salad container. She wadded up the sandwich wrappings, squeezing them into hard white balls. I folded the blanket and placed it inside its carrier while she flung her paper balls and napkins, cookie crumbs and all, into the cooler.

We started walking toward the car. "Do you want to look

over the list of waterfalls and decide which ones we want to visit?"

She shook her head violently. "I think we should go back to I-5 and get to Portland as soon as we can."

"We came all this way." I heard the whine in my voice and tried to swallow it. "Even though it seems impossible now, I *still* want to enjoy our trip. I'm going to see some waterfalls. I'll probably never drive through this area again in my life."

She sighed. I opened the trunk, and we piled our things inside. As she placed the cooler into the spot on the left, beside our bags, the car wobbled and tilted slightly. Raven wedged the cooler into place, then walked around to the driver's side.

"Oh my God. Oh shit. Abbey!" She let out a painful sob. "He found us!" She whirled around, looking in every direction, seeing nothing. She flung herself toward me and grabbed my arm. "He found us! He slashed the tire!"

This was one part of my agreement with Lance that I'd seriously questioned. Now that it was real, I felt a tremor of fear. Had I been too easily taken in? He'd said he would puncture the tire so Raven couldn't run from us. He would drive the three of us—he was very clear about that—all *three* of us—back to Medford, where we could report the damage. The rental company would provide a replacement car on the spot. I'd argued that I loved our little sports car. I didn't want to be in trouble or have extra expenses. He'd asked how much the truth was worth to me. He'd even handed me a few hundred dollars for any expenses that might come up.

I hadn't liked the idea, but he refused to budge. This was the only way to keep her from running, from calling the police and painting him as the bad guy. To the police, a crime could not be proven from innuendo and made-up names in a dead girl's diary written over a decade earlier. He was the one who would be in trouble.

"I wonder where we picked up a nail," I asked.

"It's not a nail, Abbey! Wake up. He's here!" She kicked the tire. The tire heaved a sigh as if the kick was more than it could take.

"I don't see any obvious hole," I said.

"He must be good with a knife. A tire doesn't go completely flat from a nail. In fact, a lot of times the nail stays in place, and the tire doesn't lose air for quite a while."

"Are you a car maintenance expert?" I asked.

She started crying. "It was a stupid, stupid mistake to come out here. We're all alone." She sobbed harder, her shoulders shaking. She covered her face with her hands and wailed. "And I don't have my phone!" Her cries grew louder. If she carried on like that, she might attract a mountain lion or whatever wildcats lived in the area. Maybe even a wolf or a grizzly. Then we'd be dead without a moment to discuss an escape plan or to speculate on what our predator wanted.

"Calm down. I'll call a tow truck. If you want to do something useful, go stand by the road and see if you can flag someone down."

"You said yourself, we haven't heard a car the entire time we've been here. Besides, I don't want to be alone."

"I need to be near the car to give the license number and any other details they might need."

She looked at me as if she didn't quite believe me, but her need to watch for Lance overcame her desire to stay beside me.

"It's almost six," she said. "It will be dark soon."

"Not for two more hours."

"I had no idea we spent so long walking around those graves. What a waste of time."

What was a waste was this trip. Not only the time, but the cost—the hotels, the meals, the fun little car. What Lance hadn't cast a shadow over, she was destroying, one complaining, frightened mood after the other. She refused to have fun, refused to relax even for an hour.

As she started walking toward the highway, I pretended to place the call, providing the information about the car and our location, pausing appropriately as if someone were speaking on the other end of the call. Lance had said he would arrive by seven at the latest, making sure there was plenty of time in case we took detours. I couldn't touch base with him because I'd put my phone in airplane mode when we turned off Highway 62. If anything happened with Lance, I couldn't have a digital record that I'd visited the abandoned church.

After Raven had been out by the road for a few minutes, I walked over to where she stood. She stared down the highway in the direction we'd come, looking as if it were her last moment on earth.

"I've only seen one car," she said. "They sped up when I waved at them."

"Let's go explore the cemetery some more. It will help pass the time."

"How long did they say?"

"About an hour."

"An *hour*!? It will be almost dark by then. We can't stay out here in the dark. We're sitting ducks."

"It won't be dark yet."

"We're in the middle of a forest. It gets dark earlier."

"Let's try to stay calm."

"Don't you know how to change a tire?" she asked.

"There's no spare."

"Why didn't you check when you picked up the car?"

"You didn't check either." There had been a spare, but I'd allowed Lance to remove it from the car when we'd made our final plan. By then, I wasn't disagreeing with any of his plans.

I had to let him think he was in control of how things would play out.

"It's not my car," she said.

"You're an equal partner in this trip, Raven. I'm not your chaperone."

"I'm not equal. You paid for the hotels; you bought more than half the meals. And you rented the car. It's in your name. You made all the decisions."

"Maybe you shouldn't be so trusting."

"You have that backwards," she said.

Again, we squeezed through the opening where the gate to the cemetery was stuck.

As we walked around, we allowed the peeved silence to grow between us, quietly studying the names on the gravestones. I was occupied with thoughts of the possible scenarios that might unfold once Lance showed up. I wondered if Raven was so strong in her determination to keep a secret that she still wouldn't be pressured into telling the truth. Because of the way her mind distorted reality, part of me wondered if she truly believed she had absolutely nothing to do with Lily's death. Was it possible she'd seen Lily's body, but entirely forgotten about it? The mind does unpredictable things. It's not always the reliable piece of machinery we'd like to believe it is.

Although she didn't speak to me about anything else, every ten minutes Raven asked me to call about the progress of the tow truck. Each time I reminded her they'd said it would be an hour. Finally, she said, "You need to call them right now. It's been an hour."

"Give him a minute or two," I said.

"They should be able to tell you how far away he is."

I pulled out my phone. Raven stood too close for me to feel confident pretending to make a call. "I don't have a good signal." I walked away from her. I squeezed out through the gate and moved a few yards beyond that. I mimed calling, inquiring about the location of the tow truck.

Before I could get back through the gate, Raven was beside me. "What did they say?"

"Twenty minutes."

"Oh my God! I can't believe this is happening to me."

"To us," I said.

She started crying.

I stood helplessly beside her, mildly concerned that Lance hadn't arrived yet, wondering how well I was going to manage this after all.

34

LILY'S JOURNAL
NOVEMBER 12, 2010

The Roaches are getting ready for another party. All the usual—the strong scent of their perfumes crashing into each other, making our room smell like the cosmetics section of a department store, makeup all over the bathroom counter, shoes all over the floor of our room, clothes spilling out of their drawers. They spent an hour doing their makeup, and now they're slipping their feet into high heels.

I'm sitting at my desk. I was writing an email to my parents, which I haven't done for more than a week, and I feel terrible about that. It's Friday night, and my parents play board games with the people next door on Fridays, or I would have called them.

Now, I put my laptop aside, and I'm writing in here. I have my journal inside a lab notebook so they'll think I'm doing homework. They really don't pay much attention to me anyway, so I doubt they'll notice. If they do, they won't care.

The Prince is going to the party tonight. He usually goes to all the parties. But this time is different. I feel like I'm living in an alternate reality—he said he would *see me there!!!*

As awful as the Roaches have been to me, I really don't want to show up at the party alone. I'm trying to get up my nerve to ask if I can go with them. I thought being bold enough to write in this notebook while they're in the room would increase my courage overall, but I'm still not feeling it.

In five minutes, I'll be out of time. I hate asking them, but going alone is too much. I don't want everyone staring at me —first, for showing up at all, but also for walking into the fraternity house without any friends, even props that look like they could be friends. Going to a party alone labels you an outsider, untouchable from the start. No one does that. They go everywhere in groups, like little clusters of ants scurrying and scrambling to get somewhere important, sometimes moving in circles, terrified to separate from the group.

I DID IT. I asked. And it went exactly as I should have expected. Why did I even bother? I put down my pen and closed the spiral notebook over my journal, trapping it inside. I turned around to face them as they came out of the bathroom.

"Hey," I said.

They stared at me as if I'd grown a third eye—LOL— maybe a chocolate brown one this time.

I asked if they were leaving right that minute, which was a stupid question and made me realize I'd waited too long to ask. They weren't going to want to hang around while I got ready, even though it would take me five minutes—a nicer top, my favorite boots, and some mascara and lip gloss.

Roach Two said, "Isn't it obvious?"

Roach One laughed.

I still didn't see what was coming, though. I asked if I could go with them, and they laughed. Hysterically.

I said I was serious, and they laughed harder. I stood up

and went to my closet and pulled out a white sweater with a low neck.

"Why do you suddenly want to go to a party?" Roach One asked.

"I just feel like it. Maybe it'll be fun."

Roach One's laugh sounded like a shriek. "*Maybe?*"

I didn't want to tell them I didn't want to go alone. And obviously I couldn't tell her that Prince said he'd see me there. I told them I knew it was weird after all this time. I laughed because I knew how it must sound to them. Then I was stupid enough to ask again and tell them it would only take a few minutes to get ready, like I was begging.

"That figures," Roach One said.

"We can't wait," Roach Two said. "We promised we'd go by the store and get some chips and dip, so we're already late."

"Can I meet you in front of the dorm after you go to the store, and walk over with you?"

"That won't work." She didn't explain why, because there was no reason why. They left without saying goodbye. They rushed to the door like they were running for their lives.

Now, I'm wearing my sweater and writing in here again. Trying to build up my courage. Again. I can't not go. He said he'd see me there! And I know that meant he wanted to be sure I went because he knows I've never been to a party at the University of Washington, even though it's my second year. After he said he wanted to see me there, he kissed me. It wasn't a long kiss, but it was absolutely incredible and actually felt like real love.

I knew from that kiss he wants me as much as I want him. Not just that, but from all the things he's said to me. From how he loves talking to me, how he thinks about me all the time. Because of how he learns something in one of his classes and the first thing that comes into his head is wanting to tell me about it and to find out what I think. Also, the kiss!

As he kissed me, he slid his hand down my lower back, slowly over my butt, and then rested it on my hip. I felt like I was going to collapse on the floor in a puddle of longing. It felt so incredible I don't know how to describe it.

Right this minute, I'm not sure why I've never had sex. I think it's mostly because the guy I went out with in high school was only my boyfriend for two months. Also, no one has made me feel like Prince does. It's not like I'm in a rush to get my first time out of the way, like it's on a checklist for my semester goals. I don't feel some directive to lose my so-called virginity before I'm twenty, but I do want to do it.

There's no reason to wait, and I could tell from the way he looked at me, and his hand on my butt, that he was thinking about that. While we were still close, looking at each other, his hand on my hip, he asked if I was going to the party.

One reason everyone loves fraternity house parties is because those old mansions have tons of bedrooms. People like to take advantage of that to hook up with someone.

Even if I have to walk in the front door alone. Even if everyone stares at me and thinks I'm a loser, I'm going to that party. Because Carter doesn't think that at all. I think he loves me.

35

RAVEN

Finally acting more concerned than she had for almost the entire trip, Abbey put her arm around my shoulders and gave me a comforting squeeze. Her voice was soothing. "Let's wait on the porch. We can see the road from there, so we'll know when the truck arrives."

I shrugged off her arm and stomped up the wooden steps. The top step made a loud crack as I landed on it with too much force. I felt my foot sink into empty space. I screamed, fearing I was about to fall into the basement. I grabbed the post and stepped carefully onto the porch. I felt around with my right foot, pressing the floor for weak spots. "We should wait in the car. This doesn't seem safe."

"It's fine," Abbey said. "The driver won't be able to see our car from the road. I don't want to take a chance on him missing us."

I leaned against the post, holding on to it as if it were Emmett and he was there to keep me steady. I'd fooled myself into believing I was there to protect Abbey, but now I realized that since the moment I posted on her Instagram that I missed her, I'd made choice after choice that turned out to be some of the worst decisions of my life. I'd had no idea that meeting with Abbey for a glass of champagne would turn my life inside out. I felt as if I'd been walking down a dark corridor, and each time I saw a sliver of light under a doorway, I flung open the door without thinking. And now, I'd wound my way into the depths of a building filled with countless rooms and hallways from which there was no way out.

"I had another dream about Lily," Abbey said.

I closed my eyes and tried to let thoughts of Lily melt out of my mind, as I'd been able to do in the past.

"It was raining again. The same as in my other dream. She was—"

"I don't want to hear it," I said.

"Why not? It's so strange. Think of it as a story to entertain us while we wait."

"Seeing her in your dream doesn't mean anything."

"I didn't say it meant something. I'm just telling you the bizarre story my subconscious is weaving for me."

"Dreams are nonsense."

"I don't think you believe that at all. But let me tell you what it was about; then you can decide. It's the strangest dream I've ever had." She laughed. "I need to get it out of my head."

"By forcing your subconscious anxieties into my head?"

She talked over me. "She was standing in the rain again, and I absolutely *knew* she had something urgent to tell me. It started up right where the other dream ended. I've never had that happen before. Have you?"

"No. And I don't want to—"

"The rain grew so heavy, I almost couldn't see her."

"You probably dreamt that because you've been thinking about waterfalls," I said, hoping to change the subject.

"Maybe." She smiled. "But then I was running toward her. She started running too, and I was chasing her, shouting at her to wait for me. When I didn't think I could run another step, the rain suddenly stopped. It was night, did I say that? The moon came out almost immediately after the rain stopped. It shone down on the center of an endless lawn. Carter was standing in the middle of the lawn, and—"

"Why on earth would you dream about Carter?" I was angry she was telling me her ridiculous dream when I said I didn't want to hear it. Now, part of me wondered if she was making it all up to torment me.

"Like you said, dreams don't always make sense. We have to figure out what they mean," she said.

"What they mean is that you're not sleeping in your own bed, you're in unfamiliar environments, eating different food, and we've been talking about the past. So of course random people and places are popping up in senseless ways."

As if she hadn't heard me, as if she were dreaming as she talked, she kept going. "Lily ran across the lawn, just a shadow at first, then bathed in moonlight. She threw herself into Carter's arms, and he spun her around. Her hair was dry, and it flowed out as they spun in circles. Then the sun came up, and they were surrounded by wildflowers. They started dancing in the sunshine."

Abbey was turned away from me, which I was happy about. I had no idea what the expression on my face might be saying. Part of me didn't believe a single word of her dream. At the same time, a large part of me was terrified. Was it possible that Lily's spirit was communicating to her in a dream? Or maybe this was something Lily had written in her journal, and Abbey was telling it to me like it was her own dream to see what I'd say.

After several moments of silence, she added more. As if what she'd said already wasn't bad enough. In this second part of her dream, she said that Lily and I were screaming at her to be careful. We were crying and shouting, and she didn't know why.

Finally, she looked down and saw that her belly was huge with a child. She was standing in the middle of a frozen lake. She realized Lily and I were screaming because if she took a single step in the hard-soled leather boots she was wearing, she would start sliding and wouldn't be able to stop. She would fall and lose her child. But suddenly, all the ice around her melted and she, too, was standing in a field of wildflowers.

"That's weird, but dreams always are," I said, hoping she would stop talking now.

"What do you think it means?"

"You have to figure that out yourself. You want a baby, obviously. Maybe your subconscious knows you're not equipped to care for a child. And you like wildflowers, obviously." I laughed, but it sounded hollow and sharp.

"Maybe."

"You can hardly take care of yourself," I said. "Deep inside, you know you could never nurture a child adequately because you take such terrible risks. Children need stability and security."

"Do they?"

I nodded. "They need a normal, almost dull life if they're going to thrive."

"I don't think I agree," she said.

"Well, neither of us have been given that blessing yet, so there's no point in talking about it right now. It's too upsetting."

"Don't you think it's strange that I dreamed about Lily being with Carter?"

"No. I already told you why." I wanted her to shut up. I didn't know what she was trying to do. What I really wanted to know was whether that tow truck company had lied to her.

"It's been an hour and twenty minutes. Where the hell is the tow truck?"

She shrugged. "I'm sure they'll be here soon."

"You're *sure*? Based on what? Maybe they aren't even coming."

"They're coming."

"How do you know?"

"It's a reputable company. They had good reviews."

"We're a long way away from a town large enough to have a decent towing company. Maybe the guy wanted to get home for dinner and decided to bail."

"Stop *worrying* about everything. You're driving me crazy." She walked to the other end of the porch and looked out at the forest behind us.

I hugged the post even tighter, hoping the solid, oddly intact wood might comfort me. Abbey's dream was too real. It was too close to what really happened, and I wondered if she somehow knew that. Maybe it had all been in the journal, and she wasn't telling me because she wanted me to be eaten alive with bad memories. Maybe she'd even known back then.

During the months she was sharing my dorm room, Lily had been slowly bewitching my boyfriend, the first boy I loved, with her freaky eyes. He couldn't stop *staring* at them, talking about how beautiful they were. Carter and Lily were so stupid. They thought I didn't know he came to our room every time I went out. The first time, when I caught them sitting so comfy and cozy on the dorm room floor, they said they were just talking. Did they truly think I was gullible enough to believe that?

Lily wanted Carter, and I came to see that he wanted her, not me. I had to find a way to get him away from her. I loved Carter. I loved him with the love you have the first time you fall for someone. And it wasn't teenage love or puppy love. He filled my soul, my body, my heart. He made me feel like I mattered. He made me feel normal and interesting and captivating and sexy. I loved him so much, it hurt.

After he'd been in our room *talking* to Lily, I could smell him on my comforter.

He never stopped staring at those eyes. He literally gushed about them all the time. *They're so beautiful, so unique...mesmerizing.* He said this right to my face! You'd think she was a Greek goddess come to life. It made me sick. And I could see the lovesickness in her weird, disturbing eyes, when I could bear to look at them.

Right before the Halloween party, I advised Lily to take E. But she blew me off, which I'd expected. As usual, she didn't go to the party, so it would have been a waste anyway.

Then she showed up at another party. November 12—the last party before the Thanksgiving holiday. It was so perfect. She was so clueless. She followed Carter around like a puppy. I could feel his heart slipping away from me. He was looking for a chance to ditch me. I asked her how she was liking the party. I told her she had to try the Jell-O shots. She liked the first one, so I insisted she should have more. Like every newbie with alcohol, she didn't understand how much alcohol was in those sugary-sweet treats.

I forced myself to stay in the background so she wouldn't catch on to what I was doing. When I saw her and Carter sitting close to each other in a secluded window seat, I asked them if they wanted sodas. Carter was so full of himself, he thought I didn't get what he was up to. Lily looked suspicious, but she didn't want to be her usual bitchy self with Carter watching. Also, she was pretty tipsy by that point.

In the kitchen, I dissolved an E tablet in her soda. I returned to the window seat and handed the plastic cups to them. I told them to drink up. They needed to stay hydrated because of all the alcohol.

"I only had one drink," Lily said. "And a few Jell-O shots, but those are like candy." She gave me a smug look.

I kept my own smug look to myself. She'd find out soon enough. "There might be more alcohol than you realize," I said. Luckily, Carter backed me up, and she drank the whole thing.

Then I reminded Carter we hadn't danced at all. He let me drag him onto the dance floor. I knew that once the E hit her, she would fall all over the first guy who told her she looked hot. And she did look hot. I had to admit that.

Carter and I danced for five or six songs. He kept trying to leave, but I hung on him even though it was a little pathetic. Then I felt a little off, probably from too many Jell-O shots myself. I went to the bathroom. I threw up a little bit, which was weird because I didn't feel sick. Just more buzzed than usual. I hadn't taken any E that night. I wanted to be clearheaded.

When I came out of the bathroom a while later, there was a line. People were not pleased. I ignored them. I walked all over the main floor of that magnificent, gothic-looking brick mansion. I couldn't find Carter or Lily anywhere. My heart started beating so hard, I could hardly breathe. I had to go into one of the small sitting rooms and lie down on the couch. My head was spinning, and even lying in that dark, quiet room, I felt like my heart was exploding.

36

ABBEY

After I told her about my dream, Raven stopped speaking to me. She closed her eyes, and each time I tried to start a conversation, she said, "Be quiet. We need to hear every sound. We need to know where he is. And we need to hear the tow truck coming, if it ever is."

As I'd been telling her my made-up dream about Lily and Carter, it had come to me that I should add a second part. But the second dream was real. So real, it had stayed in my thoughts for a day and a half, clinging to me like a newborn clings to its mother. It was surreal and a little confusing, so I had to tell someone.

I suppose we all think our dreams are uniquely fascinating. When a dream is vivid and detailed, there's a compulsion to share the images and confusing storyline. A person's dreams aren't all that interesting to anyone else, but we're in thrall to our own mysteries, so we'll tell them anyway. Besides, I hoped that painting a mental image for Raven of me possessing what she so desperately wanted might undo her enough that the truth would finally spill out.

"What's that?" The porch creaked as she let go of the post

she'd been hugging and put her foot carefully on the top step. She looked around wildly, like a chicken pecking its way through the yard, frantically jerking its head in a state of perpetual anxiety.

As she crept down the steps, I knew that this time what she'd heard was real. It was the sound of someone walking on hard-packed earth, approaching the building without giving much care to concealing his presence. I knew Lance was just around the corner from where she stood halfway down the steps.

Moving away from the porch, she turned back toward me, speaking in a loud whisper. "Did you hear it?"

Normally, her ridiculous stage whispers made me laugh, but not this time. Adrenaline was pumping through my body, ensuring every muscle was poised for action. I thought I had a good plan. I was trying to keep myself from mentally rehearsing it too often because there was a danger I'd over-think it. I shook my head, not trusting my voice.

"I heard someone walking," she said.

"Could have been the wind."

"It was not the wind. Come down here. We need to stay close together."

I moved toward the steps, glancing to the left to see if Lance was about to show himself to her. Why was he taking so long? I walked slowly down the steps and stood beside Raven. "We can't see the road from down here."

As if my voice was the trigger, Lance was suddenly in front of us. He was pointing an absurdly large handgun at me. Without hesitating, he kicked Raven hard right on her ankle bone. She screamed, waving her arms as she tried to maintain her balance. He grabbed her arm before she could fall and pulled her close beside him. He twisted her arm behind her back, causing her to cry out again. His moves were smooth and expert. Maybe he'd studied martial arts in preparation for his treks into the wilderness.

"What are you doing?" I whimpered and cowered in the face of the gun, which wasn't all put on for Raven's benefit. The size of that gun and the reality of staring into the dark hole aimed at me were more terrifying than I'd imagined. He'd never mentioned a gun, but I hadn't been able to work out how he would get Raven under his control without a weapon of some kind. I'd hoped it would be a knife, but I should have known better.

"How did you find us?" Raven began sobbing. "What do you want? Please let me go. I didn't do anything."

He struggled to keep Raven's arm twisted so her forearm was pressed against her spine. She cried uncontrollably while I made frightened little sounds that echoed her terror, thinking about the much smaller gun that seemed so far away at the bottom of my purse.

"Come with me." His voice was not the growl of rage I'd expected. He sounded cool and clearheaded, which was infinitely more chilling. He dragged Raven toward the side of the building, waving the gun at me. "Come on. Get over there." He waved the gun again, using it as a pointer to direct me to walk in front of them. "Keep going," he said. "Around the side."

I walked toward the corner of the building, intensely aware of the cracked, flaking paint, the rotted appearance of the siding, the sense the entire place was poised to sink into the earth. I wound through overgrown shrubbery as he continued telling me to keep going in that icy cold voice of absolute certainty.

When we reached the entrance to the basement, he yanked Raven hard. I heard a bone crack somewhere in her shoulder or arm. She screamed and bent over, cowering beside him. As he squatted to remove the padlock, tugging Raven down with him, I slipped my phone out of my pocket.

Without looking up at me, he said in that same cold tone, "Not a good idea."

He fired the gun at the hard-packed dirt several yards away.

My body startled violently, causing the phone to flip out of my hand. It crashed to the ground, landing faceup.

The sound of the gunshot obliterated my thoughts for a moment. My ears hummed with a silence that made me fear briefly that I might never hear another sound.

Lance lunged toward the phone and kicked it out of reach. "Don't move again."

Dragging Raven to where he'd kicked the phone, he picked it up and shoved it into his pocket, then yanked her back toward the basement door. He kicked at the padlock to dislodge it, but it remained stubbornly attached. He kicked again with the same result. Shoving his knee into the back of Raven's knee, forcing hers to bend, he pushed her down to a kneeling position and told her to take the lock out. She began sobbing, her entire body convulsing with the effort.

As I watched them in a tight struggle with each other, as if they were a single, writhing creature, I took a few steps backwards. Then I turned and ran, headed toward the front of the building.

"Come back here!" Even shouting, his voice maintained a calm, controlled tone.

I kept going, skidding as I raced past the porch and around the other side, headed toward the cemetery.

I squeezed through the gate and bent low as I made my way to the center where the sepulchers were clustered like a silent neighborhood of tiny houses. Crouching behind one, I turned over my plan in my mind. I was fairly certain he wouldn't come after me until he had Raven secured. That gave me at least five minutes.

When Raven and I had explored the cemetery earlier, I'd had the shivery thought that I might need to hide inside one of the small concrete buildings. I'd tried the doors and found one was slightly loose. But it would be my absolute last resort. The thought of hiding out with the bones of the deceased, no matter how purified by time and the cessation of decay, made me ill. Even thinking about it made me feel as if maggots were burrowing into my own flesh.

All I had to do was catch my breath, pull the gun I'd stolen out of my purse, and return to the basement, which Lance would not expect.

37

RAVEN

I n the midst of a fear that made my insides feel like Jell-O, there was a tender sliver of superiority. I'd told Abbey Lance wanted to hurt us, and she'd refused to believe me. She'd refused to consider one shred of caution or healthy fear. She'd mocked me and dismissed me and gaslit me.

This was the result, and I was pretty sure I was going to die. So was she, despite her temporary escape. Knowing this forced a steady flow of tears out of my eyes, such a constant flood that I no longer had the strength to wipe them away.

Lance was alternately dragging and pushing me down the concrete steps into a pitch-dark basement that hadn't seen human life in fifty years. Probably a lot longer. He clearly had a plan and was prepared for whatever torture he had in mind. I felt him shrug off his backpack. It fell on the ground, thudding on what sounded like hard-packed dirt. He was holding my arm so tightly, he was cutting off the flow of blood, making my fingers numb. I wriggled them, trying to regain some feeling. I heard him rummage in the backpack, and a moment later a small portable light came on.

His face looked calm; his eyes were focused and clear. Not angry as I'd expected. Maybe he wouldn't kill me. He didn't have the look of a madman, not that I was certain I'd recognize that if I saw it.

"Sit down."

"It's dirty."

He yanked my arm, so I stumbled and lost my balance. I sat on the ground. Holding the gun in one hand, he took zip ties out of his pack. He wrapped one around my wrists and one around my ankles, pulling them so tight, they hurt even worse than his grip had. While he rummaged through his pack again, I looked around at the shadowy concrete walls. The place was surprisingly free of cobwebs. It smelled like old dirt. There was no odor of decay trying to scare me even more, whispering that maybe he'd brought other women here and killed them over the years. He sure seemed to know his way around.

"Do you come here a lot?" I asked.

He gave a snorting laugh. "What is that—a pickup line? Not exactly the time and place." He pulled Lily's orange journal out of the pack. It was covered with insect stickers. It looked juvenile and disturbing at the same time.

He faced me, clutching the notebook with one hand, the gun in the other. "You murdered my sister." His voice was so soft, I almost didn't catch what he said.

"I didn't."

"Don't talk. I'm doing the talking. You silenced her voice forever, but now, I'm going to talk for her."

"I—"

"Shut up."

"What about Abbey?"

He laughed. "Throwing your best friend under the bus again? You haven't changed at all since college, have you?"

"I didn't. I just wondered where she is, if she's okay."

"No idea. I'm dealing with you right now."

He stood about two feet from me, looking down. I was forced to tip my head back to see his face. My neck ached, and everything looked darker because the light was so low to the ground. I opened my mouth to tell him it was uncomfortable, to ask him again what he wanted, but he saw my lips part, and he stepped closer, pointing the gun right at my mouth. I started crying.

"No talking. No crying." He took a step back and lowered the gun to his side. "I read my sister's journal after we buried her. I've read it every year on the anniversary of the day she died. But I never figured out which one of you gave her the Ecstasy. That's what killed her, you know. That, and a shit-ton of Jell-O shots." He grimaced, then raised the gun, moving it in small ovals in the air, tracing the outline of my face.

"Twins are different from other siblings," he said. "A twin is a deeper part of who you are. When your twin is gone, a piece of you is physically missing. Literally. Because that person has been with you every moment of your existence, even before you were conscious. When she isn't there, it feels as if half of you has been sliced off."

I nodded, still trying to keep my head back, locking onto his face. Surely if I was looking at his face, if our eyes stayed in contact, he wouldn't kill me. He couldn't kill me because he'd be aware of me as a person instead of the monster he believed I was.

"You and your *friend* bullied her. You deserve to be punished for that alone. But giving her an illegal drug when she'd never experienced anything like that. You knew it was risky. You knew Ecstasy, any unregulated substance, could be unknowingly mixed with more dangerous—"

"But it wasn't mixed. I took some from the same batch two or three times and—"

He rushed at me, pressing the gun against my temple. "You. Do *not*. Get. To. Talk! Are you clear about that now?"

I nodded.

He rubbed the nose of the gun across my forehead, pressing it into my skull. I felt more tears pouring out of me, but I forced myself not to allow even the tiniest sound to escape with them. He was so calm and so furious and so sure of himself. He was also a little sad, and I wasn't sure which version I should focus on.

"Maybe it was pure," he said. "Maybe, maybe, maybe. You mix that shit with alcohol, and you might as well have put a bullet in her brain."

The beam of light reflected off the barrel of the gun, blinding me with its focused glare. I couldn't believe he was going to kill me and leave me in this place where no one would ever find me. If he left me in the basement and locked that door, not even a wild animal could drag one of my bones into sight, offering me a chance of justice and a proper burial.

Emmett. I let out a sob and felt the gun press against my temple. What would Emmett think? He had no idea where I was. I would disappear off the face of the earth. He would contact my mother and find out I'd lied. The last thing between us, the last *I love yous* we'd ever said, would become a lie to him. He would hate me for tearing his heart out, and then he would start a new life without me. And my mom...I began sobbing.

"When you get a grip, we can continue hearing about how you made Lily cry, instead of your indulgent self-pity for having to finally face up to what you did. You thought you got away with it. For twelve years. You lived your happy little life and didn't think about her once." His voice rose, cracking on the last words. He took a deep breath.

For a moment, the basement was silent. It was the quiet of being inside the earth, the structure so airtight that it was quiet and cool, even with the heat that still burned outside as the sun dipped below the horizon.

"You're scared." He laughed gently. "You've been terrified every moment since you first saw me by the river, watching you."

"How do you know that?"

"Shh." He touched the gun to my lips. "Your friend told me. Your friend also filled in some of the blanks that Lily left. She was so disgusted by you two, she made up names for you. Cockroaches. Very fitting. Abbey informed me that the boy Lily called a prince in her journal, the boy she loved and wanted to have sex with, was your boyfriend."

I was having trouble breathing, my head still tipped back, mucous running down my throat and out of my nose and eyes.

"You truly are a cockroach," he said.

"Are you going to kill me?"

He laughed. He lowered the gun and stepped over to where his backpack lay on its side. He poked at it with his toe, then sat down. He crossed his arms over his knees, letting the gun dangle by the side of his leg.

I could finally lower my head to a normal position. I closed my eyes and tried to think. He wanted me to suffer, but maybe he wouldn't kill me. Did he really have that in him? Plus, he still had to deal with Abbey, and she might fight back. She might have already escaped. Maybe the tow truck driver had actually shown up. Maybe she was with him, calling the police, and help would be on its way sooner than I imagined. Maybe it already was. The tears stopped. I opened my eyes and looked at him.

He was staring at me. I didn't think he was waiting for me to talk. He'd told me enough times to shut up. He thought his sister was such an angel. I didn't know if he thought that when she was alive. Sometimes death turns people into angels in the minds of those left behind. Either way, Lily was definitely not an angel.

That little *angel* stole my boyfriend right out of my arms. She flirted with him and took advantage of his curiosity about her weird eyes. She fed his ego with all her questions about his life. Who knows what else she did on the floor of our dorm room.

November 12 was the worst night of my life. I thought it would all work out, that Lily would go flying high on E and fall all over some other guy, as long as I was clever enough to get Carter out of her way. But it didn't work out that way. One moment Carter and I were walking off the dance floor to get a drink, and then they'd both evaporated into thin air.

I remember climbing that long, curved staircase to the second floor. I remember walking along the landing, opening doors, looking into bedrooms, knowing before I saw them what I would find.

Finally, I heard something. A moan of pleasure, maybe. I opened the door. The room was dark, but I heard movement and whispers. It was the room where they kept our coats, which made what they were doing even more disgusting. I heard them whispering and giggling, I heard him saying the things to her that he'd said to me, heard him groaning. Sobs rose inside me, but I pressed my hand to my chest and bit down on my tongue. I was not going to let that girl know how badly she hurt me. I couldn't allow Carter to know he'd broken my heart, that he'd destroyed me. If I let them know, they would have all the power. Knowing you can hurt someone means you own them.

I closed the door and ran up the stairs to the third floor where there was a small reading room. It looked out over the trees, and the window was large enough to see quite a few stars. I curled up on the couch and sat there in the dark, hugging my knees to my chest. I felt like my heart had a knife in it, the ache growing and throbbing, an ache that would remain forever. He told me he loved me. Now, he loved her. I cried until there was nothing left inside me.

"I'm waiting," Lance said.

"You told me not to talk."

"I want to hear you say it—*I murdered Lily Mitchell.*"

"I didn't."

"You don't seem to realize that I have all the time in the world. I can leave to get food and sleep. You will be here until you own up to what you did. Until you admit you're a murderer."

He didn't understand what had happened. He thought his sister was so freaking *perfect*. I couldn't believe that he thought it was okay to steal the boy another girl loved. It is not okay. He had to understand that. He had to see that Lily changed. She suddenly wanted to party—to get drunk, dance, have sex. She had years of suppressed desire from doing nothing but studying. One party to end all the parties, all the parties she'd missed because she thought she was better than everyone else.

"Abbey and I are going to the fraternity open house," I said. "Did you know that?"

He stared at me, then put his hand to his ear, telling me I hadn't said what he wanted to hear.

"She had an unsettled death. I think her ghost is still in that room where she... If I can talk to her, I can explain." I wasn't sure what else to say. I didn't want to say too much, but I needed him to see that I was a good person. I was trying to do the right thing, to put her to rest, even if it was also to get what I wanted. Something doesn't automatically become bad just because it benefits you.

He glared at me. "What are you talking about?"

"She cursed me. I can't have a child and—"

"Stop babbling. It's simple—*I killed Lily*. Say it. Three words. Then maybe I'll think about letting you go."

"I'm not babbling. If I can connect with her spirit, I can tell her I'm sorry she died."

He shook his head, each shake growing harder than the one before. "No!" Although it was much louder, his voice was still controlled. "You don't get to absolve yourself of murder by saying *oh, sorry*."

"Well, I didn't mean for her to die from Ecstasy, so I'm sorry that happened and—"

"Wrong. You're not sorry. You're a killer. And you'll sit there until you admit that, or you die from your own lack of remorse."

He settled down again, his arms resting on his kneecaps, the gun resting on his bicep. He stared at me. I stared at the gun.

38

ABBEY

Standing at the top of the basement steps in my soft-soled running shoes, I reached up inside the hem of my loose top to feel the waist of my jeans. The fabric was pulled tight, the nose of my newly acquired gun shoved inside. I didn't need to touch it because I was constantly aware of its weight, of hard, cold metal pressing into my flesh. The gun was small and weighed less than a pound, but still felt incredibly heavy against my belt.

I was confident I could manage to fire it accurately, although it would probably require several shots. The gun was fully loaded with ten bullets, which made me feel I had room for a few mistakes, but not too many, since I needed to disable Lance immediately.

As I crouched out of sight, listening to Lance's accusations, I was surprised that he hadn't been able to frighten her into owning up to what she'd done. His desire was simple, and I would have thought her self-preservation would have finally kicked in. Maybe she figured he would kill her no matter what she said, so her best chance was to prolong things indefinitely.

I waited until I heard her going on about talking to Lily's ghost. Had she really joined me on this road trip with the intention of confronting a *ghost*?! I knew she believed they existed, but hearing her now, I understood she was more disturbed than I'd thought. I crept down the stairs until I could see both of them. They faced each other almost like lovers in a bitter argument.

I stepped softly onto the dirt floor. I pulled the gun out of my waistband, turned off the safety lock, and pointed it at Lance. I began moving closer to the small circle of light where he sat, his arms on his knees, the gun resting against his lower leg.

Raven turned first. "Oh my God! I knew you wouldn't leave me. I knew you..." Her bleary, swollen eyes focused on my hands. "Where did you get a *gun*?"

Lance turned and gave me a slow, enticing smile. "Don't you trust me?"

I didn't answer, waiting to see what he would do next. It appeared his plan was to remain calm. Already my arms were tired, and I hoped I was up to maintaining this pose, to keeping my attention focused solely on him. If I glanced away for even a second, I would lose my advantage.

"I knew you'd come back!" Raven cried. "Are the police on the way? Did the tow truck driver—"

"Be quiet." Lance shifted his position, moving the hand holding the gun, raising it slightly.

"If you shoot her, the police will know right away it was you." Raven's voice was filled with unwarranted confidence.

He ignored her.

Without taking my eyes off Lance's, pleased that my arms were holding steady, I spoke to Raven. "Did he tell you about Lily's leg?"

"What?"

I addressed Lance. "Did you?"

"No. What are you planning to do with that?" He gestured toward the gun.

"Just covering my bases," I said. "Did you think I would go unarmed into a basement with a man who wants revenge for his sister's death, no matter what the truth is?" I paused. I heard Raven's breathing, heavy and rapid. "I never told anyone that I moved Lily's leg off my coat, Raven."

"What are you talking about?" she asked.

"I moved her leg before I realized she was dead. It was the most awful thing I've ever felt, knowing without really understanding that she was already dead. I never forgot it, and I never will. I never told a single person about it because it felt so bad. Even though it wasn't true, I felt as if I was more concerned about my coat than a dead girl."

Lance groaned and briefly shifted his gaze away from mine.

"What are you talking about?" Raven asked.

"You were in that room with Lily when she was already dead. The only reason you knew her leg was on my coat was because you saw her dead."

Lance made another, more painful sound, but his expression remained steady.

"I...please help me," Raven said. "Untie me."

"I know you saw her before I did. You sent me into that room to get the coats so I would be the one to find her, so no one would think you had anything to do with it." I kept my voice as calm as Lance's had been, and I found an intoxicating sense of power in that adopted calm. "When Lance started telling everyone I was a killer, you let them all think he was right. You could have told them you were there too. But you kept silent. You *let* them hurt me. You have no idea what it feels like to have everyone shut you out of their lives as if you don't exist. You can't begin to comprehend the pain."

"Maybe I can." She was crying softly.

Hearing her sniffle and cry infuriated me. Lance was right about that; she wasn't going to be allowed to buy her way out of her guilt with a victim-blaming apology and tears.

She stopped crying, coughing hard to clear the mucous. "Are the police almost here?"

When I didn't respond, the crying started up. "Untie me. Please untie me! You don't even have to kill him. When the police get here..." She stopped, as if she sensed something in me. A coldness she hadn't noticed before. Maybe it was a slow understanding that if I was concerned about her, I would have immediately directed Lance to cut the straps around her wrists.

"I told Lily a thousand times it wasn't my fault she died. I told her. Every night I talk to her, and I think she's listening, but then comes the blood and another month without a baby to love, and I know the curse is still there. I don't know what she wants from me!"

Her voice grew soft. "What do you want from me, Lily? You stole my boyfriend. I loved Carter with all my heart. And he was so in love with me until you started whispering lies to him. I'm sorry, okay? I know you thought I could help you. But my heart just froze, and the rest of me froze with it. I didn't want you to die, but the pain was too much. My heart was broken. I couldn't move. And then when you said you were having trouble breathing, I didn't know what to do, and I was still hurting so bad...I wanted you to get a little taste of that. I didn't think you would actually... It wasn't my fault! It all happened so fast, and I was hurting so much I couldn't think straight. I—"

Lance flung himself at Raven. "What the hell did you just say?"

"She's here. I can feel her. You loved her so much, she must be here because she feels your love, and maybe, because you're here, she'll let me go. She'll stop trying to hurt me."

Lance grabbed Raven's hair and yanked her head back, forcing her to look at him. A wave of nausea came over me. The angle of her head and the position of his body made it look as if he'd severed her head.

I shuddered and told myself to get a grip. I had to stay focused. My opportunity was coming soon.

Lance's unnatural calm had dissipated. He was shouting now, yanking Raven's head from side to side. "What did you say? You saw her? She was alive, and you stood there and watched her die?"

"You don't understand what happened. She fucked the boy I loved! I was out of my mind, crazy with hurting so bad—"

He smacked the side of her head with the gun. The sound was sickening, and Raven screamed with such volume, my ears rang.

I lowered my gun several inches, aiming at Lance's back. I slowly pressed the trigger, ready for the recoil I knew was coming. I let out my breath and fired again. He fell to the ground, and his gun flew to the side. Blood spread across his back.

"Oh my God. Oh, Abbey! Thank you. It's so horrible, but thank you. He was going to kill me."

I walked closer and shot Lance in the back of the head, just to be sure.

Raven wriggled her shoulders, trying to raise her arms. "Get these off. You can't believe how much they hurt."

I looked down at her, waiting for her to meet my gaze. "What kind of friend are you?"

"What do you mean? We're BFFs. We always were. I love you, Abbey. You're like a sister. We're kindred spirits."

"I don't think we are."

She stared at me, her mouth opening slowly, her eyes flooding with fear as she realized what I was going to do. I shot her three times as well. I needed to be sure.

When her body collapsed on the dirt floor, I turned away.

I placed the gun on the ground and sat down with my back to the two of them. I put my head in my hands and let the sound of gunfire reverberate, then finally subside inside my head. I felt numb. I felt calm and incredibly free. The thing that I'd done was awful, but at the same time, it felt right. It felt like justice. I thought I might cry, but I didn't. I imagined that would come later. My body began shaking uncontrollably. I let it until I was spent. Then I sat there for quite a long time, my mind empty and utterly calm.

Finally, I stood. I picked up the gun. I took Lance's gun from where it had fallen. I dug his car keys, cell phone, and wallet out of his pockets, trying to keep my mind blank, not thinking about what I was doing. I stuffed all of that, along with my phone and Raven's purse, into his backpack. I turned off the portable light and placed that inside as well. I strapped the pack over my shoulders. Despite the heat, I'd worn a hoodie over my tightly braided hair to keep stray hairs from falling on the ground. I'd left my own purse by the sepulcher so that nothing weighed me down. I removed one of Lance's shoes and rubbed it across the floor, blurring any footprints I might have left.

I made my way to the basement stairs and climbed them.

It was dark out now, and the night air had cooled slightly. I took a deep breath and exhaled. I retrieved my purse, then went to the car and removed all my luggage. I took Raven's tablet and luggage tags. I piled everything into Lance's rented sedan. In one of the side pockets of his backpack, I found a complicated knife with several blades and various other tools. I went to the edge of the forest and began dragging fallen branches back toward the basement entrance. I cut some into smaller pieces, then added some brush to the pile. I reached into my pocket and pulled out a padlock I'd bought in one of the antique stores when we were killing time in Medford. I inserted it through the latch and locked it. I tossed branches around the edges of the entrance and along the side. I half-covered the entrance with more shrubs and branches. I covered just enough to make sure the door wasn't obvious to the casual observer, but not enough to draw attention to an unusually large pile of dead shrubbery.

I drove Lance's car back to the highway and headed to Eugene. I stocked up on snacks and coffee and then turned east. Driving all night, I stopped twice for restroom breaks and once to trek into the woods, where I dropped Lance's backpack, phone, and gun into a tree trunk that had been gutted by wildfire. I reached Twin Falls, Idaho, in the morning. After wiping everything I'd touched with a clean T-shirt, I left his car in an industrial area where there appeared to be several abandoned cars and trucks and a few decaying motor homes that were providing temporary shelter. I called an Uber to take me to Boise, where I booked a flight to Seattle. While I waited for my flight, I called and reported my rental car stolen. Then I walked around the terminal, burying Raven's various belongings deep in the bowels of trash cans.

Sitting on the plane as it climbed into the billowing white clouds, I closed my eyes. I slept the entire trip, feeling the cottony warmth of those clouds around my body. It was a deep, dreamless sleep.

39

ABBEY

Raven had thought it would be fun, in a way that I now saw as disturbing, for me to attend the official reunion events posing as her—dyed hair and colored contact lenses. But now, the last thing I needed was anyone giving more than a passing thought to Raven Sanders Ward. Anything beyond the casual speculation about what ever happened to her might shine a spotlight on the timing of her disappearance. It would be a day or two, at least, before Emmett contacted Raven's mother and they both discovered her elaborate lie, then called the police.

Her family would never connect her disappearance with me. They didn't know I existed. They wouldn't think about people she knew in college because she never talked about them. The police would dig through her current relationships and habits for clues. They would track her phone to the point where I'd knocked it into the pool of water. Her husband wouldn't know the extent of her lies, and her mother wouldn't know how cleverly she'd been used. Both would be left with a lifetime of unanswered questions.

All of my questions were finally answered.

It was too risky, even for a risk-taker like me, to attend the reunion as Raven. However, I did have an open invitation to enter and stroll around the fraternity house as they hosted their reception for current members and friends, alumni, and prospective pledges.

For this event, I became a woman named Laura Newton, aunt to a seventeen-year-old boy who was a good student, a soccer player, and a guy who enjoyed parties, within reason. Since my fictitious persona was from the Seattle area, I was checking out the fraternities on his behalf so I could give him some real-world insight that wouldn't be found on college websites.

They were serving champagne and beer, which was fitting for a frat house. The champagne was a concession to people in their thirties and forties, but they would go no further into the world of adult drinks. The appetizers consisted of chips and dip, bowls of mixed nuts, a few cheese and meat trays, and finger-sized pizzas. It was well done for a bunch of college kids. Maybe a few alums had helped.

I declined the champagne. I had a sudden, visceral distaste for it. I wasn't entirely sure why—maybe it was a result of all the bottles of the stuff I'd shared with Raven. I asked for sparkling water with lime. They didn't have lime, but they had orange slices as garnish on the cheese tray, so I slipped one of those into my glass.

Scanning the room for people who looked to be about ten years younger than the members of the graduating class from which I'd been expelled, I strolled through the first-floor rooms. Two college-age girls stood near the elaborate dining room table that I'd never seen used during the year and a half I was attending parties in this stately, brick mansion.

I sidled up to them and raised my champagne glass full of the wrong color bubbles. They didn't seem to notice, clicking their glasses against mine.

The girl with long black hair, wearing a sleeveless black dress and a gold snake bracelet around her upper arm, spoke first. "What year were you?"

I laughed and raised my glass to her. "Thanks for pointing out my age."

They both laughed.

"Sorry," she said. "I'm Janelle."

"Katy," said the other.

"I'm Laura. I live in Pioneer Square."

They nodded eagerly.

"My nephew lives in New Jersey, and he's applying to UW, as well as a few other schools. I'm checking out the fraternities so I can give him some real-world insight."

"That makes sense," said Janelle. "I had a friend who was in the same sorority I am, so she gave me all the insider info."

I nodded and sipped my drink.

"Is he cute?" Katy asked.

"Of course I'm going to say he is." I smiled and paused for a moment. "But yes, he's very cute. And smart. And a pretty good athlete. Should I go on?"

They laughed.

We talked for a few minutes about their chosen majors and the activities they were involved with. I changed the subject abruptly, sensing they might be tired of me already. "The only thing I'm a little unsure about is that I heard a girl died here a few years ago. It makes me wonder if the drinking is out of control. A little is fine, obviously. He likes to party and have fun, but not out of control."

They both nodded.

"The games that make you drink ridiculous amounts, toxic amounts...he doesn't want anything to do with that. All the aggressive initiation pranks..." I sipped my drink and waited.

"That was years ago. Not just a few years. Maybe eight."

"Or more," said Janelle.

I nodded. "What happened?"

"She drank too much. But they got a lot more strict with campus drinking rules after that."

"I'm glad her death wasn't for nothing. Maybe she saved other kids."

"Maybe." Janelle looked over my shoulder, now clearly bored with my dive into ancient history.

I had a few seconds of their attention left. "I heard a girl got blamed for killing her or something."

Katy shrugged. "I think there were rumors, but no one really believed them."

I wanted to smack her, which wasn't at all rational because it had nothing to do with her. She probably didn't even know the details of the rumors. It was unlikely she even knew Lily's name. She absolutely would not know about Lance or Abbey or Raven. Was that how the story had changed shape over the years? No one believed what Lance said about me? Maybe he was so popular, they believed him and followed his wishes while they were blinded by his presence, but over time, they dismissed it and then forgot.

From rumors and gossip that was only half-believed, then quickly forgotten, my life had been shattered.

I went on like this for a while, working my way through the rooms and the guests, continuing to target people who looked like current students, as well as those about four or five years older. Anyone who appeared to be about my age, I carefully avoided.

When my second glass of sparkling water was empty, I put the glass on a tray. I made my way toward the staircase. With music playing, everyone talking and laughing, disinterested in my movements, I eased my way up the staircase. I was in plain sight, but they didn't see me, just as they'd pretended not to twelve years ago.

I walked quickly up the last few steps and along the landing toward that room filled with searing, life-changing memories. I opened the door slowly. The room welcomed me with wide-open blinds, the space filled with light. The bed and nightstands I remembered were gone. The odor of vomit had been eradicated, obviously; the carpet replaced with hardwood. The room smelled faintly of roses.

It had been redone as a computer room. There were four desks, nicely spaced, a large, sleek computer sitting on each one. The chairs were simple but looked comfortable. Framed posters with inspirational quotes from tech leaders hung between the desks.

I closed my eyes and tried to remember how it had felt. Had I known when I walked in that there was another human being in here? Had I sensed the last few breaths of a nineteen-year-old girl who was fascinated by insects and their intricate connection to other forms of life? I didn't think so. And I didn't sense anything now.

Raven's insistence that Lily's unfinished life was in this place waiting for resolution was all in her mind. I knew that. I'd always known that, but still, I liked standing there, breathing in the sweet air. Imagining her letting go of her short, but powerful life.

I'd been innocent. Finding her lifeless body, seeing her eyes, had given me serious trauma. Her eyes had never frightened me in life. I thought they were beautiful. But in death, they were terrifying, as any eyes would be.

I opened mine and walked quickly out of the room. I walked down the stairs and out the front door. I didn't speak to anyone. I hoped that the few seeds I'd planted might sprout, stirring up the past, causing new rumors to spread to those who had graduated with me. It was a fragile hope, but it was all I had, and I'd felt compelled to make the effort. I hoped that some of them felt badly for what they'd done to me.

Anything is possible.

It didn't really matter because standing in the room where she died, closing my eyes, and thinking of her, I suddenly knew the shape my life would take going forward.

EPILOGUE

During the road trip, despite the distractions of Raven's guilty lying and unbridled fear, I'd given some thought to what kind of career I might want. I was utterly free to do whatever I pleased. After what I'd been through, returning to study marketing and publicity twelve years later felt like the desire of a person who no longer existed.

Standing in that room at the fraternity house, my mind had taken a new path. It was slightly dramatic, but in honor of the roommate I'd bullied, I was going to study entomology. Following her lead, I would devote myself to becoming a respected forensic entomologist. And who knew, once those bodies were discovered in an abandoned church basement in Oregon, a respected scientist like the one I planned to become might be called from another state to consult. I could steer them in a direction that would cut me out of the picture forever.

It was a fanciful, unlikely outcome, but it made me smile.

I needed all the good feelings I could get, because I would hurt for the rest of my life for what Raven and I had done to

Lily. Yes, Raven was far worse than I, and that eased my mind slightly. But I was complicit. I never once spoke up in Lily's defense. I never called Raven out. I just went along. I never showed Lily a shred of kindness or friendship.

I never recognized how badly we hurt Lily until Lance showed me parts of her journal. The words she'd written revealed an amazing human being, and I would spend the rest of my life regretting that I never got to know her. She would have been a fascinating and loyal friend.

IT TURNED out my distaste for champagne at the open house, and the nausea I'd felt several times during that last day with Raven and Lance, was caused by hormones.

I was pregnant.

Maybe the dream I'd told Raven about had been my body's early recognition of what had just begun inside me. Contrary to Raven's interpretation of my dream, I didn't have a shred of doubt that I would be a terrific mother. I completely disagreed with Raven—children *need* risk in order to thrive. It helps them develop resilience and enthusiasm for life. Life *is* risk. Making a friend, falling in love, deciding to bear a child are all enormous risks.

As I'd hoped, every part of my life had fallen into place on the road trip. Now, I knew what I wanted the next few years to look like. I knew what my career would be. I also knew I would relish every moment as a single mother.

When I'd hooked up with Dirk the first night of our road trip, he used a condom without me having to ask. But when I met Lance, before I knew who he was, I was swept off my feet, silly as that is.

I told him I was on the pill and that because he'd dedicated his life to clean living, I trusted him. A huge risk, but one I was willing to take, because I wanted a child far more than I'd ever revealed to Raven. I didn't allow her to see that vulnerable part of me. She'd hurt me enough. I, too, ached to hold an infant, smelling her sweet skin, feeling the warmth and weight and absolute love for her. I felt every sword in Raven's heart, intensely aware of that innate desire to give a child life, to hold it and nurture it, to introduce a new human being to this vast, incredible world.

I'd wanted a child for years. My husband kept telling me it was too soon. Finally, I realized it would always be too soon for him. When I saw him furtively checking his phone in the bathroom for the third time in our marriage, turning off notifications on his lock screen, I decided I wasn't going to wait for him.

It's less risky to wait for things to unfold—to meet a man, fall in love, get married, or not, and have a child. I'd been denied everything I'd wanted in my life. I was not going to be denied a child.

It's a little strange to carry, give birth to, and raise the child of a man who ruined your life, but I can shape this child into a better human being. I feel like she's a little part of Lily that has a chance to live on.

A NOTE FROM THE AUTHOR

Thank you so much for choosing to read *Best Friends Forever*. I hope you enjoyed reading the book as much as I loved writing it.

I want to take a moment to give an enormous thank you to Brian Lynch and Garret Ryan and the rest of the team at Inkubator Books. Their belief in my writing, their unique, passionate approach to developing and shaping a story, as well as their investment in getting the word out to readers, have changed my writing career in amazing ways that I can't begin to describe.

A special thank you to my editor, Line Langebek. She sees characters through a lens that's very much like mine. Sometimes, brainstorming and revising my outline with her feels like talking to myself.

I also owe a huge thank you to Shirley Khan for her thoughtful insight and incredibly sharp eye, and to Pauline Nolet for her careful attention to all the details.

Reviews are so important to us authors. If you could spend a moment to write an honest review on Amazon, no matter how short, I would be extremely grateful. They really do help get the word out.

Best wishes,

www.cathryngrant.com

Made in United States
North Haven, CT
14 April 2022

18280075R00178